RISE OF THE RAIN QUEEN

What Reviewers Say About Fiona Zedde's Work

"Zedde's explicit erotic scenes keep no secrets, and her tender, masterful storytelling will keep readers spellbound and squirming."—*Publishers Weekly*

"Fiona Zedde is a culinary artist with words, cooking up spicy, flavorful tales [to] satisfy the appetite of a malnourished audience."—*Washington Blade/Southern Voice*

Visit us at www.boldstrokesbooks.com

By the Author

Broken in Soft Places

Every Dark Desire

Desire at Dawn

Rise of the Rain Queen

RISE OF THE RAIN QUEEN

by

Fiona Zedde

2016

RISE OF THE RAIN QUEEN
© 2016 By Fiona Zedde. All Rights Reserved.

ISBN 13: 978-1-62639-592-3

This Trade Paperback Original Is Published By
Bold Strokes Books, Inc.
P.O. Box 249
Valley Falls, NY 12185

First Edition: July 2016

CREDITS
Editor: Cindy Cresap
Production Design: Susan Ramundo
Cover Design By Sheri (graphicartist2020@hotmail.com)

PART ONE

CHAPTER ONE

Tanganyika Region, 1414

Duni walked ahead of Nyandoro as if she held the most delicate treasure between her thighs. Duni had a graceful and swaying walk that was almost like dancing, hips moving beneath the *kanga* cloth tied low on her waist while her yellow and green waist beads gleamed against her skin. That skin glowed with sweat from her walk in the hot sun. The dimpled small of her back caught and held Ny's eyes as she imagined, not for the first time, fitting her hands there as she kissed the hollow of Duni's throat.

With her four brothers, Nyandoro trailed behind Duni and the clutch of women winding their way through the center of the village on their way to the river. Her eyes were only focused on Duni. The early morning sunshine seemed to gather around Duni who walked in the midst of her sister wives, graceful and glowing with the thatched basket of clothes balanced on her head. She was the tallest of the wives and, in Ny's opinion, the most beautiful with her smooth dark skin, high cheekbones, and perpetually sleepy eyes. Like she'd already seen all there was in the world and found it all boring. She wasn't bored now, though. Leaning close to one of her sister wives, Duni laughed, her fingers fluttering up to cover the flash of white teeth. Ny felt the rippling of that joyous laughter down to her very toes.

Nyandoro couldn't look away from her.

"You watch her any harder and she's going to end up with a baby in her." One of her brothers, Kizo, said with a low laugh. His thick hair, long and luxurious as a girl's, lay heavily down his back.

"You do know that's not how it happens, right?" Nyandoro shoved Kizo.

"What do you know about where babies come from?" Adli, one of the twins, asked, laughing at her too. "You still have the smell of Iya's milk on your breath." Like all the boys, he was tall and handsome, a copy of their father. He wore his hair the shortest of them all, telling anyone who cared to listen that it made the dimple in his chin, and the rest of his good looks, stand out more.

"Shut up!" Ny muttered.

She fell back with a pout, her brothers' teasing make her blush and stumble on the smooth path. Ny was used to their teasing. She was small, like no one else in the family, her hips and breasts rounded and full in a way that often attracted stares from men and women alike, and drove her to tackle the hardest physical task, try for the most difficult kill during a hunt so no one could take her womanly shape and round, doll-like face for weakness. Her brothers remained merciless though.

Up ahead, Duni stopped laughing and nodded at something one of her sister wives said, a smile curving her lips. Then she looked over her shoulder. Ny stumbled again. This time she fell into Duni's eyes that lingered on her, warm and thoughtful, for longer than a dozen heartbeats. Then Duni turned back around, not missing a single step. Ny's heart thumped like a frightened rabbit in her chest and she tried to control her breathing. If not for moments like those, she told herself, her infatuation would have died long ago. But it had been two long seasons and she still felt foolish and breathless every time she saw Duni. Her want felt like the full-grown ache of a woman, not the uncertain desires of a child who had not yet seen her twentieth season.

In Jaguar Village where she and her family lived, the people were notoriously long-lived. One hundred and ten seasons was the average age of an elder. Because of that, the maturity of the young people officially came at twenty, much later than the fifteen and eighteen seasons Ny had heard of other villages not far from their seat at the edge of the forest. A few boys were impatient with that, eager to start their new lives with wives of their choosing. But Nyandoro was okay with waiting.

Aside from Duni, who was already married and, at twenty-five seasons, had already begun her own family, no one in the village caught her interest. And even when she visited other villages with her father on his diplomatic missions, none of the women there attracted her either, at least not enough to tempt her for something more than the physical. She'd found no one she would give up her life of hunting and brawling with her brothers for. No, she was okay with waiting until she reached her twenty seasons. Especially if Duni was to remain forever out of her reach.

Ny gripped her spear with a sweat-slick hand and stared at the slim form moving easily among the sister wives, a group of women who differed as much in age as they did in temperament. Ibada, husband to the women, was a greedy man with no discernable preference. All the women had in common was their beauty, though Ny would argue that Duni was the most beautiful, and the most interesting, of the wives.

"You have to be more subtle than that." Kizo lightly gripped her shoulder, his palm hot and dry on her skin. "If her husband saw you looking at her that way, he would be the one hunting today, not you."

Ny grinned at Kizo and shrugged. "I'm only looking."

But that was not all she wanted to do. Every night, she dreamed of other things, of touching and tasting and making Duni moan her name as they moved as one on the sleeping mat, naked and wet with desire. Although Duni was six seasons older, she wanted her with every ounce of her youthful passion and impulsiveness.

Kizo snorted. "If I *looked* at a woman that hard, she'd be pinned under my spear by nightfall." He made an obscene gesture with his hips and their brothers laughed.

Ny punched him in the side. "You are *not* funny."

She scowled at him although she knew he was right. She had no business panting after someone's wife. After another quick look at Duni, she turned her back on the women and followed her brothers through the gates of the high stone wall surrounding their village.

In the surrounding forest, Ny and her brothers found plentiful game. Grunting bush pigs nosed through the underbrush while pythons slithered on high branches and monkeys screeched, flinging themselves from tree to tree. This was also the place where they found the freedom from the watchful eyes of everyone in the village. Even though her parents had taken great care to shield her from the malicious gossip, Ny knew the villagers thought she was strange. The sixth child of her parents, the only girl, and too pretty, some said, to be running wild without a husband lined up to rein her in so close to her coming of age. But she didn't care what they thought. Her family—and her mother in particular who had lovingly spoiled her from day one—didn't see anything wrong with her, and that was all that mattered.

She walked silently between her brothers, the five of them fanned out across the forest floor, talking quietly but also keeping an eye out for prey that could turn predator. Ny carried her spear easily in one hand, her gaze roving around her.

"But seriously, sister, you must be careful." It was Hakim, the other twin, who spoke. "If not for your sake then for hers. You haven't officially said you're *onek epanga*, but everyone already knows you'd rather marry a woman. You can take a wife of your own but not someone else's." Like Adli, he was vain, but wore his hair big and wild around his face. He loved it when his women oiled his scalp and played in his hair.

Ny made a dismissive noise. Why did she have to make an official declaration of what was already obvious? That archaic system always seemed stupid to her. Her brothers didn't have to stand in the middle of the village and tell everyone they preferred girls so why should she? Ny turned to Hakim. "I don't want to take her. I want her to come to me freely."

"We know you're beautiful. We're your brothers so, of course, you take after us." Hakim grinned, but the humor did not reach his eyes. "But chasing after someone else's wife is asking for trouble."

"Even if she's only a second wife and everyone knows he hasn't bedded her in months." Nitu, the gossip, shoved Ny lightly with his shoulder. He was the least handsome of her brothers, but attracted the most women because of his unusual eyes, one obsidian black and the other leaf brown. "He could divorce her and leave her with nothing if you take this any further than just looking."

Ny's brothers had had this conversation with her before, often when they caught her openly pining after Duni who seemed to barely know she existed. The girl was beautiful and seemed committed to her life as the second of six wives. But Ny said the same thing she always did: "I haven't done anything."

Kizo, the closest to her in age and her favorite, gave her a teasing look. "You boys are acting like virginal grandfathers. Ny's not going to run off with Duni or anything that stupid.

She's young but hasn't lost her mind." His teeth clenched down on his chew stick.

"Are you so sure about that?" Hakim asked. "Her eyes look a little glazed. Sure signs of madness."

"Bah!" Ny dismissed them with a wave of her hand, an affectation she picked up from her father. "Are we hunting or are we gossiping like children?" She aimed a pointed look at Nitu.

He thumped her between the shoulder blades, making her stumble. The others laughed.

The wind moved through the thick jacaranda trees, bringing the scent of far-off rain, jasmine from blooming flowers, the sweat of her brothers. Their mother had asked for a gazelle for the evening meal. Her brothers didn't think they could find one so near birthing season, but Ny had made the promise without hesitation. Her mother didn't often ask for something, but whatever she wanted, Ny would get.

She and her brothers broke through the thick forest to the wide plain that was little more than tall grass and sudden boulders, pale and massive, laid out under the sun. They clambered up to sit on one of those tall rocks, one overlooking the river that wound lazily around half the village before spilling south toward the sea. Although they hadn't seen much of the world, Ny and her brothers agreed that their village was the most beautiful. They'd traveled with their father who sometimes filled the role of ambassador to nearby villages, and had seen no other equal to it.

Ny stretched back on the sun-warmed rock to stare up at the sky, Kizo at her side while Hakim and the others scouted from the trees high above. Kizo stuck his chew stick at the side of his mouth and belted out a raucous song about a boy from Arabia. Ny laughed as each verse grew more and more ridiculous. When the lyrics came to a close, she rolled over on the rock, laughing at him.

"You *wish* you would meet an Arab boy that flexible."

Kizo laughed along with her. "Sure enough."

Although, like her, he saw himself potentially ending up in an infertile marriage and marrying another man, he also enjoyed spending time with women. His brothers called him greedy and bet each other all the time that he would outgrow this phase and choose one or the other, just like Ny had done. Although, she never bothered to remind them, she had never liked both, had never found a man she wanted to enter into a marriage pact with, a boy to dive naked with her into the river.

"Do you ever wish you could travel to the lands you're always singing about?" Her brother got his songs from the seafarers, men and women who'd traveled on giant boats to China and Arabia, even the barbaric white North Anglia.

"What would I do there except find some acrobatic boy to bend for my spear?" He shrugged, but it was an empty motion. "My whole life is here. Except for their amusing songs, I don't have any interest in these other people."

His light-filled eyes twinkled at her. Like their mother, Kizo rarely asked for what he wanted. Despite his words, Ny knew he longed to see the world, to travel to far off places just like her. When they were children and traveled with their father, they sometimes talked about letting their father return to the village while they continued the journey on, going to the East, maybe even to Pompeii as a cousin had done. But all that talk stopped as they grew older. Kizo knew his reality was to stay in the village. He had accepted it and allowed the dreams to die. But sometimes she wished the younger Kizo still existed, the one who believed in the impossible.

"If I could leave here, I would," she said.

Kizo feathered the ragged end of his chew stick across his front teeth before sticking it back in his mouth, a regimen that was part of his obsession with keeping his teeth gleaming white and his breath fresh. "Even if Duni would agree to be yours?"

The thought of Duni being truly hers punched a breath from Ny's chest. The nights they could spend making her wet-thighed fantasies come true. The love they would share, maybe even a love as deep as the one her parents enjoyed.

She turned to Kizo, shocked into giddy laughter with the images rampaging through her mind. "Well, maybe I wouldn't have to make a choice."

"There are always choices to be made, little sister." The chew stick dipped between his lips as he spoke. "Never forget that."

A sharp whistle cut through the air and Ny looked up and up to see Nitu high in the tree above them waving in their direction then pointing. He'd spotted game for the kill. She jerked upright on the rock, her pulse pounding with eagerness in her throat.

"Let's go." She grabbed her spear and nudged Kizo.

They waited for Nitu and the others to clamber down from the tree before making their way through the high grass to a small herd of resting gazelles. The animals were beautiful and sleek, soft-looking in the sunlight with their graceful legs and slender throats. The nearly waist-high grass rippled gold in the breeze around them.

One heavily pregnant female rested beneath a flowering tree. The thick white blooms drooped low above her head while another female stood nearby with a newborn foal. A male wandered farther from them, his horns long and beautiful, dark against his golden brown face as he nibbled at the grass at his feet. He was the perfect size, but was too far for Ny to bring down. She looked at the females again, a tightness in the back of her throat. They were so beautiful, it seemed sinful to roust them from their rest.

"Is your womanly softness giving you second thoughts, sister?"

Adli whispered from her right. She hadn't heard him come closer, but she kept her eyes on the prey. When his question came, she made her decision. "Is yours, brother?"

Ny hefted her spear and struck. The male gazelle cried out as he fell, blade buried in his flank, blood blooming on the pale brown pelt. Not a killing blow. The male jumped up, a mooing cry, and hobbled into a run with Ny's spear still stuck in him. His struggle was pitiful, but it gave the resting females the chance to escape. And they took it, darting quickly across the high grass despite the wobbling newborn and pregnant foal.

But Ny didn't watch them for long. Quickly, she yanked her knife from her belt and ran toward the wounded gazelle. The blood pumped in her ears, feet pounded across the hard ground, the smell of trampled grass and fresh blood rising swift and fresh. The buck's screams scraped the air.

Ny's brothers fell back, allowing her to finish her kill. She leapt over its twitching body, avoiding its sharp horns, the scathing agony in its eyes. The buck's fearful heart thumped hard through its skin, rapping against her palm. Its pelt was hot. Its eyes wide and afraid. She cut its throat, gasping as the blood rushed over her hands and she felt its heart stutter, slow. Then stop.

Her own heart was a pulsing calm in her chest. With the red on her hands, she looked up. Nitu and Adli were frozen at the edge of everything, watching her as if she was some unexpected thing they'd found in the forest. Ny didn't understand why when they'd seen her hunt before and killed much bigger prey. Kizo dropped to one knee next to her, a knife already in hand to help gut the buck and get it ready for travel back to the village. Hakim appeared at his side.

"Well done, sister," he said. But his eyes were already moving around the grassy plain, already looking for other prey.

❖

Ny and Adli carried the heavy buck through the fortified gates of the village. Each held on their shoulder one end of the long pole supporting the skinned and cleaned gazelle in the middle. She had insisted on helping to carry the kill, just in case they ran into Duni. Proof that she could provide. But they didn't see her.

Although it was dark and the long torches lit up the high stone rocks of the wall, a schoolroom of children greeted them with clapping and shouts, following them in a ragtag parade along the paved stone of the main village road. It felt good, a true triumph that made the pride swell in Ny's chest although it had only been a few seasons since *she* had been one of those children trailing successful hunters back from the village gates.

Darkness crept from the forest to enfold the entire village as they walked in front of the children, huffing from exertion, the smell of the meat and sweat from their bodies high in the evening air despite the carcass being rubbed down with green wood to diminish its scent. Ny's shoulder ached from the weight of the buck carried nearly two *maili* from the edges of the forest.

Kizo, who preferred to carry a machete and knives instead of a spear, cleaned his nails with a small blade as he walked beside Ny. It was a miracle he didn't cut off his own finger in the dark barely illuminated by the torches along the road. "I don't see Duni waiting for you to come back with meat to make for her evening meal, Nyandoro." Kizo teased her without looking up.

"Because it's not happening today doesn't mean it won't ever happen," she said, talking braver words than she felt.

On lesser days, she thought maybe Duni had desires she could never satisfy. Perhaps she was not *onek epanga* like Ny and wanted only the pleasure of a man on her sleeping mat. But there had been days when Ny exchanged heated glances with Duni, watched as she squirmed under Ny's naked longing, nipples hardening under her *kanga* cloth, her tongue flitting out to wet her lips before she looked away.

"Maybe that's not the kind of meat Duni wants," Hakim said, interrupting Ny's thoughts.

She winced but kicked out at him anyway, almost losing her balance. "Shut your hole," she muttered.

Adli let loose a big, dirty laugh. Kizo lost his place as her favorite when he chuckled along with the others. But he got it back when he rubbed her back in sympathy.

They made their way along the wide road, through the main square with the empty market stalls, past the council building where Ny's father spent most of his days, and past the tall flowering trees granting privacy to those who had chosen to build their homes on Jaguar Village's largest street. The road widened into veins of smaller streets and, as they drew closer to the family's compound—a plot of land with four houses separated from neighbors by a low stone gate flanked by honey blossom trees—the children drifted away, leaving just Ny and her brothers.

They had enough meat for the entire family, including their childless aunt Basma, who lived in one of the four houses on their compound. It had been a very good hunt and Ny was proud. The only negative, from Ny's point of view, was having to help cure the leftover meat.

Curing the meat with salt was hard and hot work, nothing she looked forward to. Her aunt was too old to do the work, and her brother Ndewele's wife too heavily pregnant and busy taking care of her own home. That left Ny and her mother to deal with the big buck on their own.

"After a day like this, I just want a soft place to plant my spear for the night," Adli said with a suggestive circling of this hips.

Ny rolled her eyes, but the others gave their versions of agreement, bringing up the names of which women or men in the village they would soon seek out. Although Ny would've loved to unwind by playing a few songs on her *kora*, she knew that wasn't going to happen.

Sometimes she wished her brothers found it as easy to help their mother as they did their father. But they had definite ideas of what was women's work, especially the twins. Ny shrugged off the familiar but unproductive thoughts to focus on the moment.

In their family compound, torches were set at the doorway to each of the four houses, round dwellings made of dark river rock, with thatched roofs and the insignia of their family—a cheetah leaping over a flowing river—stamped into each wooden front door.

Ndewele, their parents' firstborn, shared a house with his wife while the wifeless brothers (except for Kizo) shared one home and Aunt Basma had her own. There was plenty of room on the grounds for at least three more dwellings, but everyone insisted they enjoyed the space and illusion of privacy that came from having the houses spaced so far apart.

Ny and her brothers tracked their sandaled feet across the hard-packed brown dirt to the largest house in the family compound, the one that belonged to Ny and their parents. Her brothers, each born a year apart, had chosen to move from their parents' home in preparation to have families of their own. But so far none except Ndewele had found mates to their liking.

They took the buck to the smaller, separate cook house at the back of the family dwelling. It was a space her mother had designed and helped to build with her own hands. She told Ny she didn't want the smell of food to live in their clothes and in the fabric of their everyday lives. An affectation that many women in the village first scorned and now copied. They thought it showed off their wealth.

Ny settled her half of the burden on the large, raised stone slab near the water pump and window overlooking the small corn field out back.

"I see you've brought much work for me, daughter." Her mother appeared at the entrance to the cooking hut as Ny lit the last of the torches. As tall as Ny's father, she had to walk carefully not to bang her head on any of the pots and utensils hanging from the cooking hut's ceiling. Her cheeks crinkled with the force of her smile, the light from the torches flickering over the sprinkling of beauty marks on her face. She touched Ny's cheek with a soft hand. "Go and bathe. You have blood all over you."

"I'll bathe after I help with the meat."

Her brother's wife, Xolani, appeared at the entrance to the cooking hut, eyes flickering over the gazelle and small game Ny and her brothers had brought. Pregnant with her husband's first child, she was always ravenous and eyed the meat as if she would cook and eat it all. She greeted Ny with a kiss and a teasing wrinkle of her nose, a hint at Ny's less than pleasant smell. "I've made the evening meal for all of us. You can cure the meat after."

Ny didn't have to be told again. "Let me have a bath then I'll come eat."

Instead of using the bathing room attached to the house, she grabbed the basket with her soaps and cloth then made her way to the river.

The high moon guided her down the winding path that seemed to shine with an otherworldly glow. After hunting, she always felt everything more sharply, her skin tingling with life, her heart beating quickly in her breast. Kizo called it bloodlust, but her father said it was the excitement of being alive. An excitement that only came from taking another life.

But weren't that and bloodlust the same thing?

At the river, Ny found her favorite deserted spot, stripped, and quickly bathed, washing her blood-stained body and hair that was musky with sweat. She dunked beneath the gently rushing water to rinse away the soap. She broke the surface to the sound of humming. Ny held her breath, blinking away the water to watch the shadowy approach of a slim shape along the riverbank. The way the woman walked was familiar, the swaying motion of hips, footsteps that barely disturbed the ground.

Duni.

She held her breath as Duni walked past. Ny swore she smelled her on the breeze, feminine sweat, wood smoke, and a hint of something flowery. One of the oils they sold in the market.

What was she doing out here on her own? Ny stood in the water with the slippery rocks pressing into her feet, the cool water running over her skin like a caress. She wanted this woman, but was she bold enough to do something about it?

Yes. You are.

The sound of the voice, faint but so very close, wasn't a surprise. It was a voice she'd heard since she was a child. Truthfully, it was the voice that got her into half the trouble she'd found herself in over the seasons. But this was trouble she definitely wanted. She crept from the river, water running down her flesh, a rush of cooling wet over her suddenly overheated body, and scrambled up to the riverbank to hastily arrange the *kanga* over her body and tuck her bathing basket out of sight.

It didn't take her long to find Duni. She'd only traveled a short distance away and sat on top of a high rock at the water's edge. It was a rock the younger children jumped from to splash into the river. But tonight, Duni was alone. She sat high on the rock with her legs dangling over the water, a small pot of oil near her hip, combing her hair in the moonlit night. She was humming.

Duni reminded Ny of the legends she'd heard from her mother of river women, half-fish, half-human females, who spent the rainy summer days on the riverbank combing their hair and singing to lure careless river travelers close. Ny crept up behind Duni.

"Will you lure me to my death with your song?"

Duni jerked in shock, her indrawn breath loud in the darkness. Her comb tumbled from her hand and fell into the water. She gasped. "My comb!"

Ny didn't stop to think. She scrambled up on the rock beside Duni and jumped into the water after the comb. She fell in with a splash that took her breath away. The water, cold and deep and dark, churned with tides that would easily carry something as small and insignificant as a little comb away. It could be anywhere. But the moment the water covered her head, the coolness embraced her from crown to foot and she felt a confidence in the foolish gesture she hadn't felt before she dove in.

She opened her eyes under the water, discerned immediately the darkness and the rocks and the fish moving lazily beneath its surface. The moon's glow penetrated the water, a silver blade of light that illuminated everything around Nyandoro, especially Duni's pale comb. It floated slowly downstream, the white bone like a petrified smile under the water. She grabbed the comb and twisted in the water, bubbles floating up. The comb's unyielding contours pressed into her palm, and she blinked down at it, amazed she could see it so clearly. She looked up and the world enshrouded in night was floating above and past her. It was beautiful.

A voice, muffled and urgent, came at her from above, far away and easy to ignore. But it took only seconds to realize that it must have been Duni. Ny squeezed her hand around the comb and darted toward the water's surface. Duni's rock was farther upstream now, a dark shape against the darker night. But Duni wasn't there. Still, Ny heard her voice.

"Nyandoro!" Duni's hysterical cry cut through the night. "Where are you?" Her voice dropped to a harsh mutter. "If I get the minister's only daughter killed, he will kill me with his own bare hands."

"No one is going to kill you," Ny called out softly, keeping her voice low. She swam against the current, arms burning. In moments, she was at Duni's rock and Duni was back there too, leaning down with a hand toward Ny to help pull her from the water. Ny shook her head and pointed to the bank that had easier access to the shore. She held up the comb in triumph as she got out of the water.

"Your comb, my lady."

Duni grabbed Ny's hand that held the comb, took the comb back, and held it to her chest. "The comb wasn't that important." But her actions made a lie of her words. "I didn't mean for you to jump in there after it."

"But I did, and everything is fine." She wiped the water from her eyes and staggered to the rock, weighed down by the water in her clothes. It was a miracle she hadn't been dragged deeper into the water and carried off. But she hadn't been thinking about that at the time. "How about you?" she asked with a breathless grin. "Are you fine?"

"By the pearls of Yemaya, of course. You're the one who—" Then she must have seen that Ny was joking. Duni pressed her lips together. "You're making fun of me." She sat on the rock next to Ny, still gripping the comb to her chest.

"Never." But Ny didn't hide her smile.

Duni was even more beautiful from close up. Every time Ny had seen her, it had been sneaked glances, hungry looks that she'd tried not to let linger too long. But now, here was Duni, soft and stunning under the moon and stars, her narrow eyes and yam root skin glowing close enough for her to touch.

"You're gorgeous," Ny said.

Duni pulled back in surprise. She looked Ny over from her toes with their gold rings to the top of her limp, wet hair. Duni shook her head, saying nothing.

Ny felt a moment of shame. Had it been a mistake for her to be so bold?

Never. The voice prodded her toward the course she'd already chosen.

Duni shifted on the rock, her face a study in conflict, her expression shifting between gratitude and anxiety and another emotion Ny couldn't place. Ny leaned back into the cold rock, any reminder of the sun's bright heat buried beneath the surface.

"You *are* gorgeous, you know."

Ny committed herself to the course again and worried at her lip with her teeth. Duni, though, sat next to her, dry and concerned. Arms wrapped around her raised knees, only two small braids done, and the rest of her hair loose and sticking up toward heaven. The emotional tides drifted from her face until she only looked thoughtful, evidence of some decision settling into the smooth contours of her skin.

Ny wanted to tug at Duni's woolly hair, twist it between her fingers and learn its texture, offer to finish braiding Duni's hair while she rested her cheek on the solid line of Ny's thigh. Braiding. Yes. She wanted to braid Duni's hair. She had to laugh at herself.

"Is it wrong to say I find you beautiful?" Ny asked.

Duni squirmed, her tongue flicking out to wet the corner of her mouth. "I have a husband," she finally said. "You know that."

Ny grinned at Duni in relief. She was concerned about her marriage, the appearance of things, not about being pursued by another woman. Her smile widened.

"People have divorces all the time. You can decide you no longer want him and leave." She slid closer, but slowly, not wanting to frighten Duni away.

"Then what would I do? Leave my comfortable home to live with you in your mother's house? It doesn't work like that. You are a child." Duni touched Ny's jaw, a glancing brush of fingers that might have been nothing, except for the way her gaze dropped to Ny's mouth, a look that sparked something new and dangerous under Ny's skin.

"I am no child," Ny said, emboldened. She leaned closer, close enough to sip the air from Duni's lips. "Didn't you see the buck I brought home today? I killed it myself."

After a moment's hesitation, Duni drew back. "You are a child who killed a gazelle then."

Ny opened her mouth to argue again, but the sound of footsteps and a low voice calling out her name pulled her attention from Duni. She scrambled to get up.

Ny cursed. "I promised I would help with the meat." She stumbled to her feet, rearranged the soaked clothes over her skin to the sound of Duni's soft laughter.

"Yes, go, child. Your mama needs you."

Ny pressed her lips together. She wanted to disprove Duni's claim that she was only a child and good only for teasing. Swiftly, she leaned in to press her mouth to Duni's. Duni froze, her eyes flickering wide. Then she drew in an open-mouthed breath that invited in the flick of Ny's tongue, a serpent's lick. She made a startled sound, whimpered, and dove into Ny, lips parted, breath hot, a devouring suck and lick that tugged Ny's nipples hard and dripped a shock of wetness between her thighs. Ny moaned in helpless want. It would be easy, *maybe*, to slick her fingers between Duni's thighs as she'd so often done in dreams, stroke and kiss until they both lost their breath and—

Shuddering, Ny pulled back. Her entire body *ached* with lust. But she didn't know what to do. Inexperience and indecision locked her helplessly into place. Then a sound too close by freed her from her paralysis. She stumbled off the rock and ran toward her things downriver. Ny got there in time to see Kizo searching for her with a torch held high, the flames flickering orange light over his serious face. His look was suspicious.

"Mama is wondering where you got off to."

She grabbed up her basket with her dirty clothes, oils, and soap. "I was taking a bath."

Kizo lifted his torch higher, eyes searching around the clearing and farther up the riverbank. "You're not a good liar, sister."

Ny grabbed his arm. "Come. Mama is waiting, and I'm starved."

He looked beyond her again. "I'm sure you are."

The family, already gathered around the low fire with the evening meal, greeted Ny with greetings of concern, mock annoyance.

"Are you clean enough, sister?" Nitu had the nerve to look like he knew exactly what had distracted Ny at the river.

She shouldered him aside to get to her place by the fire and to the bowl that was already waiting for her. "Cleaner than you at least." She wrinkled her nose and the scent of the forest and the day's hunt that still clung to him.

They ate their meal, laughing and sharing stories about the things they'd done that day. Ny, of course, said nothing about meeting Duni although her brothers gave her laughing looks over their food. The meal wound down into soft silences and sighs of contentment, bellies patted, and shared plans for the next day.

Ny's lashes were fluttering low when her mother gently nudged her shoulder. "We have things to tend to before you fall asleep, my rain and sun."

She stirred at the familiar love-name, the one her mother called her when she didn't want to say Ny was her favorite, her only girl child who Yemaya had gifted her with. "Yes, Iya."

Offering wishes for a good sleep, she and her mother left the others for the cooking hut to tend to the gazelle. The meat was still fresh, beautiful and glistening in the night. Her mother lit the torches and pulled the stools out for them to begin their work. She'd already prepared the brine for the meat while Ny and her brothers hunted so all they had to do was wash the meat again, cut it up, and settle the pieces in the large jugs of brine where they would lay for several days.

"Your brother tells me you were watching the married women today."

Ny hissed. She could kill Nitu. He was always talking, especially about what everyone else was up to, when he should just shut his mouth. "Yes. We saw them heading to the river on our way to the hunt."

"One day you will be married too, my daughter. You just have to decide if you want to be with a man or a woman. Once you decide, I'm sure it will be easy to make a good match for you."

Ah. Aspirations to marriage. If Nitu had told their father the same story, Ny was sure Baba would've guessed correctly, not about her want for marriage but her desire to bed a married woman. She loved her mother's soft and kind spirit. She would never even consider the idea that her daughter had impure motives.

"I already decided, Iya. When the time comes, I'll marry a woman."

"But that time is far away, Nyandoro. You're still a child."

This again. Why did everyone seem determined to see her as a child? "I'm *not*, Iya." She lowered the piece of meat into the brine, careful not to let it touch her hands and begin to roughen the skin. "I'll have twenty seasons very soon."

Her mother flinched. The meat fell into the cask, splashing up and into her mother's face. She cried out, hands flying up toward her eyes.

"Iya!" Ny grabbed her hands before they could make contact. "Don't move."

She grabbed a pot of clean water, tilted her mother's head back and poured the water over her face, into her eyes. Her mother was never this careless. Never. Ny picked up a clean cloth from the stack on the table.

She gasped, eyes red and running with water. "I don't know what's wrong with me tonight." Her mother put a hand out, blindly fumbling for something to wipe her face. Ny gave her the cloth.

She touched her mother's hair. "Are you sure you're okay?"

"Yes, yes. I...I wasn't paying attention to what I was doing." She patted her skin with the clean towel Ny gave her.

"You should go outside. I'll finish here. It won't take me long." At her mother's doubting look, she gave a rueful smile. "You can come back and check on the quality of my work tomorrow." She took the now damp cloth from her mother. "Go and have a bath. Rest."

Her mother looked as if she might protest, then she touched her cheek with the tears still rushing down its creased curve. "All right." She stood up, seeming older in that moment, a hand pressed to her back as she rose from the low stool. "Thank you for doing this."

"It is my duty to see to your comfort, honored one." She bowed before her mother, a subject to her queen. She rose with a teasing grin.

Her mother pinched her hip, an effort at a smile twitching her mouth. When she stepped through the doorway of the cooking hut and disappeared into the night, Ny's tentative smile disappeared altogether.

When her mother left, she finished the curing of the meat, carefully slicing the last of the batch how her mother preferred and sealing them in the barrels. She was exhausted, but it wasn't the kind of exhaustion that wanted sleep. She wanted instead another chance at the river, another kiss from Duni, another *everything*. But she made do with a bath in the outdoor tub her father had installed for the family many seasons before, another eccentricity her mother insisted on.

Instead of soaking like she would at the river, she quickly washed any remnants of brine from her body, the sweat and stink of the meat. In her room, she smoothed jacaranda oil over her skin and quickly plaited her hair.

Her brothers were all gathered with their father in the sitting room when she arrived, seated on low stools and re-wrapping their spears while their father sat in his customary chair, smoking his pipe.

"Baba." She sat on the animal furs near his feet.

"Nyandoro, your brothers tell me you have been into mischief today." His eyes twinkled in the torch lights.

Never wanting to limit her life experiences (in his words), her father was always the first to encourage Ny in whatever foolishness she was doing.

"My brothers talk too much," Ny said.

She'd brought her spear from the room to tighten the leather and sharpen the edge of the blade. But she'd also brought her *kora* in case she felt like playing. Her father was in a storytelling mood, she realized from the teasing start to his conversation.

"Do they only talk too much when they tell your secrets?" He chuckled.

He was a diplomat, the official who organized trade with nearby villages, often brokered difficult marriage contracts. But at heart he was as much of a gossip as Nitu.

"It's only human to want something that doesn't belong to you." He pulled the pipe from his lips. "Did I tell you that when I met your iya, she wasn't meant to be mine?"

Her brothers groaned.

"You've already told this story, Baba," Kizo said. He was the only one who had the courage to say it.

Ny laughed but played her part. "No, Baba, I did not know that." Since she was a child, he'd told that story, or at least various versions of how he'd met their mother. The story always seemed to change and reflect the point he was trying to make.

He looked at her with approval, smoke puffing from his pipe toward the open roof of their hut. Her brothers cut their eyes at her.

Her father pretended not to notice. "On the evening I met her, I was supposed to get engaged to a girl from another village. The arrangements had all been made. The girl's family was a more powerful one than mine with closer connections to their chief, but my family had more money. It wanted to buy itself two more paces closer to the position of chief."

He paused to blow smoke rings into the air, his eyes at a thoughtful droop. "My family badly wanted this match," he said. "I was unattached and had no woman resting in my heart so the arrangement was fine with me. But while at the feast where my engagement was due to be announced, I had a sudden fever." The smoke wound around his head like the heat that must have flowed from his body on that long ago day. "I left the circle to find water to splash on my face, but couldn't find any nearby without asking some servant to break their enjoyment of the festivities—there was dancing and food, acrobatics, joke-telling—I left for the river only a small distance away."

He told the story of walking through the unfamiliar village in a daze, his head swimming and heavy as if the sun Orisha, Obatalá, had clenched hands around his face to blind him to everything but the path to the river. At the riverbank, he dropped to his knees breathing heavily in a panic, his heart squeezing hard enough to burst. He dunked his head into the river, almost falling in. When his head came from the water, his mind was clear and their mother was standing there.

Tall but delicate, with her long neck and pale *kanga* cloth, she looked like a true vision. He thought he was hallucinating, after all, all the women and girls of the village had gathered for the festivities and were nowhere near the river.

"Are you well?" she asked him and offered him a cloth for his face.

Their father paused. The pipe in his hand forgotten as he stared into the past with a smile. "She smelled like the rain." His smile widened, and he put the pipe back between his teeth. "I knew then she was the wife for me, the only one. I could not marry the girl of that village even if it would cost my family their two paces closer to the chief."

In another version he'd told before, he said how his younger brother stepped in to marry his original betrothed. But he only told this part of the story when he was trying to impress upon Ny's brothers the importance of responsibility, especially to family.

"It was easy for me to leave that girl behind because I knew your iya and I were destined for each other, and that we would love each other until the end of our days." Her father looked at Ny. "Can you say the same about you and that married woman?"

By the blood of Yemaya. Ny dropped her face into her hands, and Kizo laughed at her. "Baba…"

"I remember what it's like to be young," her father said. "Youth hurts blindly when in search of its own pleasures. And the pleasures of youth are often as fleeting as they are strong."

"I wouldn't do anything to jeopardize her marriage," Ny said. "I have nothing to offer her if he decides to divorce her. Besides, I'm not certain she desires women the way I do."

Ndewele looked up from sorting his bags of cowrie shells. "If you already talked with her, and she looked at you with your big, mooning eyes and did not run away, then she is interested in you."

"We are beautiful, however," Kizo said. "Maybe that has blinded her to the fact that you have no spear between your legs."

"I have many spears," Ny said with a smirk. "In as many sizes as she could want."

"What are you talking about?" Adli chortled and nudged his twin. "You've never even had a woman."

Her brothers laughed, knowing it was the truth.

Ny flushed with embarrassment and wished it was easier to keep a secret in her family, or even in the village.

Or maybe she should've been more sexually adventurous. By her age, all of her brothers had already experienced at least one lover. The twins alone, only four seasons older than she was, already had over two dozen lovers between them. Sometimes literally.

"I don't need to have done it to know that I can," she said.

"Practice makes the spear fly true, sister," Hakim said. "You didn't wake up one morning knowing how to bring down a gazelle from twenty paces. It's the same with making love to a woman. Or a man." He looked at their father. "Right, Baba?"

Their father broke in. "This is not a conversation I wish to have with my children." But he chuckled, his pipe waggling between his teeth.

Serious Ndewele joined in on the teasing, asking their father just how true his spear had flown before he found their mother on that riverbank.

As they talked, their mother walked past, a strange visual aid to their conversation, although she did not stop aside from sharing a quick smile with her husband. Her hair was coiled on top of her head, skin glistening with oil, and her sandaled feet still damp from her walk through the wet grass.

She slipped through the beaded curtain separating the sitting room from the rest of the home. It wasn't long before Ny smelled smoke from her incense, the one she burned at the altar to her Orisha, Yemaya, who held power over the seas, lakes, and motherhood. Her father she knew, was joined to Obatalá, the Orisha of wisdom and compassion, and had his own altar in a separate part of the house.

When she was younger, Ny's mother tried to teach her about Yemaya and the other Orishas. But unlike most of the village that faithfully practiced Ifa and were faithful to the religion of their people, Ny turned her back on it all. Seasons before, she'd watched her favorite aunt, her father's youngest sister, a faithful priestess of Ifa and village healer, get eaten up from the inside out by a mysterious sickness that kept her in constant pain the last few seasons of her life.

Ny frowned at the beaded curtains still swaying in the wake of her mother's passage. It was strange for her mother to pray so late at night. Ny thought again of earlier when her mother had accidentally splashed brine in her face, the flinching terror in her eyes.

Even now, she didn't know what she'd said to make her mother drop the meat so quickly. Despite her concern, she turned her eyes away from the curtains. Maybe her mother would tell her what was on her mind tomorrow. Maybe by then, whatever it was would be better. Ny picked up her *kora* and strummed a few notes, willing the instrument to soothe her thoughts.

"Will you play something for us, Nyandoro?" Her father stopped her brothers' raunchy story seeking with a wave of his hand.

"Of course, Baba." She grinned and looked over at Kizo. "I actually heard this song today."

She strummed the *kora* again and began to sing the ridiculous ditty Kizo taught her that morning.

Her brothers laughed, even Ndewele. "That wasn't exactly what I had in mind, daughter." Her father's voice was firm, but the seriousness did not reach his eyes. They were like merry stars in the torch lights.

"But wait," Ny laughed. "There's more."

❖

Despite her easy dismissal of her father's words, Ny couldn't ignore them so easily. It was true. She wanted Duni with a sharpness that kept her aching and wet deep into the night. But she didn't know what that meant for the future. If anything.

Yes, she wanted to undress her and taste the firm fruit of her breasts. But she also wanted her to be happy. Her husband, old and selfish Ibada, didn't treat her well. At least that's what the town gossips said. Because of his great wealth, he was allowed up to six wives. He took younger and younger wives each year, and didn't lay with the older wives except in an attempt to have more sons. He already had two girls and one boy, and three of his six wives were pregnant, but not Duni. Ny prayed never Duni.

As long as Duni was only someone's wife and *not* someone's mother, Ny held out hope that something could happen between them. Slim hope, but hope nonetheless.

Ny shifted on her sleeping mat, the covers, soft and smelling of the lavender and limes her mother used in the wash, slid over her bare skin. Her fingers fluttered low on her stomach, but she forced them not to go any lower as thoughts of Duni melted her from the inside out.

The first time Ny noticed Duni was on her wedding day.

Other than that, it was a day like any other. Kizo chattered at her side, anxious to get to Sky Village because he'd heard they petitioned the Rain Queen and, after being dry for nearly three seasons, had been granted their wish. The rains came in the morning, the drums announced, and Kizo said he missed the feel of mud under his feet. So they were on their way to play in the mud and celebrate with the people of Sky Village.

But on their way, they had to pass a wedding, a bride making her slow way down the stone path with her two closest female relatives by her side, ceremonially holding her up as she walked the short distance to the house that was obviously the home of her new husband.

Ny wasn't sure why she stopped. She'd seen plenty of weddings before and had never been impressed. But something about the way the two older women held up the bride seemed more than ceremonial, as if the bride would topple over or run away without them.

The women, dressed in wedding whites, were a stark canvas to the bride in her black kanga, swathed in the ceremonial manner from head to toe. She could only see through the strip left uncovered over her eyes.

"Who is that?" she asked Kizo, gesturing to the bride.

"Some unlucky woman." Her brother shrugged. "Ibada isn't good enough for a good fuck, much less marriage." Apparently, he knew the husband-to-be well enough.

Ny shrugged too and began to walk away from the small wedding procession.

Kizo tugged her arm to hurry her along. "If you walk any slower, the mud will turn into rock-stone before we get there."

Ny didn't bother to argue about how unlikely that was. They'd heard the drummers late in the morning and the sun was still in the middle of the sky. The mud wasn't going anywhere. But to please him, she began to walk faster.

Then the women began to unwind the cloth from around the bride. Ny's feet stopped. This was the part of weddings she always enjoyed, the slow unwrapping of the black shroud to reveal whatever color the bride chose to wore underneath as she presented herself to her new husband. Like a slowly spinning top with black threads attached to the white-clad women, the bride began to turn and walk forward at the same time.

Her bare feet were deliberate on the stone path, while the women, each pulling an end of the black cloth, unwound her and slowly bared her to the gaze of the sun and her new husband. The two pieces of cloth parted first at the waist, revealing the bride's deep brown skin, a double drape of waist beads, and her flat stomach. Her steps were measured. She did not stumble as she walked toward the man in white, her husband, who stood at the open door of the stone house, the top of the doorway hung with streams of red and white flowers. Two of his male relatives fanned him with giant palm fronds, stirring the folds of his white robes.

The bride kept her eyes on the man, even as she turned to help peel away the black cloth and reveal more of her skin. Then the cloth parted over a strip of yellow, a bright kanga in two pieces, a skirt worn low on her hips then a mere strip of color covering her ribs and breasts. The black cloth unwound to show more of her. Bare shoulders hunched protectively forward and glistening under a sheen of honey oil and sunlight, a long neck, and then her face. Ny stopped breathing.

It wasn't just the bride's beauty, even though she was beautiful. No, the reason Ny stopped so suddenly was the expression in the bride's eyes. Terror and determination both. A fearsome look as if she stared into the abyss of her future with this man and was determined to face it. It was a steely resolve that would've been inspiring if it didn't make Ny want to rescue the bride from the man she was steadfastly walking toward. But since that felt too foolish to say out loud, she turned to her brother.

"I wish she was my wife," Ny said.

But Kizo only made a sound of impatience. "Come on. There are prettier girls in Sky Village without husbands ready to kill you for lusting after what's theirs."

And although that should have been it for Ny's instant and paralyzing infatuation, it wasn't.

CHAPTER TWO

At first light, Ny checked on the curing meats with her mother before meeting with the men and women of the village council to take the last of a series of tests that would determine if she could follow in her father's footsteps as an ambassador or even administrator if she chose. She wasn't sure which of these paths she wanted to take, but she knew what she *didn't* want.

Ny respected her mother and the work she did at home, but that was not where she saw herself. Being trapped in the village without having a chance to see the rest of the world would feel like death. In less than one season, she would be twenty and an adult in the eyes of the village. That was all the time she had to decide both her personal and her political future. It was too bad the path to both was as dark as a moonless forest.

With her future weighing heavily on her mind, she left the council and headed for the market to buy her mother some *kanga* cloths. Three village women just had babies, and her mother wanted gifts for them, as well as some cloth for herself.

Dust rose up under Ny's sandaled feet as she walked the crowded stone path through the market. The village hadn't seen rains in over a season. Too long had passed with the ground dry and packed tight, on the verge of cracking from lack of life-giving moisture. From what her father said, the elders were in discussion about petitioning the Rain Queen, a figure only half of them believed in. Ny wasn't a believer herself. She only trusted in the things she could see or experience for herself and, so far, a crowned woman with rain at her beck and call had not made herself known.

If the elders agreed to ask this queen for rain, then she would demand as payment one of the young virgins from the village. Once the payment was received, then the rain would come. As an escape from the monotony of village life, many virgins had volunteered themselves, but the elders were still undecided.

Ny gently pushed her way through the market crowd, half-smiling at the everyday pleasure of friendly bodies pressing close to hers in passing. She was still flush from the victory of kissing Duni the night before. Everything felt good. Her bare arms were warm from the heat of the sun, and her muscles ached pleasantly from the previous day's hunt. Even the combined smells of sweat, perfumed oils, and just-ripe fruit were sweet to her. A pair of boys, no older than she was, shouldered past her, reminding her to adjust the leather purse with the money at her waist, putting it in front of her in case of thieves.

Vendors called out to her as she passed, mostly women and teenagers, saying their yams, broad beans, cho-cho, oranges, pineapples, jackfruit, and papayas were the sweetest of all at the market. Ny shook her head at them all and slipped between other shoppers to the stall belonging to her mother's favorite cloth woman.

She stood holding up a fold of freshly dyed *kanga* when she heard someone call out a name. Ny looked up.

"Does my *kanga* please you, miss?" The cloth woman, wearing her own bright yellow *kanga* wound tightly around her body from breasts to hips, asked. "I can give it to you for a good price. Only for you."

But Ny wasn't interested in the cloth anymore. She searched quickly through the brightly dressed women, the heads gracefully holding up wide baskets, dismissing the ones with children strapped to their backs. Then...*Duni.*

She refolded the cloth and dropped it back in its pile. "No, I'm sorry," she told the cloth woman. "Please, excuse me."

Ny slipped through the crowd until she was close to what she wanted. Duni. Glowing in a pale green *kanga* knotted behind her neck and flowing down to her knees, and with a basket balanced gracefully on her head. She stood with three other women who looked her age or younger. The sister wives, all except one. The youngest and newest wife must have been at home underneath their husband.

"Duni."

She glanced up at Ny with little surprise. "First light greetings to you, Kweli's daughter."

Ny's face warmed with heat. *Kweli's daughter.* She called Ny by her father's name, reinforcing how much of a child she thought Ny was. But she didn't let the embarrassment put her off. "It's good to see you, Duni."

"Is this by chance?"

Ny was blank for a moment, then she realized what Duni was asking. She lowered her voice. "If I wanted to hunt you, I would go to the rock where I'm guessing you dream every night away from your sister wives and husband."

Duni bit her lip and looked away. But a smile hid beneath the clasp of her teeth.

They spoke too softly, too quietly, Ny thought, to be heard above the noise of the market. But Ifeyalo, the woman behind the stall who she'd known since birth, gave her considering looks while she talked with Duni. Ny remembered her father's words. Or at least her version of what he meant. *Caution*.

Ny smiled widely at Ifeyalo. "Two yams, please."

"Only two?" Ifeyalo said with a similar smile. Equally insincere. "Your family is so big, Nyandoro. They would not be content with just two yams." Her smile sharpened.

Ny clenched her jaw. "How many do you think would make them contented?"

The woman seemed surprised, as if she hadn't thought to get this far in the negotiation. Then her uncertainty dropped away. "At least twelve. Don't you think so?"

Duni gasped and stepped back, catching on to what the woman was doing. She glared at Ny, then at the woman.

Ny practically threw the money at the woman and took the yams, juggling them in her hands since she hadn't brought a bag. Duni backed away from the stall, and she followed.

"Are you trying to make this thing we *don't* have between us into a dirty secret?" Duni hissed the question at Ny. "Because if you are, you should walk away now. I'm not someone who would ever do that."

But the knowledge of what happened on the riverbank pulsed between them, heavy and thick.

"I didn't kiss myself last night!"

The words escaped Ny's mouth before she could catch them. Her father's temper pricked her rarely, but when it did... She dropped the yams on the ground and was vaguely aware of them scattering around her feet, heard gasps, saw from the corners of her eyes hands scrambling to pick them up.

"What kind of person do you think I am, then?" The frustration at wanting and not getting spurred her, and she grabbed Duni's arm, jerking Duni toward her. Duni cried out, a hand rushing up to steady the basket on her head. "Don't play with me like a child and act shocked when I bite back like

an adult," Ny said, ignoring the sudden onslaught of stares.
"Because, believe me, I *do* bite."

A calloused hand clasped the back of her neck. She smelled
the familiar scent of cinnamon chew stick, sweat, and flint.

Ny grit her teeth. "Kizo, let go of me."

But his touch was enough for her to let Duni go. Duni gave
her a sharp look, then reached up to hold her basket steady as
she turned quickly away to find her sister wives.

"Sister, you're not thinking clearly." Kizo tightened his
grip on her neck and shook her lightly, just once. "If you care for
Duni, don't let her become the talk of the village. Her husband
will *abandon* her." He emphasized the word with a sharp click
of teeth.

Ny looked around her at the quickly averted gazes, heard
the whispered conversations in the crowd, and felt keenly the
possibility of someone telling Duni's husband what they'd seen.
"Shit…"

Kizo seemed to relax then, his teeth releasing their clench
around his chew stick. "I hope you're not planning on kissing
our iya with that mouth."

At the mention of their mother, her regret deepened. She
cursed again.

"Come," Kizo said. "Get what you came here for or leave
these women to their market day. I think you've done enough
for the day." He grabbed the only two yams not stolen by
enterprising beggars and dropped his arm around Ny's shoulder.
Ny nodded, not knowing what else she could do. She looked
around, and yes, the villagers and vendors were still looking
at her, some slyly, others with knowing and direct stares. Her
father was going to send a blade straight through her stupid
head.

"I think I need a drink," she muttered.

"I know just the place."

He took her to a bar she'd never been before. Filled mostly with men, it was a lodge on the far edges of the village with the dried carcass of a monkey hanging from the eaves of its small verandah. A group of men sat on stools trading old stories while two women sat nearby sharing a jug of liquor.

No one on the verandah looked up when Kizo guided Ny through the doors of the lodge and into a wide room littered with tables, only half of them occupied. The place was filled with the stink of drink and sweat, a cocktail of sorrow and regret. Or maybe that was just what she was feeling.

Light poured in from the single large window looking down the mountain. It would be easy, Ny decided, if someone wanted to drown their sorrows in drink then end their life in the same place. A quick jump out the window and tumble to the rocks into the forest canopy below.

Kizo ordered drinks for them both then took Ny out the back door to a smaller verandah, this one empty except for a few empty chairs and tables. A baobab tree fluttered its leaves overhead. She drew a grateful breath of clean air.

"What the hell were you doing out there?"

"Making a mess of things?" She wanted to drop her head to the surface of the table and groan out her frustration at herself.

But Kizo didn't let her. He shoved the mug between her head and the table, giving her a look of brotherly disgust. "Drink."

The drink was honey-colored and looked sweet, almost pretty, in the rough-hewn wooden mug. Ny took a single gulp. And gasped. The liquor burned her tongue and her throat going down. "What the f—?" She gasped again, unable to go on. The drink scoured her belly as it settled.

"It's a drink." Kizo drank from his own mug and gave her a look of utmost patience.

Ny pressed a hand to her chest, willing the burning to go away. She swallowed again and looked away from the awful drink, wishing her deepest wish for a cup of water. A tub. An entire river.

"Stop being so dramatic." Kizo slapped her on the shoulder, but Ny squirmed under that brief touch. Even her skin burned.

"Fuck..." Ny dropped her head back and blinked at the open blue sky, at the occasional bird that floated by. She breathed until the fire was gone and she could talk again.

She licked her lips and the taste of spice lingered on them. "Okay. I think I've actually survived this assassination attempt."

"Assassination? You're not that important, sister." He drank again, licking his lips in a way she knew he did just to fuck with her. At her annoyed look, Kizo rolled his eyes then held out his cup to her. "Here, have some of this."

She took a sip, then stared at him. "You asshole!"

He was drinking *water*.

She tried to glare at him while guzzle-gasping from his mug.

Kizo laughed in her face. "I'm not the one who almost dragged off someone else's wife in the middle of a crowded market. Why would *I* need a drink?" He took his water back from her and took another deep drink.

"I didn't almost drag anybody off."

He ignored her. "Yesterday you promised our baba you wouldn't shipwreck the girl's marriage, but today here you are practically shouting to the entire village that you want to fuck her." Kizo sighed like he was the most put-upon brother in the world. "And she didn't exactly look like she was telling you no."

Ny felt her face warm again. Her second round of embarrassment for the day. "That's not what I meant to do."

"But that's what happened." Kizo could look as serious as their father when he wanted to. He apparently wanted to now. "Do you think she'll even talk to you now?"

"Shit. I hope so."

"Put yourself in her place. Would you?"

Ny drew her cup closer, sniffed it, then took a cautious sip. She winced. It wasn't *that* bad. "It depends on how much I wanted the woman who did that to me."

"That's a load of shit. No lover likes being rough-handled in public with so much at stake."

Ny loved her brother, but he was really making her feel like crap. She sighed and stared down the mountain. The heavy trees, summer thick with green leaves despite the absence of rain, wavered in the breeze. Far, far off, the peak of the mighty mountain Kilimanjaro hovered among the clouds. Ny knew she was being a child about this. One denied a sweet that she had been *almost* able to taste.

"I don't really know what happened to me."

"Yes, you do." Kizo gave her one of his searching glances, the one that said he wasn't buying whatever garbage she was trying to sell. "You have to realize the power you have here," Kizo said. "If you do this, she could lose *everything*."

Something about the way he said the last word flashed Ny back to her grandfather, a small man drunk on his small power.

He had had more money than their father, more influence, and every day it seemed he had bought a new woman, or bought the courts away from some trouble he'd gotten himself into. And he had the temper of a storm newly unleashed. Young with an endless capacity for destruction. Even as an old man, he'd been terrifying in his efforts to keep Ny's parents apart. When they came and stayed together despite his wishes, he'd simply dedicated himself to making her mother's life miserable. Telling her how worthless she was. How she could never compare in looks to the woman her father should have married. Ny had been glad when he died. Furiously glad.

And, all too often, her father told her how like her grandfather she was. Ny didn't want to be that small. She swallowed the lump of hot stone that suddenly appeared in her throat.

"I have to apologize to her," she said.

"You have to stay away from her."

Kizo shoved her drink back into her hands and Ny drank from it but did not wince this time. The burn was no less than she deserved.

CHAPTER THREE

The village was small enough that it was nearly impossible to avoid someone, but Ny tried. She did errands for and with her mother, helped her father in the usual ways, spent time with her brothers, but did not seek out Duni. She was trying to be better. Over a week passed.

The only thing she did not give up in her quest to be a better person was the late nights she spent at the river. At her usual place, she purposefully did not think about Duni.

She sat on the wide and worn rock on the river's edge, thinking of everything but the night she'd finally been able to talk with Duni, touch her hand, steal a kiss. Ny toed off her sandals and lay back on the rock, her bare back pressing against the stone, her breathing light and even. She closed her eyes.

A handful of moments later, her eyes opened at a far off sound. She stared upriver, craning her neck in a vain attempt to see around the curves and hidden branches of the winding snake of a river. Where her sight was limited, her hearing was not. She knew the sounds reaching out to her from beyond the shadows. It was Duni's song. Ny closed her eyes again and listened. The humming melody from the last time she had seen Duni on the river.

She sat up, tense, on her rock, fighting equally strong urges to stay where she was and to find the source of the song.

Stay away from her, Kizo had said. *Stay away.*

But the sound coming from upriver was truly a siren song, impossible for Ny to ignore. She slipped from her rock and followed the sound to its source. Duni lay on a patch of grass near the water, her slender form outlined in moonlight. Ny's desires made flesh. The melody she hummed was constant and sweet, rising into the night, mixing with the sound of the wind moving like its own kind of music through the trees. She was so beautiful that Ny's breath stopped in her chest.

"It's dangerous for you to be out here by yourself at night," Ny said once she could breathe enough to speak.

Duni didn't seem surprised to see her this time. Her humming song stopped, and she rolled her head to glance at Ny before she turned her attention back to the sky. "Do you think only you have the right to the night?"

"That is not what I meant," Ny said.

"It doesn't matter what you meant." She sounded resigned, unhappy. "Why are you here? Will you lie to me again and tell me you're not hunting me?"

"Bathing, not hunting." Ny crept closer to Duni, sank to her knees in the grass near her feet, but still kept a respectful distance between them. "Even though I wasn't searching for you here, I'm glad I found you. I—" She took a breath. "I want to apologize for what I did at the market. I had no right to say those things to you. I had no right to touch you."

"Rich men and women have been doing what you did since long before I was born." Duni dropped her gaze from the sky to the water, to the rocks scattered along the riverbank. Anywhere but at Ny. "That time was no different and you are no different."

"Please, don't—I wouldn't want you to believe I'm like that."

"And it's always about what *you* don't want, right?" Duni made a scornful noise. "Until you show me differently, there's nothing else for me to believe."

Ny nodded. The futility of what she was trying to do, get forgiveness from a woman whose life she could have destroyed with her careless actions, struck her like a blow. "I'll leave you alone." She stood up and brushed off her knees. "I *am* really sorry about what happened."

She turned around to leave.

"Why did it take you so long to find me?" Duni was now giving all her attention to Ny, the rippling of the river that had so transfixed before, forgotten.

"I didn't want to hurt you any more than I already had."

Duni nodded. "Okay. Thank you for that." She pressed her lips together. "I want to apologize too…for denying what happened between us. You kissed me, but I kissed you too. We both were part of it. Whatever that makes us, we are the same." She pushed out a noisy breath, then looked away.

"Apology accepted," Ny said.

When Duni only nodded again, she backed away. Thinking they were finished, Ny turned again to leave and had made it a few feet down the path before she heard Duni call out to her again. "You can stay."

She'd never moved so fast her entire life. Duni laughed at her as she skidded to a halt near her. Ny, trying not to force herself too much on Duni, sat on the small rock closer to the river and took off her sandals. She dangled her bare feet into the water and sighed at its cool eddies lapping at her ankles. The water was almost as soothing as Duni's presence.

Duni sat up and smoothed down her hair. It was a loose cloud around her face, big and soft and smelling of the honey oil Ny remembered. Under the moonlight, her eyes were large and shadowed. "Since you were not hunting me," Duni said, "what have you been doing in the days since the market?"

Small talk now? Okay. She could do that.

Ny shrugged. "The usual. You know there's nothing very much to do in the village except have babies, tend to the animals, and swim in the river."

"That is true for most, but not for you. I've been asking around."

Ny couldn't stop the jolt of pleasure that Duni had been trying to find out more about her.

"I need to know more about the one who I might have to report to the council."

The sweet feeling died as quickly as it was born.

Duni laughed at whatever look she must have seen on Ny's face. Her laughter was soft and musical, even if it was at Ny's expense. "I was only joking, Nyandoro." She slid closer to Ny. "Will you be an ambassador like your baba? Did you pass the tests?"

The tests. Truthfully, she'd forgotten all about them. She told Duni as much. After the market, her mind had been consumed with regret about how she'd treated Duni. The tests and their possible results were barely second thoughts.

Besides, they were easy. She was her father's child. She'd traveled with him since she could string meaningful sentences together and knew nearly everything about his position. If ever it came time for her to take a similar post, she was more than ready.

"The tests mean nothing," she said at the end of it. "Either I will be an ambassador or I will not." She smiled at Duni. "For tonight, I'm happy to be here with you."

Duni rolled her eyes, but she was smiling.

"What about you? What have you been doing since that unfortunate day of the yams?"

Duni smiled again. Relaxation curled into her slender body, and she tossed her head, as graceful as a lynx. Then she waved her arms to encompass the river and everything around them.

"This is it. I go to the market. I clean my husband's hut and teach the younger wives to do what he says, then I come here to escape."

"That's not too bad," Ny said.

"Would you say that if you were married to a man and had this kind of life? You have the freedom to do anything you want. Become an ambassador or your iya's help at home. Marry your own wives or travel the world. Choices like these sound like heaven to me."

Ny heard the echoes of need in Duni's voice, the desire for her own freedom. For more. "Is that what you want to do?"

"What I want doesn't matter anymore. I have the only life that I'll ever have." The sadness flickered so quickly across her face that if Ny hadn't been watching her so carefully she might have thought she imagined it.

"You can have more than this, Duni. If that's what you want."

Duni dipped her head to the water and looked away, but not before Ny saw the quaver in her chin and the way her eyes grew bright with moisture. Moments passed. When she lifted her head again, her chin was firm but her eyes were still wet.

"I want a room of my own," Duni said. "I want open skies. I want to go to the river in the daylight and sit with no one around me. I want only my own company for miles and to not feel afraid someone will come and take my solitude from me at any moment." Her mouth tightened. "Can you give that to me?"

Although Ny would have liked to give all that to her, and more, she could only tell the truth. "No."

"Pity." A smile, more a grimace really, twitched her mouth. "Then, tell me, Nyandoro. What is it that *you* want from your life? Maybe it's more of a possibility than my ridiculous dreams."

Water rippled around Ny's ankles as she moved her feet back and forth in the water. She wanted to pursue the question of Duni's own dreams, but knew the time for that had passed.

"I won't be any man's wife," Ny said. Again, Duni didn't seem surprised. "I'll have a wife of my own—"

"Only one wife?" Duni asked.

"Yes, just one. Just like my baba. She will be all I need." Ny stopped at the longing that drifted across Duni's face, an unvoiced need that Ny read as easily as any of her father's reports. "She'll help me," Ny continued. "We will help each other. And we will live in a house as big as this entire village."

"This village?" Duni laughed at her, but not unkindly. "And how will you get the wealth for this?"

"I don't know, but it will come." Ny said this with a powerful certainty that rumbled her chest.

She didn't need a village shaman to cast bones for her to envision her future. She saw it as plain as day. The only mystery was how to go about making it happen.

"You don't know anything about life, Nyandoro. How do you expect success to just come to you? You are a child."

"I may be a child in this moment," Ny said. "But I won't be a child for long. And I'm free to do what I want. The life I see for myself is the life I'm going to have. I know it."

CHAPTER FOUR

Despite the brave words she spoke to Duni, Ny still had her doubts about her future. About how she would get there. If Duni had a place in it. After the night with Duni on the riverbank, she felt consumed by those thoughts and questions, barely able to pay attention to the things actually happening in her life.

"This is stupid." Kizo sat up on the large tree branch they were sharing on a day that finally seemed as if it would rain.

"You're telling us." Adli and Hakim shared a look of understanding from their own perch a few feet higher up. The twins passed a pipe of sweet-smoke between them while the sun glistened on their bare shoulders, still sweaty from an impromptu wrestling match.

The brothers had gotten news of a group of wildebeests making their way north. Ny had never seen one. She, Kizo, Nitu, and the twins had made their way into the forest to lie in wait for them. So far, they were perched in a wide-branched tree, watching and waiting.

"What are you talking about?" Ny frowned at her brothers.

"We're talking about you," Kizo said. "You've been moping for days and that doesn't suit you."

"Not to mention it ruins our good time." Adli blew a cloud of smoke from the corner of his mouth.

He and Hakim had fewer opportunities for play than their younger siblings. He was to follow immediately in their father's footsteps and take charge of a post in a nearby village while his twin had agreed to marry a girl from a place so far away that few knew the name of it. The match was not for love but for duty. It was a sacrifice Hakim was happy to make.

"So are you going to tell us the reason you're acting like this or do we have to guess?" Kizo asked.

Nitu, who had been perched highest up in the tree and keeping watch on the far horizon, dropped down next to Ny with only a whisper of his sandaled feet through the leaves. The thick branch bounced from the addition of his weight. "Yeah, does her name start with Duni?"

"Does it end with 'married woman'?" Kizo added.

Ny snorted. "You all think you're so damn funny."

"Not think. We know," Adli said as he passed the pipe down to Kizo who promptly passed it along without smoking from it.

Hakim squinted down at her. "Seriously, sister. What do you have going with this woman?"

Ny exchanged a quick glance with Kizo, trying to tell him with a single glance that she didn't want to talk about it. Not in the open, not yet. He dipped his head. Yes, he understood. Ny breathed in relief.

Before she could say anything, Adli chimed in. "It better be good with all the misery you're going through."

I'm not miserable. Ny opened her mouth to say it, but something else entirely came out. "She thinks I have nothing to offer her, that I'm a child." She blinked, instantly irritated at herself for revealing she'd talked to Duni. And for talking about what she absolutely *didn't* want to talk about.

"She has a point," Hakim said. "What can you offer her now?"

"Can you rescue her from her terrible marriage?" Nitu asked.

"No. Not yet. I—"

Adli stood up on the sturdy branch to twist his hips. "Can you make love to her until she forgets everything and everyone else but you?"

She could try, but even about such a thing, there was no certainty. "You know I can't give her any of that, not yet. Maybe later on…"

"Then you should leave her alone," Hakim said. In that moment, she hated him a little.

"But what about love?" she asked a little desperately. "Isn't that worth something?"

Adli coughed out a laugh. "What do you know about love? You're still living in our parents' house."

"That doesn't matter." Hakim made a dismissive motion, and Ny could have kissed him for defending her. But when he opened his mouth again, she knew she'd thought well of him too soon. "Do you love Duni or are you infatuated? You don't even know her."

His twin chimed in. "What makes her cry when she's at her most vulnerable? Where do you kiss to make her scream out your name in pleasure? What are her most enduring desires?" Adli jerked his chin at Ny, knowing she didn't have the answers to his questions. "These are things a lover should already know or at least be willing to know," he said. "Just last week you were talking about wanting more freedom and leaving this village behind for good."

Her brothers all hummed in agreement, even Kizo who had been silently supporting her.

"You can't have it every way, sister," Hakim said, though his voice was soft with sympathy.

Ny squeezed her eyes shut, knowing they were right but not wanting them to be. She had craved Duni for so long. And now, for the first time, she was actually within reach.

"But if you insist on going after her," Kizo finally said, his tone a low warning, "you have to show her you're serious about being a partner and life-half to her."

"But you're not ready to do that," Nitu said. "Instead you're out here with us."

"Being out here doesn't mean we're not serious about the other things," Hakim said with an annoyed frown.

"I'm talking about Nyandoro, not you," Nitu muttered. "She tries to be everything to everyone and ends up being nothing to no one."

A rush of heat, then cold swept through Ny's body. She turned to Nitu, a snarl on her lips. "That's not true! Take it back."

But he just laughed in her face. "I won't eat my words for a child who gets frightened by the sound of them. Are you a child afraid of words or are you the *onek epanga* who will rescue delicious Duni from her dead marriage bed?"

Suddenly, it was all too much. Ny scrambled up from the tree limb, ignoring Kizo's call and climbed down and off the tree to drop the last five feet to the ground. She turned her back on her brothers and slipped into the cool comfort of the forest, away from the hot sun and the blazing furnace of their teasing. She wasn't ready for their questions, for her lack of answers, for any of it.

She felt like the earth, scorched from the lack of something it needed. Rain. Understanding. Duni. By the time she got back to the village, the clouds were still heavy with rain's promise. But it was a promise that would remain unfulfilled.

❖

Ny knew what she had to do. It was time she stopped taking from those around her, like a child, and learned how to give. So, she changed the things she did. She stopped hunting so often with her brothers and instead helped her mother more.

Sitting with her mother at the wide table in their receiving room, Ny helped to organize upcoming parties for visiting diplomats and plan naming day ceremonies for the three babies recently born into their extended family. She even tried, and failed, to weave baskets, a task her mother immediately pulled her from when she saw the mess she was making.

When her mother was sick of having her underfoot, Ny went with her father to his village meetings and sat in on the boring but necessary discussions about crops and family alliances and the potential threat of foreigners from the sea. She sat in the circle of elders, slightly behind her father since she had not yet earned her place among them. The white-haired men and women spoke in self-important, droning voices that were like lullabies to Ny's ears. If she was bored, she rationalized, then it was only her childishness that made her bored. If she fell asleep, she chided herself to try harder.

Days passed. Then weeks. Her brothers complained about her abandoning them, but she assured them she wasn't. Being an adult took sacrifices, and like they told her, she had no experience with sacrifice. It was time she learned.

Being an adult was exhausting. At least the kind of adult that did women's work, men's work, and everything in-between with no time for games and pleasure. Resentment ate at Ny because of it, but she was determined to stay the course.

It was late when she and her father finally returned from a tribe meeting two villages away. Before leaving Jaguar Village, Ny had asked her father to consider using one of the zebras she and her brothers had tamed for riding, just like the Arabians had done to their horses. But her father, staunchly old-fashioned and leery of the zebras' powerful kicks, refused. So they walked the many *maili* to the village and back. Ny was used to this much walking and more, but she would have rather been home in time for the evening meal and a bath. Now, all she wanted to do was wipe the travel dirt from her skin and fall into her sleeping mat.

"It was a good day," her father said. "I think these old-fashioned men are getting used to seeing you at the meetings."

"And, you, are you getting used to seeing me at these meetings, Baba?"

"I am, daughter, and I am proud of your interest."

Ny felt a rush a happiness, and guilt that she hadn't thought to do these things with her father more often. She felt embarrassed that it took the chance at getting between a woman's thighs for her to give her father the support he needed. Her oldest brother, Ndewele, had no interest in politics. Instead, he worked to create a way for the fields to produce more crops than they did now. Adli and Hakim had already committed to leaving the village and do their duty by their father. Nitu was often off chasing women, and Kizo was still himself a child although he had long since reached the majority age. Hunting, joking, and dreams were his passions. Ask him about anything else and his eyes glazed over.

"I want you to be proud of me, Baba."

"I am proud, my daughter." He rested a hand on her shoulder, a warm and reassuring weight. The exhaustion she'd felt before didn't feel so crippling anymore, and her feet felt strong enough to walk another half day. Well, almost.

They continued walking the quiet road through the village, greeting passersby and dissecting the events of their day. Soon, the family compound was a dim light down the path. Two torches lit at the entrance, welcoming light from deeper inside the wide ring of houses. Home.

A movement just behind her paused Ny's footsteps. Her father was talking about the meeting they had earlier that day, policy changes that needed to be made, but Ny was distracted and barely heard the rest of what he had to say. At first, she thought it was Kizo, coming to waylay her for ignoring him for so long. But the softly treading steps and smell of honey oil told her it wasn't her brother.

"Baba, forgive me. I think I'll stop by the river after all to wash away the travel from my skin."

Her father's eyes were a sharp glimmer in the starlight. He turned to peer briefly behind him, seemed ready to say something that would keep her at his side. But in the end he only nodded and tightly clasped a hand on her shoulder. "See you soon, Nyandoro."

As soon as her father disappeared through the entrance to the family compound, Ny turned to the woman half-hidden in the shadows.

Duni tugged the *kanga* cloth even more around her face, turned, and walked toward the river, obviously expecting Ny to follow. Duni took them on the smaller path, winding through the high trees, and away from any potential prying eyes. Ny forced herself to be calm and not read too much into Duni's actions.

At the riverbank, Duni walked past Ny's usual bathing place to the rock where they'd had their first real conversation. Wordlessly, she pulled the long *kanga* cloth from over her face, tugged it from her shoulders, and dropped it at her feet. Her hair was pulled back in neat corn rows away from her face, and a curved comb, white and wide like a fan, sat anchored to the crown of her head. She looked like a queen under the silver moonlight, her skin like obsidian, remote and untouchable. But she dipped her eyes and stepped back, then looked briefly at Ny. A seductive woman once again.

With a graceful motion, she climbed the high rock, more than twice as high as she was, to swing her legs over the moving water. Ny sat beside her, copying her pose.

Duni's gaze latched on to her right away, a strong pull she felt like a literal touch. "Don't throw your youth away," she said. "Not for this."

Happiness fluttered in Ny's stomach, and she grinned. "I'm not throwing anything away, just reaching for what I want." Her smile widened. "I'm happy you noticed."

"It's hard not to. The whole village is talking." A frown wrinkled Duni's forehead. "Even my husband says you're stepping up like you've never done before. And I often see you in the market with your iya. Where do you find time to help them both?" She sounded worried instead of impressed.

It was Ny's turn to frown. "I'm being an adult. Isn't that what you said I wasn't before?"

"But adults also make time for their families. I know you miss being with your brothers."

"Of course I do. But this is only temporary. Until I get—" Ny stopped, feeling herself on shaky ground.

"Get what? Get me?" Duni pulled away from her to sit farther back on the flat rock and clasp her arms around her upraised knees. "I'm not a prize you have to win, Nyandoro. Do this for yourself, not because I might chose you over my own husband."

Ny clenched her jaw at the mention of Duni's husband. All month while she'd been changing herself, she thought about Duni's husband. Wondering if he was really a fool and ignoring Duni's beauty in favor of the other wives. Or if he was pumping between her legs every night, easily getting the privilege Ny was working so hard for. As useless as those thoughts were, she couldn't stop having them.

"I *am* doing this for myself," she said. "My parents like having me around, and my baba tells me that he's proud of what I'm doing."

"What about your brothers? You're practically ignoring them, but for what reason?"

"Duni, don't pretend that when you said those things to me, you didn't mean for me to change and become the woman you want." Ny balanced her hands on her thighs, hoping and praying she was right. In her eyes, Duni had practically dared her to grow up. "So, tell me, am I now the woman you want?" She felt Duni close to her, the heat of her body just a touch away. Her breath smelled of a recent dinner and mint leaves. "Do you want me?"

A sigh left Duni's lips. "I…" She drew back and took her breath, her lips, and her heat with her.

Ny straightened her spine against the disappointment. At least her father was proud of her now. At least she knew her mother better than she had before. At least—

Duni kissed her.

Ny gasped and drew in the taste of Duni into her mouth. Mint and sweetness and the press of her soft lips. Ny's heart thudded in her chest, and her lashes fluttered with surprise. Then she realized what was happening. *Duni was actually kissing her!* Ny quivered and kissed back. She and Duni crashed together, mouths pressing firmly, hands grasping in heated intent. Ny tingled every place they touched.

Her head spun with the reality of what was happening, her fantasies no longer confined to her sleeping mat, but made real under moonlight with the quiet rushing of the river nearby. Emboldened, she touched even more than she ever had in dreams, her fingers slipping under the thin *kanga* to skate over Duni's waist beads, her warm skin. Duni shuddered and pulled back with a moan. She licked her lips, took a moment to regain her breath. Her eyes dipped down. "This is dangerous for me."

Yes, it would be dangerous if Duni's husband found out. But they would be discreet, they would only touch when they were alone. They would only speak of their intimacies to each other.

"We need to be careful," Ny said. It didn't even cross her mind to give up what she'd just found with Duni.

"Yes." Duni's tongue appeared to wet her lips, and Ny stopped thinking.

She leaned in again to press a kiss back to Duni's mouth, entranced by the softness of it, the plump dampness like ripe fruit. The faint taste of oil and honey berries lingered on those soft lips. Had Duni worn the oil for her?

It excited her, the thought that Duni had enticed her to the river not just to talk, but to kiss. Like this. Ny licked the enticing flavor on Duni's mouth, the sweetness of the berries and the much more delicious taste of her mouth's natural essence. She wa like a fruit Ny had only hoped of tasting, always hanging high on the vine and out of reach. And now, here she was, practically in Ny's lap. She groaned and pressed closer.

Duni drew back, smiling. She curved her palm around Ny's cheek. "Like this."

She kissed Ny again, lips pressing as delicately as flower petals, leaving Ny slightly dizzy, a hunt in the forest that pushed her body to the very limit. The feel of her was intoxicating and weakening, strange in a way she'd never considered. She'd been interested in kissing girls before, but too nervous to try. Nervous in a way she hadn't been about jumping from cliffs or diving into the river. Duni's lips parted. Her tongue gently breaking the seam of Ny's mouth. And her thoughts flew away, a flock of wild birds.

Heat pooled in her belly with each stroke of Duni's tongue. A shiver rippled through her body. It felt dangerous, this kind of kissing, her heartbeat speeding up too fast to be safe, her breath stolen, palms wet. But she didn't want to stop. Duni taught her everything she needed to know. That a kiss could be a greeting, an apology, an unmaking. Duni's tongue slid against Ny's, firm and slick. Her hands gripped her waist, sinking into soft flesh. Her thoughts were gone. Everything was only sensation. Wet agitation between her legs. A sound like pain from her throat. Or was it from Duni? Soft noises, squirming against Ny on the rock, their chests pressed together, nipples rubbing, aching. Ny pulled away with a gasp, desperately needing to breathe.

Duni's breath puffed against her lips. "Are you all right?"

Ny shook her head. "My heart is beating in my chest. It feels like I'm going to die."

"Die?"

"Yes. No…I can't explain it properly. It…it feels good." Her hands drifted down to Duni's hips. "You feel good." She dipped her head into the curve of Duni's neck, smelled her, that soft place where neck met shoulder, the scent of her hair, of wood fires and honey flower oil. Ny licked her throat, and Duni shivered against her.

"I knew you would be a fast learner."

Ny drew back. "How do you know I haven't done this before?"

Duni laughed, trailed a hand down Ny's bare back. "There are no secrets in this village, Nyandoro." She flicked a thumb across Ny's lower lip. "Besides, your touch feels too tentative for you to be anything but untouched. And I am surprised. I thought you…you would have had many offers."

"I've had offers. But there's never been anyone I wanted, no one but you."

"You humble me."

"Does that mean I can taste you now?" She dropped her gaze to Duni's hips so there would be no mistaking her meaning.

Duni smothered her laughter in Ny's shoulder. "A very fast learner. And eager too." She lifted her head, eyes still shining with mirth. "Not here. Not tonight."

"Then where? I…"

Was there some way she could tell Duni that she ached? Her nipples hurt, but the pain was sweet. Between her legs was slippery, and an ever deeper ache was there. She wanted to touch herself but knew it would be even better if Duni touched her. "I want to touch you, and I want you to touch me."

"I know. Soon." The humor vanished from her eyes. "Remember, we must be careful."

Ny shivered at the seriousness in her voice. The lust drained from her, common sense slowly replacing it. Duni could lose everything, she realized again. Was this worth it? "Are you sure?"

Duni shook her head. "No. You don't get to chase me then change your mind when I say yes. Now, *I'm* the one saying yes." She leaned in to kiss Ny once again, her gaze flying to the path far up the river. "I have to go. They'll miss me if I'm away much longer." She pulled the comb from her hair. It was the same one from the first night they met by the river. "Take this and think of me."

"I always think of you." But she took the comb anyway and slid it into the neckline of her *kanga*.

With another look at the path, Duni clambered down from the rock. In the dark, Ny could feel Duni's gaze on her mouth, on the slope of her shoulders. "See you soon."

Duni was quick. Bare feet slapping quietly against the hard ground, then she was gone.

On the riverbank, Ny splashed water on her face and took a moment to gather herself. By the time she stepped through the doorway of her father and mother's hut, she was calm again, her heart was back to its normal pace. Her father was in the sitting room, smoking his pipe. He looked up at her, his sharp eyes missing nothing.

"Did your visit go well?" he asked.

Ny's face grew hot and she looked away. She only just restrained herself from pressing her cool hands to her hot face. She didn't bother denying she'd been at the river to meet someone. "Yes, Baba."

"You will be careful?" He leveled a gaze on her, filled with concern and love.

"Yes, I will. I am."

"You will be careful of what, Nyandoro?" Her mother wandered into the sitting room, the edges of her hair wet from a bath. She looked tired, like she'd had a long day too. With a low sigh, she draped herself on top of her husband, resting her head over his heart. He pressed a kiss into her palm before taking another puff from his pipe. Smoke wreathed the air above his head, trailing toward the ceiling.

"She will be careful to invest where there is a high probability of a positive return for everyone involved." Her father glanced at her before turning his gaze once again to his wife.

"Is that right, Nyandoro? You have been investing unwisely?"

"I'm not sure about the wisdom of it, Iya. But it's something I'd like to do."

A delicate wrinkle settled on her mother's brow. "All right. As your baba says, be careful."

"Of course." But any care she would take was balanced precariously against the lust that sparked between her and Duni on the riverbank. "It's time for me to get some sleep."

"Rest well." Her father gave her a meaningful look.

She left them to clean up and find her sleeping mat. After the long day's walk and negotiations by her father's side, Ny's body was tired. But her mind was not. She couldn't stop thinking about Duni's kisses and the way they had moved into each other on the riverbank, the sweetness that swayed between them, the way her heart beat so fast she thought she would not survive the next kiss.

But here she was. Alone on her sleeping mat, and aching. She squeezed her legs together, holding her breath as the tightening only amplified the sensation. The eucalyptus leaves and lavender blooms in her mattress rustled as she rolled over, releasing more of their scent. Ny held her breath.

When all she heard was the quiet murmur of her parents' continuing conversation, she squeezed her thighs tightly again and again, slowly building the honeyed feeling, the slick between her thighs, her deepening breaths. Ny held herself still on the mat, only moving her internal muscles while her imagination explored what her hands had not been able to.

She thought of Duni's mouth. The sensation of her body through their clothes, the drifting pearls of her waist beads under her fingers, the plump fruit of her bottom. A quiet gasp ghosted past Ny's wet lips. She imagined parting Duni's thighs to find her wet and eager, her nipples hard under her tongue… Heat crashed over Ny in an unrelenting wave, and her throat clutched from an imprisoned cry. She bit into her fist and squeezed her eyes tight as her core fluttered with release. Long moments later, her breathing slowed and she drifted into sleep.

A woman walked at Nyandoro's side. Although she wanted to, she couldn't look away from the woman's feet, slender with bones as delicate as a bird's, their beauty only enhanced by strapped sandals. The ground was dark and brown, healthy from a downpour of recent rain. Nyandoro wore a cloth that covered her from throat to ankles, a soft fabric of bright blue that was soft on her skin and swirled like butterfly wings around her bare feet.

"Do you know what you want?" The woman's question pulled Nyandoro's eyes from her feet, up her body, to the waist

cloth that dipped with the elegant and sensual sway of her hips, naked waist, and her long collar made from thousands of different colored beads hiding her breasts from Nyandoro's gaze. The woman had a slender neck, a narrow face, hair braided in an intricate style like a crown. She had eyes as vicious as the ocean.

"Of course I know what I want," Nyandoro said. Once she found the woman's eyes, she could not look away. They were roiling and white, but oddly soothing.

"Then take them." A corner of the woman's mouth curved up, a double-edged invitation. "Make no apologies for the things you desire."

"If only it were that simple."

"It is. Take what you want. Because the rest of the world will take what it wants whether or not you are ready."

They walked through the grass of a rich and fertile field. Giraffes bounded across the earth with a joyous pounding of hooves, scattering birds from a nearby leafless tree and into the bright blue sky. The sweet salt smell of the ocean drifted on the air. A tall mountain wreathed in clouds hovered over everything, a familiar giant Nyandoro had seen on the horizon of her life since she was born but had never been this close to. It was a beauty she'd never experienced in her waking life and was sure she'd never see again. A breeze rose up and brushed sensation over Nyandoro's sensitive skin. She shivered in the wake of it, but from pleasure, not from cold.

"What will it take from me?" She parroted the woman's word back at her.

"Everything you're not ready to give." The woman's eyes were like half-moons, narrowing with the sadness of her smile.

When Ny woke up, only remnants of the dream remained. The woman's pretty feet. Her dagger-sharp smile. But the sensations she'd felt while in that world—unlimited freedom, curiosity about everything—lightened her every step. With her mind still on the mysterious woman of her dreams, Ny tidied her sleeping mat and shook out the thin blankets to hang outside in the sun.

Still distracted, she nearly bumped into her mother who looked ready for the day with her hair in neat braids, her oldest cloth wrapped around her waist and pinned up between her legs like the pants men and women of Arabia wore. The scent of incense clung to her. Her mother steadied her with an unfocused smile.

"Iya, I'm helping you today."

Her mother seemed to shake herself. She touched a hand to her cheek and blinked at Ny. "I don't have anything for you to do to today, Nyandoro."

Her mother's use of her whole name brought more of the dream back to her. The woman had called her that, right? Ny forced her attention back to their conversation.

"Are you sure?" she asked. "I have time today."

"Yes, I'm sure. Go ask your baba if he needs help if you're so desperate to be of use today." She squeezed Ny's shoulder and walked away.

It was only when her mother came back with her hands full of bananas and mangoes did Ny realize she was making obeisance at the altar of Yemaya. It was the fifth time she'd noticed in the last three days, and the increased attention to the shrine seemed strange. Usually her mother made her offerings only once a week.

Because she couldn't think of what else to do, she went in search of Kizo. She found him on the steps of his new favorite bar, a cup of liquor by his side, and sitting in a ring of mostly older men playing a game with dice. He looked clean and fresh, like he'd just climbed from the river, his hair still wet. Kizo wore a new beaded bracelet around his wrist.

"Ah, is this a stranger that I see?" He squinted up at Ny like he didn't recognize her.

"Quit playing around." She shoved his shoulder.

Kizo made a dismissive noise and tossed his cowrie shells into the small pile already in the circle. "I'm finished," he said.

The men only nodded and carried on as if he didn't just forfeit the equivalent of a day's pay for some. Kizo picked up his drink, gestured for Ny to follow, and jogged up the steps into the bar. Ny ordered a drink for herself this time then followed him out to the rear verandah.

"So what pulled you away from Iya and Baba today? Did the house burn down?" He put his feet up on the root of a tree and sat back in the chair, looking remarkably unconcerned for someone who just asked if the family home just burned down.

"No. I decided to stop being an idiot about this whole growing up thing."

"And since you are no longer trying to be a grown-up, the first person you came to find is me?"

"Exactly."

Kizo's mouth tilted in a smile. "How are you, sister?"

"Tired of being an adult." She sighed.

"If you'd asked me, I could've told you there's nothing redeeming in it. But why listen to me? I wasn't the one you were bending over for."

"Stop. Don't say that." But she could tell he'd been hurt by her absence.

Her relationship with Kizo wasn't the same as with her other brothers. If she hurt any of the others, or vice versa, a good wrestling match or the passage of one day would put the hurt behind them. But what she had with Kizo was a stronger, more deeply rooted bond whose hurts could not be superficially bandaged. Ny swallowed the lump of self-disappointment in her throat. If she hadn't had her head so far up her ass, or Duni's to be more accurate, she'd have realized just how much she was hurting her brother. Ny put her drink down and grasped his arm, strong and firm, just below the elbow. "I *am* sorry."

Their eyes met, and he gave her a real smile this time. "I know you are, sister." He grasped her arm in the same place and they leaned forward to press their foreheads together.

"Do you forgive me?"

"Absolutely. But next time, I won't make it so easy."

"There won't be a next time." She didn't want to be that stupid again.

"Good."

They sat together, drinking in silence while the sounds of the bar floated behind them—men swearing, dice rolling in a cup, raucous laughter. The sky before them was clear and blue with only a few ribbons of clouds. A bird cawed in the distance. From even farther away, a lion roared in warning.

"So what have you been doing since you've had to stay out of trouble without me?"

"Who says I was staying out of trouble?"

"No new scars." She looked him over with a smile. His pretty face glowed with light sweat from the hotter than normal day, and he wasn't walking with his shield or spear, just a young man out for a day in town.

"I'm better than you at avoiding getting hit, sister."

They grinned at each other. Since they were young, their father had sparred with them and taught them more than the basics of fighting and self-defense. Kizo wasn't the best fighter of the siblings, but he was the one who avoided conflict the best, either through his speed or wily tongue.

"Yes, you are," Ny laughed into her cup.

They shared the cozy privacy of the balcony, trading mild insults and laughter until a rowdy group stumbled out to claim the two empty tables nearby.

Kizo put aside his empty cup and jerked his chin in her direction. "Are you ready to go?"

"Whenever you are."

"Good. We have much more interesting things to do with our afternoon." A wicked grin lit up his face.

She finished her drink in one quick gulp, winced at the burn of the alcohol down her throat and in her belly. "Lead the way."

It turned out he had his weapon after all. On their way out of the bar, he dipped his hand into a hidden corner and plucked up his spear, clean and recently sharpened. He carried it easily beside him, sharp end up like a walking stick.

"Are you sure you still know how to use that thing?" she teased him.

"Try me and find out. It hasn't been that many days since we've been hunting, has it?"

They left the bar and headed away from the village, walking under the canopy that hovered just below the verandah they just left. Through the wreaths of fern and the wide tree limbs, Ny could see that someone had already taken the table she and Kizo had shared. Two women. They were leaning close and laughing. Something about the way they spoke to each other reminded Ny of Duni. She looked away.

"What's on your mind so heavy, Ny?" Apparently bored with carrying his spear like a normal person, Kizo began to carelessly twirl his spear in front of him. "Or shouldn't I ask?" The spear stirred the air with a low whooshing sound.

"It's the same reason as the last time."

"Does that mean you've at least taken her to bed already?" He asked like he already knew the answer.

Ny made a rude gesture at him with her fist.

It was sad, but everyone knew her exploits were non-existent. She was a good girl, and the only scandal she caused was being related to Hakim and Adli. The twins were good enough in the village but were so very bad elsewhere. They visited the divorced woman who, even though unmarried with no children, managed a household and a herd of goats just from the "patronage" of local men alone.

Hakim and Adli were not the woman's only visitors but were the most visible, especially since they both visited her at the same time, left her at the same time, and were never shy about entering and leaving her luxurious, if small, hut. Just as everyone knew this, everyone also seemed to know that Ny was a virgin. She just hoped they didn't also know who she was hoping to lose that cumbersome virginity with.

"I wish I wasn't so inexperienced," she said.

"There's only one way to get experience." Kizo gave her a laughing look, still twirling his spear. "Get a practice lover. That way, when it's time to finally enjoy your time with Duni, you'll know what to do."

Ny scratched her neck, uncomfortable at the very idea of touching someone else that way. "I'm not sure if I can do that."

Kizo grinned, all trouble. "Let's go give it a try."

Their path through the forest took them the long way around their closest neighbor, Elephant Village where Nitu was to find a wife within the coming season. The drummers of their farther neighbor, Sky Village, were rumored to be the best and, on certain feast days, the sound of their djembes could be heard for miles, joyful and loud. The women were very pretty, and many of them were luscious enough to have entertained the twins a time or two.

"Hakim and Adli have worn out our family's welcome here in Sky Village." Kizo laughed.

"But I bet not among the women, or some of the prettier men," Ny muttered.

It was market day in Sky Village, and the long stretch of road leading into the village gates overflowed with stalls spread out on both sides. Vendors, mostly women, called out to Kizo.

"Come, boy with the pretty skin. Come and see these firm yams you can take home to your iya."

"I don't want to buy any yams at the moment. Can I just get a squeeze?" Kizo flirted back, laughing and flashing his white teeth while the women hung their breasts over abundant piles of yams, cho-chos, and melons.

"Your spear looks like it needs a warm place for the night, young man." A woman held up a thick melon with a laughing smile. "I have the perfect one for you."

No one said anything so suggestive to Ny. They called to her, sang out sweetly. "A pretty cloth for a pretty miss." But nothing nearly as entertaining as the offers Kizo got.

"They never tease me the way they tease you." She mock-pouted after they left the market women behind.

"But you don't want them to tease, and your face says so." Kizo adjusted his waist pouch, making room in it for the mango he'd bought from one particularly persistent woman. "You're not as unreadable as you think, sister."

Ny's father was teaching her to keep her emotions hidden, to become a better diplomat, but it was difficult to learn something that felt like a lie. *It is not a lie,* her father had tried to reassure her. *It is a mask you wear, like in war. Once the battle is over, pull off that mask to reveal your real self once again.* Ny still had a long way to go. She had not yet learned to wear a mask.

She and Kizo walked under the wide archway into Sky Village. Crossed spears and the dried head of a lion perched in the village insignia (a circle of clouds broken by twin lightning bolts) warned away those who wished to do the villagers harm.

Sky Village was beautiful with clean and well-swept roads, plentiful animals, and well-maintained houses. On the wide main street, she and Kizo passed girls and women with baskets on their heads and children strapped to their backs, old men sitting beneath shade trees and fanning themselves with wide green leaves. The smell of eucalyptus and ripe fruit played on the breeze.

This was one of the few villages that had asked the Rain Queen for help. Although the queen was primarily a figure of speculation and myth, everyone agreed she was a godling consort of Yemaya, and an old, ugly woman who surrounded herself with beautiful virgins to distract anyone who saw her from her terrible looks. She granted rain to any village who paid the proper respect by sacrificing to her their most beautiful virgin daughter. Sky Village had made its sacrifice and now flourished with rains that pounded its rich dark earth with the regularity of the full moon. It was a lush and green village, the only one for many *maili*.

"It's nice here," Ny said.

A group of women, most around Duni's age, sauntered gracefully past, heading into the village with water gourds balanced on their heads. They were young and sweet looking, their flesh soft and plump with youth, their white teeth flashing as they laughed and talked together.

One woman, her rounded hips swinging with each step, paused to look at Kizo. Her waist beads were low on her soft belly and her breasts looked inviting beneath the cloth. She adjusted the gourd on her head, lifting her hand to show off the rise of her breasts and the dipping curve of her waist. The other women with her turned sly looks to Kizo and Ny.

"It is," Kizo said. "*Very* nice here."

The women giggled and preened under Kizo's interested gaze, some even eyed Ny in blatant speculation. A tall and voluptuous woman with the wild beauty of the Serengeti in her face, touched the tip of her tongue to her mouth and gave Ny the most intense eye fuck she'd ever experienced. Heat prickled in Ny's face and down her spine. She couldn't look away. Her hands hung heavy and awkward at her sides, and she wished suddenly for something to do with them. What was wrong with her? She wanted Duni, not this stranger.

"Relax, sister," Kizo said with quiet laughter in his voice. "I think she's just looking."

Ny backed away.

The girl was nice to look at, a true daughter of Oshun with her burning gaze that promised the sweetest honey between her thighs. But her forwardness was unsettling. Ny was the one used to making the advances. This woman looked like she would happily throw Ny in the street, throw up her skirts, and feast between her legs under the hot sun.

The women kept walking, but their paces were deliberately slow, hips swaying, glances tossed over their shoulders at Ny and Kizo.

"You can practice on her all night if you want."

Ny almost tripped over her own feet when the girl looked back again and snared Ny with her eyes, slowly drawing a hand down and over her backside. The invitation couldn't be clearer.

"I think she would eat me alive."

"I think that's the idea, sister."

She shivered and slowed her footsteps to put more distance between herself and the sensual woman. "I'm not quite sure I'm ready for that."

Kizo laughed. "With that attitude, you'll stay untouched until the day Duni wrestles you to her husband's sleeping mat."

She shoved at his shoulder, annoyed at his mention of Duni and her husband. "Don't be a dick."

"I am what I am." Kizo grinned.

He wasn't wrong. Her brother had always been uniquely himself. His long-legged strides easily caught him up with the women. From where she hung back, Ny watched him silently flirt with them, walking in a way that emphasized the sleek musculature of his body, the thrust of his sex under his loin cloth. He smiled and dipped his head, suggestively gripping his spear until Ny thought she needed to give him some time alone.

"These women would teach you everything you need to know about pleasing your married woman." He didn't look away from the women who seemed like they were silently stripping him bare for their feast.

Ny shook her head. "I don't want that," she said. "They are not for me."

Kizo glanced at her, then back at the women. "All right." He shrugged and abruptly quickened his pace to pass them. Just like that, he was finished. "In that case, I know a guy here who can get you a new, longer blade for your spear. Interested?"

Ny glanced back at the women who were falling farther and farther behind. But Kizo didn't. If she wasn't interested in having the women teach her about making love, then he seemed content to dismiss his own desires.

"Yes, I am interested."

"Good," he said. "Maybe we can get some sparring in while we're here. One of my spears might as well get some action."

Ny rolled her eyes.

CHAPTER FIVE

After the day spent with Kizo, Ny swore to find a balance between the life she had and the one she wanted. She didn't want to lose her family, her brothers, to win Duni's heart, and she didn't want to keep living as a child and lose Duni.

When she found time for herself again, she searched for Duni among her sister wives on washday at the river. On the riverbank, she waved at the women she passed, including Duni, calling out and teasing them about the sheer amount of clothes in their baskets, and kept going. The rocky river's edge where she and Duni met that first night was quiet and empty. There, Ny put aside her small basket of clothes and tied her skirt around her thighs like her mother often did when she was doing her most difficult housework.

Then she walked quickly down the concealed path that ran parallel to the river and was sheltered behind high bushes. Through the bushes, she saw Duni on the riverbank with the youngest sister wife, the basket held between her legs as she sorted through the clothes, head bent beneath the bright light of the sun that kissed her skin the way Ny longed to.

She seemed to be teaching the young one to properly wash the clothes. The little one was younger than Ny, too young to be a wife. But the village elders had allowed the marriage. Only because the child's parents had little wealth and seemed able to do nothing but sell their child to a lecherous old man. The child's head, neatly braided and tight around her face, barely came to Duni's shoulder.

At one point, Ny thought the young wife looked up and saw her. But she must have been wrong because the child looked up at Duni with a blinding smile then quickly dipped her head back to the clothes.

Ny watched them for a long moment before the child moved toward the other wives to tend to the small basket Duni entrusted her with.

Once Duni was alone, Ny whistled softly to get her attention. Her sharp eyes quickly found Ny. After a brief glance around to make sure no one was paying attention to her, she slipped away from the water and crept into the bush.

"What are you doing here?" Duni asked.

"Washing, like you." But Ny didn't stop her hand from touching, a light stroke of Duni's bare side. Duni shivered and swayed toward her, eyes falling closed. Temptation and beauty. Ny ached to touch her even more, to kiss her. But the other girls were too close.

"Come with me."

Duni bit her lip, looking uncertain, tempted. She peered through the bushes at her sister wives who sat together, laughing and splashing water more than washing clothes, their conversations like separate but complementary songs on the breeze.

"I can't stay long," Duni said.

"This is just for a little while, I promise."

When Duni finally nodded, Ny tugged her quietly down the hidden path and to her secluded bathing hole. Although the place was easy to find, there was no one else there, just the sun falling like prayers over the smooth black rocks, the quiet gurgle of the river running faster here than anywhere else near the village, the staccato chattering of birds. The air smelled dry, no more false promise of rain in it. But rain wasn't what Ny needed now.

"I missed you." She breathed into Duni's soft throat, hands sinking into the damp fabric over her hips.

She felt Duni smile against her temple. "You saw me just yesterday."

"But I didn't get to touch you."

It was true that she could see Duni every day. The village was a place of habits and routine. Any day she wanted to find Duni, she knew where to look.

Monday was wash day. On Tuesday, she helped take the goats to pasture. Wednesday was the day the wives did a majority of the housework, and if Ny walked by at the right time, she could see Duni or one of the other wives shaking out the mats just outside her husband's hut. Thursday was the day Duni helped out at the school. Friday was market day. On Saturday, their family worshipped at the large Shangó shrine at the center of the village, and Sunday was the day they cleaned and prepared most of the meat for the rest of the week. And every night of those days, Duni escaped to her rock for peace and quiet and dreams.

"Can I touch you now?"

Duni pulled back, a smile in her eyes. "Yes, but I have to get back soon." She tugged Ny down into the soft grass with their backs against the rocks. "I am here now. Why aren't you touching me?"

She didn't have to ask twice. Ny stroked her face, caressing the miracle of softness with careful fingertips. Her heart thumped hard in her chest, filling her with warmth and uncontrolled agitation. "You're so beautiful." The unfamiliar power of the emotions she felt for Duni made her heart beat faster, her throat a little drier.

Their mouths met, already parted and wet. Ny shivered. She groaned into the heat of Duni's lips, hands curving around the slender and sun-warmed shoulders to pull her close and closer. Pleasure and excitement fluttered in her stomach.

There was something in the way Duni fit her hands around Ny's hips, how she whispered soft words of encouragement when Ny lost her shyness and let her own hands wander, that reminded her of the woman from Sky Village, the daughter of Oshun. Her enticing heat and overt sensuality. But instead of making her feel uncomfortable, this heat made Ny want Duni more.

Her fingers sank into Duni's shoulders and her tongue timidly flickered out. Duni groaned softly and gripped her tighter, sucking on Ny's tongue and making her gasp. Ny jerked back and slammed her thighs together against the flood of wetness between them.

"Oh!" All of her tingled with astonishment.

"You like that?"

Duni didn't give her the chance to answer. She licked the corner of Ny's mouth, startling her lips apart again, and Ny kissed back, eager to experience that sharp stab of pleasure again. Their kiss was longer this time, a breathless moment of sensation, the slick mating of tongues, lips bruising against teeth, shallowing breaths.

Duni pulled back with a wet sound. "I have more for you."

She took Ny's hand, watching her face, and slowly guided it between her thighs. Ny shivered when her fingers encountered hot flesh, wet flesh. Duni trembled against her, jerking wordlessly from that single touch. She opened her thighs wider, and Ny explored the slick wet with her fingers.

"Duni, I…" Ny slid her fingers deeper and Duni bit her lip, breathing quickly.

"I know." Duni moved her hips in slow circles. "Give me more."

Ny stroked more of the silken flesh, guided by how she touched herself in secret, and firmly caressed the firm bud between Duni's thighs in tandem with the curling thrust of her fingers. Duni whimpered, her lower lip caught between her teeth. Her head fell forward onto Ny's shoulder. "Yes... more. Do it like...like that." Her words were whispered, urgent. Quick. But Ny didn't want to rush. It felt too incredible. The sun pouring over her shoulders, a slow sweet burn, the light gilding Duni's skin, the rising musk of her sex between them, her urgent breaths. The soft wetness around her fingers was a blessing she never expected, but now that she had it, she couldn't get enough. She was wet and aching just from the feel of Duni's most intimate flesh around hers, from the sounds she was making.

Ny curled her fingers down the back of Duni's neck, needing that grounding touch while her other hand pulled the wet, kissing sounds from between Duni's thighs, the gasps from her mouth.

"You're so good to me," Duni hissed. "So good..." She bit Ny's shoulder, a sharp and unexpected pain. Her hips jerked and rocked with each breath.

Ny shuddered, slid her fingers more firmly in long and hard strokes that had Duni's heated breath puffing against her skin. The heat of it, the moisture that slid even more from between her thighs. In moments, Duni was shivering against her, teeth buried in Ny's shoulder, a pain that pushed Ny's hips into the ground and moved her fingers faster inside Duni. Faster. Duni's muffled scream of completion vibrated through her. A wild motion. Ny felt her body jerk hard in a sudden and sympathetic pleasure that left her stunned, her mouth hanging open as she swallowed hard and her lashes fluttered against damp cheeks.

Duni's breath was loud in the bush, puffing and hot and intimate, echoing the frantic drumbeat between Ny's legs. Ny swayed in the aftermath of her pleasure, a deeper lethargy than when she touched herself in the dark secret of night. She lifted her head and reluctantly dragged her damp fingers from their sweet haven between Duni's thighs.

"I knew you'd be a fast learner at this too." Duni's smile was drugged and beautiful. "I want you to do this to me again. And I want to put my mouth on you, to show you how wonderful it feels."

Ny shivered. "I want that too." Her voice was low and rough. It didn't sound like her at all.

"You would—" Duni's voice cut off at the sound of a high voice far down the river but closer than it should have been. She leapt to her feet with a soft curse. "I have to go."

Ny nodded dumbly, her mouth already wet from the desire to drag Duni back down and taste the heat directly from between her legs. But that wasn't being *careful*. "Okay." But before Duni could move, she grabbed her hand. "Right now," Ny said, "I am happy."

Duni looked down at Ny, a smile touched with sadness on her lips. "You are beautiful and you are strong. No one has ever denied you anything. You've never suffered. Of course you are happy." She gently pulled away. "Now, I really have to go."

Duni smoothed her cloth down over her hips, then, after a quick glance over her shoulder at Ny, dashed through the bush and toward her co-wives downriver. Ny sat pressed into the rock, her body still singing with the aftereffects of their kisses, the explosive touches they shared. It was a long time before she was able to stand up and pretend to wash her clothes.

After finishing her small amount of laundry, Ny practically danced her way home. Her happiness was uncontained. After singing out a "hello!" to the fifth person who looked at her as if she'd lost her mind, she realized she needed to leave the village or risk giving away her secret. She changed into her hunting clothes, loincloth and the single band of cloth tied over her breasts and around her neck, and left for her favorite tall tree on the edge of the village. She sat on its sturdiest branch, the breeze of the late afternoon breeze brushing her face and throat, when she felt the vibrations in the trunk, someone else climbing up the tree. Ny looked down. Kizo's worried face peered up at her. She frowned. He was never worried.

She swung down to a lower branch to meet him halfway. "What's wrong?"

The branch jumped as Kizo landed next to her, his chest gleaming with sweat as if he'd run all the way from the village. "Duni's husband. He just threw her out."

The tree trunk scraped Ny's back when she unconsciously flinched away from the news. Her heart leaped in her throat. "Why?"

"Don't play games with me, Nyandoro."

"But we haven't…we haven't." She shook her head, her tongue too heavy for her to speak. But they were careful!

"Well, he thinks you have. One of the wives told him Duni met a lover at the river and hiked up her skirts for him. Or her. Is that true?"

Ny shook her head again, still unable to speak.

"I don't know whether to say congratulations or curse you for a damn fool." He grabbed her arm. "Come."

They clambered to the ground, their feet dropping quietly on the thick but drying grass. The family of gazelles Ny had been watching jerked their heads toward her and Kizo, still nibbling at the grass but watching them carefully.

"What's going on?" Ny asked as she scrambled to catch up to her brother. Her thoughts raced from one useless idea to the next. She had to set things right. "I should go to her."

Kizo stopped so fast she almost ran into his back. "You shouldn't do a damn thing that could make her situation worse."

"But isn't this bad enough?"

"The wife didn't tell anyone it was you." Kizo nodded in approval, then started walking again.

"That's good." Ny chewed her lower lip. That was very good. But... "I wonder why."

"The stupid girl probably didn't see any of what happened between the two of you," Kizo said. "Maybe she just smelled Duni's wet cho-cho and knew something happened at the river, but not with whom. I'm surprised her husband didn't put two and two together, especially after what happened with you and Duni at the market. Then again, he was never the smartest monkey in the tree."

It wasn't long before they reached the village. Even from its outskirts, Ny could hear a commotion that told her things weren't quite as she'd left them. The sound of women crying. The agitation of raised voices. A chorus of spiteful laughter from young children. Was all that because of Duni? Because of her?

"She needs me," Ny said, walking faster. A spike of fear darted down her spine.

"No. You can't afford to be seen right now."

"But nobody knows that I'm the one."

"Yes," Kizo agreed. "So let's keep it that way. The game will be up the second you show up in your hunting skins offering her a shoulder to cry on and a nipple for her to suck."

He took her to his house at the very edge of the village, a secluded home where he could maintain his privacy away from the villagers' prying eyes. Kizo's choice not to live in the family compound had always hurt their parents, but he kept a sleeping mat at Nitu's house simply to appease them, even if he seldom actually slept there.

The path to his house was mostly dark, lit only by the torches from other houses they passed along the way. No one on the path looked at them twice, only nodded in greeting or made some comment on the coolness of the evening or likelihood of rain. Most of the villagers, it seemed, were walking in the opposite direction toward the main square and the sound of all the excitement. A man's angry voice, the words mostly indecipherable, rose and fell in the night.

Ny and Kizo exchanged a look.

"That stupid man doesn't have the sense the almighty Olodumare gave a chicken," he said.

Ny shivered from more than just the evening's coolness. "But even the most stupid of men have power here."

Kizo made a distressed sound and kept walking. At the front door to his house, he stopped.

"Wait here," he said before disappearing through the doorway.

Even though Ny had left the village to find quiet, and had relished it perched high in the marula tree overlooking the savanna, the silence Kizo now left her with made her uneasy. The relentless shriek of insects scraped over her nerves, and the more accustomed her eyes grew to the darkness, the more she imagined seeing Duni, crouched in the dirt, cowering away from slaps and pinches, tears rolling down her bruised face. In the gloom, she wrapped her own hands around her shoulders, trembling. Ny felt sick with what she had caused. If it wasn't for her and her endless wants, Duni would still have her sister wives, she would still have a place to sleep tonight. She would still have a good life.

Her dull nails found enough sharpness to dig into her shoulders. Ny hissed from the pain. It was only a little bit of what she deserved.

A light flickered on in the house, outlining the small shuttered window, then the door creaked open.

"Come in," Kizo said quietly.

Inside the house, a pair of candles illuminated the small gathering room, revealing its low table, couch, the impala hide—Kizo's first kill—stretched across the wall, and her brother's serious face. He gave her one of the candles and waved her toward his sleeping room. "Back there."

Ny frowned and opened her mouth to ask him what he was up to, but he made an impatient sound and shoved her toward and through the open doorway. The heavy wooden door slammed shut behind her.

She stumbled into the room, the candle gripped in both hands. "Kizo! What—?"

But a low sniffle nearby cut her off. She spun around, candle raised high. Ny drew in a surprised breath.

Duni huddled on her brother's sleeping mat, her face ravaged with tears. The candlelight flickered over her body that was pulled tight on itself, making her look smaller. Shadows and light crawled over the lost expression on her face.

"He threw me away like garbage," she croaked. "Just on her word alone." She didn't say who "her" was, but Ny had a pretty good idea who she was talking about. "Now I have no place to go."

Ny sank down next to Duni on the mat, her knees weak from both relief and worry. Duni wasn't in the middle of the village being publicly beaten by her husband, but she'd lost everything now. Absolutely everything.

Despite the few conversations she'd had with Duni, Ny knew nearly everything about her. She knew that Duni's parents had been old when she was born and they died not long after she married Ibada, relieved that she had a man to take care of her. All she had in the village were distant relatives. No one who would be willing to take on the responsibility of a divorced and penniless woman.

Duni wiped her face with trembling fingers. "He said he will keep my dowry, the goats my baba and iya gave for the marriage." It was his right but was still a bastard thing to do since Duni had no one else to care for her. She didn't even have her own piece of land to grow crops for the market.

"I'll be fine," Duni said like she was trying to convince herself. "I know I will, but right now I just feel like even the Orishas have abandoned me."

"You haven't been abandoned, Duni. I'm here. I won't let anything happen to you." Ny moved closer, but Duni jerked away from her.

"I knew I shouldn't have given in to you." She growled the words, like a cornered lion, brutal and angry. "I knew it, but I was stupid and blinded by your beauty and that damn charm of yours."

Ny flinched. It was nothing she hadn't thought herself, but it still hurt coming from Duni. She steeled herself against more vicious truths, but the fight drained from Duni as easily as it came. She clenched her hands in her hair, so hard that it must have hurt. Ny took her hands and gently pulled them from her hair.

"Please don't hurt yourself. Please don't. Everything will be all right."

"Of course it will. No thanks to you."

A soft knock sounded on the door. At her call to enter, the wooden door creaked open and Kizo stood in the faint light.

"I'll spend the rest of the night with Nitu," he said in their mother's Ndebele language. "You can stay here and take care of Duni." The corners of his mouth twitched. "Give her *whatever* she needs."

Even though Duni didn't understand what her brother said, Ny darted a glance at her, embarrassment climbing hot and fast in her cheeks. "Kizo!"

"What? She's hurt and needs comfort beyond empty words. Besides, I know you want to feast your fill of her cho-cho." He chuckled, a low rumbling sound at odds with the heavy tension of the room. "See you tomorrow."

The door creaked shut, then he was gone. The only remnants of him the low sound of singing as he made his way through the small house and out the front door.

"What did he say?" Duni asked although it didn't seem like she cared. While her tears had stopped falling, misery still lined her face.

"He said you can stay the night here. No one will bother you."

"Please thank him for me."

Duni straightened her spine and got up from the sleeping mat. A quick swipe of her hands across her face took care of the remnants of her tears, then she was walking away from Ny, taking careful steps around the small room. Her breaths were loud, tremulous.

Ny wrapped her arms around her upraised legs, rested her chin on her knees, and allowed Duni the space she needed. She couldn't imagine being without the only family she ever knew, having nowhere to go. Being humiliated in front of an entire community that thought it knew her and found her guilty without any sort of inquiry.

But isn't this what you caused, Nyandoro?

She ignored the annoying voice inside her head.

"I haven't been alone in a long time," Duni said. "That's what I always complained about, having those child wives around me, crying and asking advice, telling me I need to please my husband more. And now, this…silence. It's wonderful. But it's terrible too. This is not how I wanted my freedom to come."

"We don't get to choose how the Orishas grant our wishes." Ny trotted out the old aphorism her father threw at her when she complained about getting what she wanted but not quite in the way she'd envisioned. She winced and shook her head. "Sorry. That was stupid."

Duni stopped pacing the room and simply watched her.

Ny scrubbed a hand across her face and over her tight braids. "I want to fix this but feel so helpless. Part of me thought it would come to this but…but not so soon. Not when you and I haven't even…" She stopped, her words ending in a pathetic whine, convinced she was saying more stupid things.

This wasn't the time to talk about how she and Duni had never actually *been* together, how the small intimacies they'd shared at the river didn't feel like enough for Duni to lose her entire world over. The air shifted around her as Duni crouched close. Duni pressed her forehead to Ny's shoulder, her breath puffing warm against her bare shoulder.

"It's all right," Duni murmured.

Now she was the one comforting Ny. The one who'd lost everything.

"Please." Ny wrapped a hand around Duni's shoulders and tried to lift her up. "You should be the one sitting here, not me." *You should be the one getting comfort.*

Duni didn't move. "I can't blame you for my recklessness. I wanted you too." She lifted her head, sadness in every curve of her face. "Until you, no one had ever courted me." She pressed her lips together, forced a mockery of a smile. "When my parents knew they were dying, they investigated every eligible man in the village. They were the ones who approached Ibada about taking a second wife.

"They forced enough goats and cows on him that he would have been a fool to say no. On our marriage night, I was just another goat in the pen. I knew what I was getting. It was better than having nothing and no one when my parents died, but as Yemaya knows, I wanted so much more." Duni drew a trembling breath. "I prayed at her altar for something more, and that's when she sent you. I knew I would have to pay for it somehow, but…" Duni's hand tightened briefly on Ny's thigh before she moved away to sit cross-legged on the floor. "Maybe I should've been more specific when I asked for what I wanted." The corner of her mouth jerked up in a puppet's smile, sad and false.

Ny didn't have anything nearly as useful to say. She knew where most of the blame lay. On her own shoulders. If she hadn't been so relentless in her pursuit, Duni would be in her own bed right now, listening to the chatter of the other wives or tending to her husband's meal or even sitting by the river in peace. She wouldn't be in danger of starving to death on her own.

"I'll take care of you," Ny said. "I won't let you become someone's servant or slave just because of what I did."

"No, this is happening because of what *we* did." Duni squeezed her fingers together in her lap, chewed on her already swollen lower lip. "But I'll survive this. I can...I can ask Iya Angaza for a plot of land to rent and grow vegetables for the market. Maybe even take the cows to the field for women who are too old to do it themselves." She chewed so hard on her lip, Ny thought it would bleed. "I'll do something..." Her words trailed off into uncertainty.

Ny frowned at Duni's lowered head. *Her* woman selling goods in the market? Taking care of someone else's animals? Never.

Ny took a breath, careful not to say the things that wanted to spill hot and haughty from her mouth. She left the mat and approached Duni as carefully as she would an unbroken horse.

"Stay here with Kizo," she said. "Let me find a place for you with my family. Soon, I'll be of age and I can make you my first and only wife."

Duni frowned like she couldn't quite understand what Ny was saying. Then she smiled sadly. "The idealism of the young. Nyandoro. No. You have a life beyond the gates of the village."

"You had a life before I touched you, Duni. You had to give it up because of me. We can be equal in loss with this, and equal in gain." She breathed deeply and clasped her fingers together in her lap when all she wanted to do was grab Duni and make her see what was best. *This* was best. "I will take care of you." She pressed her fingers to Duni's mouth when she tried to protest. "We will take care of each other."

Duni drew a quick breath, the warmth of it scorching Ny's fingers. Her lips parted under the pads of Ny's fingers and she pressed a kiss there. "All right," Duni said.

A wave of feeling swept over Ny. A light but electric burn through the senses that energized her fingers and her legs, made her want to reach out in comfort and be more for Duni than just words. Words meant nothing if actions didn't support them.

But she didn't know what actions Duni needed from her. She didn't know what to do. Her hands were calloused and clumsy with delicate things. Holding a spear was easy. Leaping on the back of a zebra just as effortless. But the thought of touching Duni, even in comfort, frightened the breath from her lungs. But she had never wanted to touch so badly in her whole life.

Next to her, Duni breathed softly in the quiet. Her chest rising and falling with her gentle breaths, head tilted to one side as she watched Ny. The candlelight caressed her face, made unknowable pools of her eyes, a glistening welcome of her faintly swollen mouth.

"Nyandoro?"

The question seemed to only have one answer, but Ny wanted to be sure.

"Duni, let me care for you." She licked the nervousness from her lips. "I'm young, true, maybe even a little bit foolish, but I've only ever wanted you. No one else."

"Your convenient short-term memory is lovely." Duni touched her face with that now familiar sad smile. "You want more than just me. But that's one of the best and worst things about being young: right now is all that matters."

"Then allow me to create a beautiful now for both of us. Tomorrow will take care of itself."

"You talk real pretty for such a child," Duni said softly. But she was joking, a light struggling to flicker on in her eyes. She was sadness itself, but trying to wear a mask of acceptance.

Ny touched her knee, squeezed it, and leaned close. "Let me do this for you."

Duni laughed, a puff of breath against Ny's mouth. "So selfless."

"Fine." Ny smiled, rueful at her own eagerness. "For us."

Their mouths touched. Lips parted. Tongues gently explored.

Ny kissed Duni like she wished she'd done before. With deliberate intention, her mouth moving slick and heavy against Duni's. Her body arched into the slowly building pleasure, but she couldn't quite leave her head yet.

Even with Duni warm and trembling against her, knowledge of her own inexperience held her captive in her head. She wanted to please. Didn't want to do anything wrong. Her brothers often talked about the women they made love with, the stretch and burn the women described, the first few moments of pain, then, if they did it right, or if the girl allowed herself to relax, the pleasure would come, hot and slow. She wanted that for Duni, a hot and slow unfurling of lust that left her trembling and breathless, her legs sprawled across the sleeping mat in exhausted abandon. And she wanted that for herself too.

It would be different between two women, she knew that. No over-eager man in a mad rush toward an immediate gratification that left the woman behind. Between two men, it was different too, it—

The stroke of her nipple brought Ny back to herself.

"Stay here with me," Duni whispered into her mouth.

Ny shivered, the thoughts that had nothing to do with what was going on in the moment scattering in the wake of the sharp bliss darting between her nipples and her lap. Duni tugged at her nipple again, and Ny realized Duni had wet her fingers with the slick from between her thighs and touched Ny with those wet fingers, painting her breasts with desire. Her belly clenched tight, and she whimpered.

She clutched Duni's hand and jerked to her feet. The sleeping mat. Their bodies together. She needed that. Now.

"Yes." Duni stood up, mouth curving, a calmer incarnation of desire.

She leaned in and Ny eagerly met her mouth as they stumbled backward toward the mat. Duni's tongue a snaking wetness that plumped Ny's sex and made her want to grab Duni's hand and push it there for her to grind down on, twist and shake until she came apart. But she squeezed her thighs together and forced herself to go slow.

"I want you so much…"

Once on the sleeping mat, their kisses became sloppy and wet, a rush toward what was a certainty. Their bodies finally pressed close through the two layers of cloth, Duni's thigh falling between hers and pressing against her. The heat of expectation rushed through Ny, her heart beat faster, and the breath hitched in her throat.

Thudding hearts. Long and deep kisses. Hands pulling at the cloths that covered their bodies.

Duni pulled back. "Sit up."

The bedclothes shifted and whispered beneath them as they moved to face each other, the smell of eucalyptus rising in the room, the dried leaves in the mattress crackling.

Ny licked her lips, faced with the challenge of Duni sitting close to her, her body offered. "What do you want me to do?"

"Undress me."

Ny's fingers fumbled with the folds of the cloth. How could they not? Finally, finally, she had arrived at the moment where she could touch Duni the way she had always imagined in dreams. Was her skin as soft as she thought it would be? Would she arch up into her with her wonderful laugh? Would the reality of their touches come anywhere close to what she often imagined?

With her clumsy fingers, she finally pulled loose the yellow cloth that covered Duni's breasts. The cloth fell into her hands, soft again her palms, down Duni's belly, and slithering down to the mat. Her hips revealed. The dark thatch of her pubic hair, her soft thighs. The smell of her, musky and salty, drifted up to Ny's face. Her mouth watered. Her fingertips tingled.

"I want to touch you," Ny breathed.

Duni closed her eyes, bare body swaying in the candlelight to her own inner music. "Please..."

Duni's breasts were plump and tender under her exploring fingers, the nipples hard and scraping Ny's palm. From throat to wrist, bellybutton to toes, every touch was a revelation. Even after so many hours enclosed in the darkness of the hut, enclosed in the rawness of her own pain, Duni smelled like the sun.

Ny had never experienced anything so beautiful. Her body was tense with need, the desire in her pulled tight at her nipples, sucked pain into the little bud of her sex, made her groan with each pleasured sigh that Duni gave. It was a pleasure and it was a lesson. She wanted to make Duni forget about her shattered life. She wanted her only to focus on the beautiful things they were sharing together. Ny dipped her mouth to her nipples, tasting one after the other, licking and sucking and moaning her own bliss while Duni twisted against the pallet, her fingers clenched in Ny's hair, her legs falling open and begging Ny to touch her there.

She smelled like a remembered dream of the sea. She wanted to dive in and coat her face with the heated wetness, cover herself in Duni's musk. So she did. She tasted like every wonderful thing Ny had ever wanted in her mouth, she moaned as if she were dying. She trusted Ny. She lay under her clumsy hands, gasping when the touch was good, guiding Ny's hands when it was not, writhing in pleasure and praising Ny with every moan that rose from her lips, every arch of her back, every drip of moisture between her legs.

Duni's hips bucked in her tight grip. She cried out Ny's name and shuddered deeply in her bliss. She opened her eyes and her lashes fluttered wildly as she stared up at Ny. Her gaze was blank, everything obliterated by pleasure, what her body reveled in. But in moments, the blankness cleared and awareness claimed her again. Her brown eyes glittered with tears. The water of her sorrow leaked down the sides of her face and into the mat. Her mouth wavered into a silent cry.

Ny gripped Duni's shoulders and turned her over in the mat, lifted her hips to bare the drenched bush and swollen wet pink of her. She tasted of salt. When Duni cried out again, it was with pleasure, a gushing rain pouring from between her legs and over Ny's face, the wet sound of it rushing so fiercely, so cleanly, that Ny felt it on her shoulders, heard it pounding on the roof of the small house. This time, she cried too.

Nyandoro knew she was dreaming.

Clear blue water rippled under her feet. Bluer than the river. Clearer than the skies. Crystalline. The vessel she was on, a boat, floated in the middle of a vast sea, land nowhere in sight. She'd never been this far out before, but—and she looked down again into the water between her knees—she wasn't afraid. The small, shallow boat rocked as she shifted to plunge both feet into the water. She sighed at its coolness over her ankles, her legs. Its soothing tongue lapped her calves.

She was naked.

"Wanting is only a pleasure if we know the want will soon be satisfied."

Nyandoro looked up from the rippling water, unsurprised to see the woman from before. This time, she wore a tunic of peacock feathers, a rippling of bright color over one shoulder, over her breasts, belly, and down to her knees. A bright blue cloth wrapped, high and regal, around her head.

"Was there ever any doubt I would get what I wanted?" Nyandoro asked.

The expression on the woman's face shifted, one moment a neutral but curious look, the next, like another mask sliding into place, a smile of amusement.

"And how was the taste?"

"Like rain," Nyandoro said, imagining the thing that the village and everyone in it had longed many seasons for but could not get. "She tasted like rain."

The woman's mask shifted again. This time, it was sadness that touched those unnaturally beautiful features. It didn't seem any more real than her laughter from before.

"Not quite, my little warrior," she said. "But soon you'll know true rain, and it won't be as sweet."

CHAPTER SIX

Early morning leaked through the slats in the window, warming Ny's face. She turned away from it with a groan, rolling into the soft heat of Duni's naked body. A long and luxurious moan rumbled from her throat, and she wrapped her arms around her new lover.

All mine, she thought with a smile.

Duni snuffled in her sleep, rubbed her eyes, and opened them to smile tentatively at Ny. She looked so beautiful, so delicious, that Ny did the only thing she could. She kissed her.

She luxuriated in the feel of Duni's lips under hers, the warm decadence of her body. As an adult, or close enough to one, she'd never woken up next to another person in her bed. It was luxury indeed, luscious bare skin on display for her to touch and kiss and suck until they fell once again under lust's heated spell. Duni moaned into her mouth, and Ny moved her hand low, squeezing the wondrous flesh of her bottom, stroking the wet cleft between her thighs.

"You don't have to go home, but you can't stay here."

Duni flinched against Ny at the sound of Kizo's voice ringing out from the sitting room. Her lashes flickered against Ny's throat and she pulled back with a soft gasp, sitting up in the pallet.

Damn him. Ny silently cursed her not-so-favorite brother. She touched Duni's hip. "It's okay. He's just joking."

But she slid from the bed and quickly tied her cloth over one shoulder and around her waist. In the sitting room, Kizo was waiting for her, a wide grin firmly in place.

"Did it go well?" he asked.

Two covered dishes sat on the low table next to three spoons, and the smell of porridge, rich and sweet, perfumed the room. Kizo looked freshly bathed, but like he'd been up for hours.

"Stop it!" Ny said with her voice low. "She's not ready to be teased yet."

"She better be ready for more than that." He uncovered one of the bowls, told Ny that their mother had made her favorite porridge. Green bananas mixed with plum juice and sprinkled with crushed macadamia nuts. Kizo picked up a spoon. "Everyone is speculating where she ran off to. A bunch of gossiping fools, our brother included."

He didn't have to tell Ny which brother. She often wondered if Nitu had been born in the wrong body and at the wrong age. Everything about him said he was a gossiping old woman.

"Do our parents know?"

"Papa might suspect something. He didn't ask too many questions when I showed up for dinner without you." Kizo blew cooling air over a spoonful of porridge before putting it in his mouth. "Mama was worried, but I told her you needed time by yourself to study for that ambassador's test. She sent the porridge as a reward for you being such a good girl." He smirked. "I should ruin a marriage or two every once in a while. Maybe then she'd make my favorite food."

The door to the bedroom creaked open, and Duni walked shyly through it, darting a shy glance at Kizo then at Ny before sinking into a small chair opposite the couch. Ny couldn't look away from her. Duni was beautiful. Too beautiful to have been the same woman in her bed just a few short hours before.

Kizo stared at Duni as if he'd never seen her before. His considering eyes on the gorgeousness of her face. Her full mouth, eyes still lazy from sleep. Although her yellow cloth was tied high at the throat and fell nearly to the floor to reveal only her arms and her bare feet, she was breathtaking.

From the plumpness of her lips to the drowsiness of her eyes, the lazy grace of her movements screamed that she's just been properly made love to. Ny wanted to pull her down into her lap and kiss the sleep from her face, slide up her *kanga* cloth and bury her face between her thighs. And she wanted to punch her brother in the face if he didn't stop staring.

He caught her frowning at him and shrugged. "What? It's only natural." He took another spoonful of porridge and only reluctantly pulled his eyes from Duni.

The bastard.

"What are you two going to do?" he asked.

Ny slumped on the couch. "What can we do? I think the best thing we can do is wait it out," she said. "No one knows who her lover is. And there are no parents to look for her and demand that Ibada do the right thing."

"What is the right thing, Ny? In the eyes of this man and probably most of the village, she was unfaithful and deserves nothing more than contempt."

"But they're wrong."

Kizo shrugged again. He turned to Duni. "You can stay here as long as you like. I'll make sure you have enough food then keep checking on the village decision about your marriage."

"You don't have to do this." Duni shook her head, looking both distressed and determined. "I can handle things myself."

Ny stood up. "With what?" Duni had no resources. No money. No family. Ny was uncomfortably aware of all these things. She looked at her brother.

He made a dismissive motion in Ny's direction, looking more than ever like their father. "It's done." He grinned. "Besides, if I know my sister, you'll be part of the family very soon."

Ny's face warmed. Marriage. Days of making love to Duni without anyone saying she couldn't. She barely kept her eyes from skittering away when she turned to Duni. "Please stay here. Between the three of us, we can think of a plan to keep you safe and out of the poor house."

"I'll do what needs to be done." Duni gripped the edge of the resting couch, her knuckles turning gray. "What will you do in the meantime?" Her anxiety was obvious, and it made Ny want to stay, want to protect her woman.

"I'll go find my iya," Ny said reluctantly. She couldn't stay away for much longer while the divorce scandal was going on. The rest of her family would start suspecting something. "I think today is her market day."

Kizo lifted his head and sniffed the air with a jackal's smile. "I'd suggest you take a bath first. One whiff and Iya will definitely know where your mouth was last night."

Ny blushed and wished again her brother wasn't such an ass.

❖

It *was* her mother's market day.

Ny left Duni at her brother's but took Kizo with her. He laughingly went along with her, saying he hadn't quite realized what a fine piece of distraction she'd found in Duni.

"Has she always been that pretty or did you do something to her last night?" Kizo chuckled, dancing out of the way when Ny tried to hit him.

At their parents' house, her mother looked over her with a sharp eye, hugging her with a greeting that seemed extreme for Ny spending just one night away, but didn't ask why she didn't come home. "Did your brother give you the porridge I sent?" Her mother bustled through the cook room, getting her money and basket ready for the market.

"No. He ate all of it." She felt no shame about lying. He had eaten most of the first bowl and she had left the second one for Duni.

Her mother lightly slapped his arm as she passed, tucking cowrie shells into her waist pouch. "Kizo!"

"It's not my fault your cooking is so delicious, Iya," he said, frowning at Ny behind their mother's back.

"But you should take care of your sister," their mother said. "You know she needs to eat too."

Ny instantly felt guilty. "He does make sure I eat, Iya."

"I sure do." Kizo gave her a meaningful stare, then made an obscene gesture with his tongue and two fingers in case she missed what she was saying.

Ny itched to punch him for real this time. Ny rubbed a hand over her still-wet hair. Her bath had been quick and rushed, but got the job done. The memory of the night she spent with Duni was seared into her mind forever, but at least it wasn't smeared all over her skin for anybody to smell. "Are you ready for the market, Iya?"

"Almost, darling. Just let me put away these oranges Iya Angaza gave me this morning." She grabbed an overflowing grass bag of oranges from the windowsill and dumped them into a basket on the table. "Her tree is bearing out of control. She can't give away the fruit fast enough."

"It's always good to have more than you need." Ny backed out of her mother's way, tucking her hands behind her back.

"And to share so willingly." Kizo gave her a teasing look. "Good things like that are always meant to be shared." He skipped out of the reach of Ny's fist and made his way to the door. "I will see you for the evening meal, Iya. Sister." Then he was gone.

"What is he up to?" Her mother stared at the doorway Kizo disappeared through.

"The usual, Mama. No good."

Her mother smiled and wrapped a hand around Ny's waist. "Unlike my baby, yes?"

Ny mumbled something she hoped sounded convincing. Despite the wrinkle of worry between her brows, her mother didn't press her.

"Are you ready, love?"

Ny nodded, and they left for the market. Her mother carried the empty basket on her head, the wide, open weave container barely moving with each of her steps.

"Did you hear about what happened at the home of Ibada?" she asked Ny.

Ny's throat tightened to hold in the lie she had to tell. "Kizo said something about him throwing out his wife, but I don't know exactly what happened."

"It was Duni, his second wife." Her mother made a noise of disgust. "I feel sorry he was her family's only choice of a husband for her. He probably doesn't beat her, but what a beast he is. Two seasons with Ibada must have been torture for Duni."

She brushed a light hand over Ny's shoulder, like she was telling herself no matter how desperate she was, she'd never give her daughter to a man who didn't deserve her. Or that's what Ny liked to think. Despite her worry for Duni, her mother's touch soothed her in a way she didn't think she needed. It reminded her of those half-forgotten memories from when she was a child, her mother rocking her to sleep with Ndebele lullabies before her altar to Yemaya, sprinkling river water on her forehead with a smile that held so much happiness that Nyandoro never completely forgot it.

"Ibada is just dreadful." Her mother continued the story, telling Ny everything Kizo had told her, and more. "Instead of taking Duni to the village high priestess and setting her aside. He took to the road."

Ny cringed.

There were two ways to break a marriage in the village. The first was for the couple to see the village *Iyalawo* together and arrange with the priestess for the quiet dissolution of the spiritual bonds of their marriage. The second way was to walk through the main road of the village, calling out the name of the wife or husband before every house, throwing down a stone each time. The second was humiliating and reserved for when someone had been done a great wrong. It was ultimately up to the village elders whether or not the divorce would stand, but when someone took to the road, especially a wife or husband with any wealth or influence, the elders rarely stood in the way of the divorce.

"Everyone knows he never wanted Duni in the first place. He saw the goats her family promised and his eyes grew big. I doubt she truly has a lover. Ibada is only doing it this way so people won't think badly of him when he brings Dabiku's youngest child home in place of the old wife. Dabiku should be ashamed for allowing him to take her daughter. He will sour that little girl in no time."

Early morning birds sang in the resulting silence. The wind whispered through the leaves. Though Ny didn't know Dabiku's daughter and didn't even remember the girl's name, she felt a sharp pang of sympathy for her. But maybe, unlike Duni, she wouldn't want more than her new husband offered. A bed to sleep in, sister wives for company, children of her own one day. Just maybe.

"Is there anything we can do for Duni, Iya? If the elders allow the divorce to stand?"

Her mother looked at her, an odd expression on her face, like she saw through all the untruths and half-lies Ny had ever spoken about her and Duni. Her face seemed carved from rock. Cruel. But she turned to look back up the dirt path toward the market, and her face seemed like her own again.

"All we can do for her is pray."

Pray? Ny barely stopped herself from making a disrespectful noise. When had prayer ever gotten them anything they needed? She thought of Duni huddled in Kizo's house, waiting for the lions to be set loose on her.

"I worry something like that will happen to you," her mother said.

Ny glanced at her, startled. "You think some man will throw me out, Iya?" She tried to keep humility in her voice but knew she failed. The day some man thought he would determine her fate was the day he lost his balls.

Their footsteps mirrored each other as they made their way through the village that had long since been awake. The sound of children singing from the school nearby rose in the morning air along with the cries of goats and conversations from front gardens.

"Not exactly." Her mother paused. "I worry about the day you will—you might be at someone else's mercy. That's not something easily gotten used to."

"I have already told you, I would rather take a wife, Mama. Men do not suit my taste."

Her mother pressed her lips together, was silent as their sandaled feet slapped against the dry dirt road. The dozen or so bangles on her mother's arms, a decorative custom only the women in her far-off village practiced, chimed softly with each step.

"I want grandchildren from you, Nyandoro. It is a hard thing for me to accept, you choosing the life of the *onek epanga* without really knowing what it means."

"It's not a choice, Iya. I've already told you that. If you would like grandchildren to sit on your lap, my brothers are more than happy to provide them."

"But I want a child from my daughter. Blood born from your blood." Her mother's clan passed everything through the females. Property, names, power. It had taken her many seasons to get used to how things were in her husband's village. "It's not the same coming from your brothers." Her mother stared into the distance, a wrinkle between her eyes. Although she spoke the words Ny was long familiar with, she didn't seem invested in the argument, like whatever decision Ny made, having children would be the least of her worries.

"I should start looking for a wife soon," Ny said, just to prick her mother from the strange mood she was in. "I will officially be an adult next season."

"*Next* season?" Her mother stopped so fast, her basket almost pitched into the dirt. "But you're still a child. My child. And a virgin."

Ny bit the inside of her lip. She didn't want to lie. She was no longer a virgin and had the ache between her legs to prove it. The memory of Duni's fingers deep inside her, the stretch of faint pain then the pleasure, confronted her under the hot sun. This conversation didn't seem as funny anymore. "I am not a child, Mama. I'm not."

Her mother's eyes searched her face. Ny felt her gaze like a touch, rippling from the top of her head, over her breasts she had chosen to cover that morning, to her hips, her feet. Her mother's eyes widened in surprise, then narrowed. "You're too young, Nyandoro. Being a grown-up is complicated business. Your cho-cho may be ready, but your heart is not."

"Mama!" She couldn't stop her face from prickling with embarrassment.

"It's true." Her mother's narrowed eyes were trained like twin spears on her face.

Ny grit her teeth. She was tired of people telling her how young she was. "I'm old enough to have a child if I wanted. And if Papa decides that it is okay, I can marry today."

"No." Her mother was agitated, her steps falling quicker and harder on the dirt road. The basket lurched again on her head and she grabbed it before it could fall. "Don't be so wicked to your own iya, Nyandoro."

"I'm not being wicked. I'm just telling you the truth. I have been with someone. And she is someone I want to marry very soon."

Her mother drew in a sharp breath, her face going faintly gray under the early morning sun. "It's too soon, Nyandoro. Don't be in such a rush to take on responsibilities that may be too difficult for you."

"I'm not too young to love, Mama. Just like I'm not too old to go to the market or attend council meetings or kill an antelope and clean it before bringing it home. Those are also the things that make an adult life, yet you and Papa insist I do them."

Her mother's breath came quickly, like she was fighting a panic of some sort. Her hand fluttered up to her face before dropping back to her side. The silence between them was poison. "I'm just not ready to let you go." Her mother's voice was barely a whisper.

"I'm not going anywhere, Iya. I'll be mostly by your side and will only move as far away as Ndewele," her brother lived two houses over on the family compound, "and then you'll get tired of seeing me every day."

A shaky smile tilted on her mother's mouth. She took Ny's hand and gently squeezed. Ny was relieved when they arrived at the market, breathing in with ready familiarity the smells of ripe fruit and meat, honey, and the sweat of so many people in one place.

"Greetings, sister!" a woman Ny had often seen traveling to the village called out to her mother. Her mother, a big believer in not revealing the soft underbelly of her family's troubles for others to sink their teeth into, replied with her widest smile and a greeting of her own.

And so it continued as they walked through the loud and raucous market, women waving at them to buy what they had to sell. A few men brushing past and admiring the sway of her mother's hips, looking Ny over as if she was also for sale. She gave them her stoniest face while her mother simply ignored them. Her mother put on her public face as they went from vendor to vendor, getting the small things they came for. Yams. Carrots. More scented oil for her mother's hair and skin.

Gradually, the rhythm of the market soothed the tension between them. Her mother bent to look at a piece of *kanga* cloth with the symbol for "daughter" etched along its edges, drew it between her fingers, and touched Ny to draw her attention to it. "I think Ndewele's wife is going to have a girl. She would like this, I think."

"A girl?"

After all these seasons, Ny was still surprised when her mother knew things before everyone else. Whether it was her persistent nosiness or the fact that people told her things they would never confess anyone else, her iya always had the news before even the most voracious gossips in the village. Ny imagined her sister-in-law with two small babies draped in the identical folds of the soft green fabric. "That would be nice," she said, touching the cloth where it still drooped from her mother's fingers.

"Yes." Her mother bought the cloth from the vendor and put it in the basket on top of her head.

"Iya, let me carry that for you." Ny gestured to the half-filled basket.

"I'm not old and helpless yet, Nyandoro." A smile creased her mother's cheeks. "But if you insist, you can take the basket when it gets full. There's barely anything in it now."

Ny laughed. "Okay."

Just like that, things were right between them. The tension fell away, and they were once again their usual selves. During the meandering morning, they sampled fruit, laughed at the jugglers in the small square, and watched the dancers performing in their colorful robes and costumes for money and patronage.

At the stall selling gourds of all types, Ny's mother passed over the now heavy basket and Ny took it, laughing. She twisted a cloth on top of her head and balanced the basket there, settling the heavy weight in a way that did not strain her neck.

As she lifted her hand to steady the basket, she caught a pair of masculine eyes focused on her. Used to being stared at by men, she ignored him. But the longer she felt his stare, the more she realized he wasn't looking at her like other men. Instead, something truly predatory lurked in his unblinking gaze, a promise of blood and screams. She frowned. Then the man looked away.

At her side, her mother was bargaining with the vendor woman for two of her best drinking gourds. She didn't see the man with screaming in his eyes. Ny shifted closer to her mother, about to open her mouth and mention the stranger when she clenched her teeth.

What was she going to say? After talking with her mother about almost being an adult, now she was running to her about the scary man in the market? Either she was a child or she was a woman. She didn't get to choose at different times of the day whether to be one or the other. Ny kept her mouth shut.

Her mother bought the gourds and loaded them into the basket. After a quick word to Ny, she slipped through the crowd to pick up the sandals she'd ordered a few weeks before from the leather merchant.

Ny looked up. The sun, warm on her arms and back, had moved to the middle of the sky. As usual, she and her mother had been at the market for a while. The morning was almost gone, and although she'd been having a good time, with the appearance of the stranger, she now wished desperately to be indoors. Preferably with Duni, a cool sheet draped over their bodies while they talked about the future they would share together. She scanned the market. The stranger was nowhere in sight, but that didn't mean he wasn't watching her, hiding behind the shifting crowd so she couldn't see him.

When her mother reappeared with her new shoes, Ny sighed with a tiredness she almost felt.

"Mama, let me take the basket back home for you. It's getting heavy. And I know you want to spend a little more time out here."

Her mother went on her tiptoes to drop her sandals in the basket on Ny's head. "I suppose I shouldn't be surprised you want to leave. You lasted much longer than usual today." She squeezed Ny's shoulder, the corners of her eyes crinkling. "Thank you."

"You know I love being with you at the market, Iya."

"Yes." Her mother laughed. "Almost as much as your baba does."

Ny rolled her eyes. "Almost." Her father hated the market with a passion he reserved for few things.

"Go on home," her mother said. "Let me enjoy the rest of this market day before coming back home to slave in the kitchen."

But she knew her mother loved cooking for the family. One of the many ways she showed them her love.

"Okay. Wonderful." Ny smiled and kissed her mother's cheek. "We'll be waiting impatiently for dinner when you get back."

At home, she put away the food and left the cookhouse with her mind on Duni, and on the stranger at the market.

"I'm glad you came home today, daughter."

Ny's footsteps faltered. In a daze, she had wandered into the common room, nearly stumbling over her father who lay on his favorite chair, his legs stretched out in front of him and into the sun from the open window.

"Today is market day," she said, as if that explained everything. "Why aren't you with the council?"

Her father grunted. "I wanted to be home to see my wife and children."

He was smoking his pipe and looking through the ledger that recorded the productivity of the village's crops for the year so far. Even at home and at rest, he was still working. But it had been a long time since he had last been at home before the evening meal. If he returned from one of his trips to other villages, he often left to report his findings to the chief, to sit with him, and his advisors until Iya sent one of the neighborhood children to let him know it was time to eat.

"The council members are squabbling like babies today," he said. "I can get my work done here and in peace." He puffed lazily on his pipe and put the ledger beside him on the chair. "Where is your iya?"

"Still at the market." She sat in the chair across from her father and stretched out her legs, mirroring his posture. "I don't know where she finds all the energy to stay there so long then come back here and make the evening meal."

"She is blessed by the Orishas with the beauty and strength of a hundred women," her father said with a soft laugh. "Maybe even two hundred."

Ny smiled. One day she hoped to love her wife—love Duni—as deeply as her father loved his. She smiled even more at that secret happiness, then tucked the thought of her new lover away for later.

"Iya deserves to rest, just like you do, Baba. One day, the boys and I will cook the main meal so you two can sit together all day and play love songs on my *kora*."

Her father chuckled although the sound seemed hollow. "A glimpse of paradise," he said. "I can't remember the last time your iya and I just sat together with nothing else to do."

Now that she'd said it, Ny was convinced that she should do this for her parents. Her brothers wouldn't mind. Nitu was actually a better cook than she was and would happily take over the cooking of the evening meal if he had someone to do the chopping and mortaring for him.

"Good," Ny said. "We'll do that sometime soon."

She sat with her father until her mother came in from the market carrying a small grass woven bag over her shoulder. Her mother stood in the entrance to the common room, her body haloed in the late evening sunlight. Her warm smile flashed, and she came into the room smelling faintly of her mint body oil and the sweat of her walk.

"My two favorites," she said and danced her fingers over Ny's hair.

Her father put aside his pipe and, still stretched on his side on the couch, invited her mother with open arms to sit in the cup of his reclined body. She sat and leaned into him with a sigh, closing her eyes. "The day has been long, husband."

Their easy intimacy, something Ny had simply taken for granted as a child, now pulled a different cord in her. Her parents' love, though not always perfect or peaceful, was constant and unwavering. Seeing it now, instead of making Ny embarrassed or just tolerant, made her want a love of her own. She left them to go find it.

She rushed a bath and a change of clothes before taking off at a jog for Kizo's house.

"Slow down, Lady Nyandoro. Where are you going in such a rush?"

It was the local washer-woman, large and friendly with big eyes and an even bigger smile. She carried a bundle of wet clothes from the river in her basket. Ny nearly kept running past, but her manners forced her stop. She straightened her wind-tossed *kanga* and made her breath even out, her heart rate slow down.

"It's a pretty day, Iya Kipenzi."

She had always been nice to Ny, even if she was a bit of a gossip. Her husband threw her out seasons before Ny was even born, but Iya Kipenzi had recovered her life and seemed happy. She had always called Ny "Lady Nyandoro" even when Ny was a child. Back then it made her feel special. Now, it just made her uncomfortable.

"Pretty enough to slow down and enjoy the butterflies then, no?"

"You're right, Iya Kipenzi." Ny struggled to find a smile, not wanting to be rude and dismiss the older woman but eager. "I'll see you later."

Iya Kipenzi chuckled like she knew a secret. "Yes, child. Later."

At Kizo's hut, the window of the main room was open, the door propped open to let in the last of the sun. The faint trails of gray wood smoke from the back of the hut rose in the air. Someone was making food. She called out to him before she walked into the hut.

"Where are you, Kizo?"

She followed his voice to the small cook room at the back of the house, a room with three walls open to an overflowing vegetable garden. Her brother stood at the preparation table over a big serving bowl of food, scooping the last of the fou-fou from the cook pot. Next to the fou-fou in the serving bowl he already had three portions of seasoned meats wrapped in banana leaves and three apples from his tree in the garden. The fire was out, only dying smoke rising from the smothered logs with the scent of the meal he'd just made.

He looked cheerful and well-rested, skin glowing with sweat from the fire, amusement glinting in his eyes. "Come help."

Ny took the apples and empty plates Kizo pointed her toward while he carried the hot food into the small common room and arranged it on the table. He adjusted the slats of the window to allow in the dying light but shade them from the prying eyes of passersby.

"Where is Duni?"

He ignored her question. "I hope you're hungry. I made enough for all of us."

All? She crossed then uncrossed her arms, shifting restlessly. "Isn't it too early for the evening meal?"

But a look from him made her sink into the low chair next to the table. She tapped her fingers against her thigh and glanced toward the closed door of the sleeping room. Kizo caught her eye and she looked away, her face turning hot. Ny took a breath to refocus herself, think about other things. From outside, she could hear the sound of bleating goats and a lone voice singing, a herder taking his animals in for the night along the small path nearby.

Even slightly isolated as Kizo's house was from the bulk of the village, Ny could still hear the noise of its heartbeat, the things that made it live. She'd always loved her brother's house, the way it sat apart and yet was still part of the village. Like she sometimes felt.

The door to the sleeping room creaked open, yanking Ny's attention back to where it belonged. Duni walked into the room. "I heard your voice," she said.

"I'm here," Ny confirmed with a swift smile.

Duni's hair was freshly braided, a different style from what Ny had seen that morning. Strain tugged at the corners of her eyes and her bottom lip looked swollen like she'd been chewing on it throughout the day. But she smelled of honey oil, and the kanga covering her from breast to ankle was one Ny had never seen.

It felt like she hadn't seen her in days when it had only been a few hours. The memory of Duni's soft skin was seared into Ny's tongue and hands. She wanted to feel more of it. She wanted to confirm that what she'd experienced the night before was no dream, but instead a reality she could enjoy over and over again.

The wood of the chair pressed into the backs of her thighs as she shifted against it, restless and impatient to pull Duni into her arms, to nuzzle her throat and beneath her breasts for the source of that sweet oil tugging on Ny's senses, and to pull her back into the sleeping room, down to the mat and press her meaty thighs open and sip on the hot slick of her cho-cho. On the other side of the room, Kizo shared out the food, a smirking smile on his face.

"The weather was nice today," he said out of the blue. "I wonder if the twins went fishing. They like to catch something fresh when the sun isn't too hot and it feels like the rain would come. What do you think, sister? Would you like to catch something fresh too?"

He put a bowl of water on the table along with three small hand cloths. Duni stood uncertainly near Ny, looking between her and the empty seat next to Kizo on the couch.

"For the sake of heaven!" Kizo laughed. "Sit on the floor at Nyandoro's feet. Unless you're going to start your honeymoon in front of my eyes. In that case, sit far away from her so you won't be tempted."

Ny bit the inside of her lip to stem any obvious show of embarrassment, but her face burned anyway. "Kizo, why are you doing this?"

"Because I'm hungry, sister. Why else?"

But once Duni sat down on the chair next to him, he cleaned his hands with the bowl of water and a hand cloth. The playfulness vanished from him.

"People are still talking." Kizo reached for his bowl of food. "They don't know where you are, Duni, but they're talking like they do. They say you're with your lover."

Ny, too keyed up to eat, didn't even look at her bowl. She shook her head.

"Do they think *you* are my lover?" Duni asked the question, her chin lifted.

"They know better than that." Kizo looked amused again. "In the meantime, your husband—"

"He's not her husband anymore," Ny interrupted.

Kizo shot her an exasperated look. "The man you once shared a sleeping mat with, Duni, has already negotiated marriage with Dabiku. That ceremony will be in three days."

"That poor little girl!" Duni lost her look of defiance, her face falling into lines of worry and sadness again. "I should've refused the divorce, then he wouldn't be able to marry her." Even the richest man in the village was only allowed six wives.

Kizo unwrapped his banana leaf, releasing the scent of spiced meat in the air. The succulent juices, a beautiful orange from the palm oil, swam in the shallow bowl. He picked up some fou-fou with his fingers and dipped it in gravy. "Once he said you took a lover and one of the wives supported his story, there was no way you could refuse the divorce."

"But I didn't have a lover." Her eyes dipped to Ny, then away. "Not really. Not until he threw me out!"

"In the eyes of the village, that doesn't matter." Kizo glanced at Ny with the same fond amusement she'd been used to all her life. "You have a lover now." He took a bite of the meat and hummed in appreciation. "Iya will be proud of me for this. I think I finally got her recipe right."

Ny knew what her brother was trying to do, distract her from things she could not change, focus on the small but still meaningful things in her life. Like him taking care of her woman while the tide resulting from what they'd done rolled over them. She followed his lead.

"Hm. I'm not sure about that." Ny took a bite of her meat, rolled it over her tongue although it tasted like stone. "Okay. Maybe."

She felt Duni's eyes on her, but Ny didn't risk looking at her for too long. The pain in them was too plain. Too naked.

But Duni wouldn't let her look away from her misery. "This is humiliating." She poked at her food, not eating it. "The *whole* village knows Ibada is a worse person than me. They know! It's shameful that I'm the one looking for a home and begging for scraps from any table that would take pity on me."

"You don't have to beg," Ny said. "Marry me and that will solve all our problems."

"*Our* problems?" Duni crossed her arms. "No. This one is all mine. I won't be a burden to you or your family. Besides, you have nothing to support a family with."

Ny and Kizo exchanged a look, her brother lifting an eyebrow in question.

"I do have something. Or at least I will when I marry." Ny pushed back her bowl and carefully wiped her fingers on a hand cloth. "When I marry, I receive the twenty goats and a piece of land in my family compound. These things are for me, not a dowry. I will marry you and we will build a house together where you can farm our garden and help me take care of our home." Ny shrugged. "Simple."

"I told you, I won't allow you to take me on as your burden."

"You're not my burden. I'm in love with you."

Do you even know what love is? The familiar voice sliced through the confidence of her declaration.

Duni gasped. "What?" Her bowl clattered on top of the table, splashing gravy on its gleaming surface. She looked abruptly ashamed and scrambled to clean the table with a hand cloth. "You barely know me."

Kizo cleared his throat and stood up. "I think this is my cue to leave." He picked up his bowl along with an apple, never one to allow a meal to go to waste. "You love birds sort this out. I'll spend the night with Nitu." He nodded his head at Ny. "Sister. Good luck." Then he was gone.

Once Kizo left, silence dropped around the room like a heavy blanket. His absence was what Ny had so desperately wanted. But now that he was gone, she longed for a distraction from the tension between her and Duni. Ny drew a deep breath and, to buy herself some time, took the seat that Kizo had left empty.

"I love you, Duni," she said again. "We can marry and work together to build a life that suits us both."

Duni tipped her head down, plucking at the gravy-smeared hand cloth. Ny watched the top of her head, the swirling pattern of the braids in her hair, moving from the center of her head like the current in a whirlpool.

Her scalp gleamed with health. Ny wanted to touch the thick hair and trace the pale veins of her scalp she could see through the troughs of hair. Although no one outside their family knew it, her papa often braided her mother's hair. There were many nights Ny had walked through the common room to see her mother sitting on the floor between her father's spread knees, humming a song while he braided a simple style in her hair and smoothed mint oil into her scalp. Ny had always associated hair combing, hair braiding with intimacy. The feel of love and connection.

She tapped her fingers on the table, nervous, waiting for Duni to say what she wanted. But then, she had never been a patient person. "Please say yes. Please tell me you'll have me."

Duni lifted her head. "I know I shouldn't." She bit her lip, pulling the lush flesh between her teeth. She was nervous, Ny knew. But the sight of her white teeth sinking into the swollen lower lip made her suddenly, achingly want to touch her. She drew back and laced her fingers together on top of her thighs.

"You're so young," Duni said. "You don't even know how this decision will affect you. We aren't meant for each other. It's as plain as the wood on this table." She laid her hands on the table, palms down on either side of the nearly full bowl and stained hand cloth. "But I've never had anything beautiful of my own before." She drew a deep breath and turned away from the table, leaned close to Ny, and put her hands on top of hers. "I will marry you."

"You will?" Ny held her breath.

Duni laughed, a shaky sound. "Isn't that what you want?"

"Yes, I—" Ny giggled, unable to believe Duni actually said yes. She'd been prepared to argue with her all evening, all night. But this... The happiness spread hot and fast through her chest. "You won't regret this. You won't."

"I'm not at the regret phase yet," Duni said with a faint smile. She gripped Ny's hands. "This won't be easy for you. People will say you were the lover that destroyed my marriage, or worse yet, that I took a lover while with my husband and will make a fool of you too."

"Those people won't be on my sleeping mat." She touched Duni's cheek with trembling fingers. "You will and that's enough for me."

Duni stood up and held out her hand to Ny. "Then come, wife-to-be."

Ny shivered at the word. *Wife.* She would soon be someone's actual wife. She would soon have a family of her own, a love that belonged to her and no one else. She took Duni's hand and got to her feet. Her legs felt like slender blades of grass, unable to support her whole body, not the body of a wife and lover and a woman who was about to get the thing she'd wanted for so long.

In the sleeping room, they sank into the mat together, kissing with a reverence and tenderness usually felt, in Ny's mind, only on a marriage night. Their mouths pressed hotly together, the heat and pressure and pleasure of their kisses inciting wetness between her legs. But there was no urgency to it. They had the rest of their lives.

Then Duni gripped Ny's hips hard and pressed a firm thigh against her quim. A sudden wave of overwhelming desire startled a whimper from her throat. She reached desperately for Duni, squeezing her breasts, her thighs, any inch of skin she could feel.

"Yes," Duni gasped. "That's good." She touched Ny more urgently, licking her throat and sucking bruises into her skin, leaving Ny a squirming mess on the mat.

Ny knew she had to be quiet. This was Kizo's house, and although they expected this of him, she didn't want to call out Duni's name though her entire body panted it with each liquid slide of Duni's tongue over the firm seed of her desire. She bit her lip, clenched her teeth. But whimpers leaked from her throat.

She tightened her fingers in Duni's hair as Duni moved lower, a snaking incarnation of desire, to lick between her legs. Duni raked her fingers down Ny's thigh, pushed one leg high in the air and draped it over her shoulder. And Ny, limber from seasons of running, hunting, and climbing trees, arched her back, bending herself nearly in two as she whispered her thanks, her pleas, to the ceiling while Duni took her apart with her tongue and fingers.

She came with the sound of her own voice rattling in her ears. She was still trembling, electric shocks of sensation darting through her body, when Duni spoke, a breathless whisper against her lips.

"I...have a present for you," she gasped. Then she turned around, sinking her bare and dripping quim to Ny's mouth. "Put your tongue on me, wife. Please me while I please you." She bent her head, and Ny eagerly did what she was told.

Afterward, she fell into a dream.

It was raining. The wet slid down Nyandoro's face and bare shoulders, licking her skin with the sensation of warm tongues. She looked up into the sky and closed her eyes, enjoying the touch of the water that was like the sweet after-love feeling she had in Duni's arms. Duni who seemed so far away from this place, like she didn't even exist.

The woman beside her spoke. "If you want her to be here, she can."

Ny opened her eyes and looked down to a valley. To the large, white building in its center, like a palace from Arabia and attached to many smaller buildings, also white, that spread out in a semi-circle and faced a high stone archway. There was no fence around the buildings, but Nyandoro sensed an invisible border of some sort separating the compound from the rest of the world. Something that prevented those on the outside from seeing it.

"If Duni comes, will you leave?"

"No, I will always be here." Under the rain, the woman's mouth curved into a smile.

A feeling of gladness opened her throat. She didn't know why. She only knew that the stranger was a constant and welcome presence, like the three gold rings on her toes, gifts from her mother for each five-year cycle of her life. Nyandoro examined the feeling, like a bug under glass. Why would she feel this for a stranger? A woman she'd only met in dreams?

"Who are you?" she asked.

"Who are you?" the woman asked her in turn, smiling again.

Nyandoro found herself smiling. This game, question for question, she often played with her brothers. "I think I asked you first."

"You like games, I see." The woman actually laughed at Ny. Then her smile faded. "I like it here. I laugh here and it feels good."

Did that mean the woman had a real world too? Nyandoro wished the rain would stop so she could properly see the woman's face. She remembered her being beautiful enough to *stop her breath. But the rain seemed like a shield of tears, and she did not want to see her coated in a layer of sadness. The woman stood up and stretched, with each sleek and eel-like movement of her body, the rain drained more and more from the sky.*

"Did you make the rain stop?"

At Nyandoro's question, the woman laughed again. Drops of rain kissed her face, her throat, bare shoulders, her belly. The water clung to the cloth that sat on her hips. Her teeth flashed in her face, bright lightning. "Your strength is beautiful," the woman said. "It will be even more so when you realize it for yourself.

Nyandoro turned to look at the woman. And woke up.

She drew in a deep breath, and almost choked on the smell of sex and sweat. The air in her dream had been different, sharper with a hint of euphoria she always associated with the rainy season. At her side, Duni shifted on the sleeping mat but did not wake. They had made love late into the night, way past time for the evening meal. The little of the sky that came though the window was dark and the moon was bright in the sky. Night insects squeaked and buzzed. The birds were long gone.

Her parents would start to worry. She needed to go home.

But wouldn't it be nice to open Duni's legs and kiss her awake?

She ignored the temptation, but it was a near thing. In the small bathing room, she made quick but thorough work of cleaning herself up. She didn't want a trace of what she'd been doing to linger on her body. At least not until she had the chance to tell her family what she had planned. To marry Duni. To have a family of her own.

In the sleeping room, she kissed Duni's shoulder and softly called her name. "I'm leaving."

Duni made a soft noise of protest, sweet and kittenish, and curled into her lap. "You should stay with me."

"I can't." She brushed a thumb over Duni's cheek, and Duni shivered into her, smiling. "Not tonight," Ny said. "But that will be the last time we sleep apart. Afterward, everything will be out in the open and we can spend all our nights together." Saying the words filled Ny with a giddy pleasure. She kissed Duni's shoulder again, her mouth.

Smiling, Duni rubbed her eyes. "All right." She sat up and the blankets fell to her waist, baring her breasts and the bruises Ny had left on her skin. She looked thoroughly loved. Thoroughly hers. Ny kissed her mouth again, breathed in her sleep scent, even the sourness of her breath that was like ambrosia to her.

"I'll come back in the morning."

Duni clutched her tightly before reluctantly letting go. "I can't wait for you to be in my bed all night."

"Our bed," Ny said.

"Our bed," Duni agreed.

Ny left her with a smile on her face, the throb of gladness in her veins.

The night was beautiful in its darkness. Every sound seemed to echo Ny's happiness, a chorus of sighs as she made her way back to the family compound. The rest of the village rang with its usual evening time rhythms, a lower tempo of noise, wives laughing softly around the yard fires after the babies had gone to sleep, old men drinking palm wine and sharing gossip on the verandah of the lodge. Torches on the front of nearly every house Ny passed lit her way.

Her footsteps were quiet as she walked beneath the honey blossom tree she had played under as a child, the tree that marked the beginnings of her family's property. Ny smiled into the darkness. Soon Duni would be her family too. Her new wife would live here with her and her brothers and her parents. Ny paused.

The path between the trees leading to the compound was oddly dark. Oddly silent. By now, the torches that blazed from the front of each house should begin to light the way. But the darkness was complete. No lights outside her parents' hut, nor her brothers'. Not in the center of the compound where they would have left a light burning for her to find her way. Ny called out softly to her parents.

"Baba? Iya?"

All she heard in return was silence. Were they angry at her for missing the evening meal? Had they all left for a party she'd forgotten about? But even as she tried to rationalize the strangeness of it, she knew better.

She drew in a steadying breath and smelled...metal? A familiar wet scent that she denied the moment she recognized it. Her heart hiccupped in her chest, began racing, pounding hard enough to make her shake. Ny pressed her lips together to stop herself from crying out again into the silence.

Silently, she ran past the orange tree with white blossoms hot with scent. She gagged, but swallowed thickly, brushed aside the low branches that dipped toward her face. The thorns scratched her arm, but she barely noticed the pain. Ny straightened and stopped running. Walked instead. Still silent but with something like terror ripping through her chest.

Her night felt torn in half. *She* felt torn in half. The dirt was wet and warm. Silent. Blood squelched under her feet. She felt it now, sticky and undeniable between her toes. She stopped her near run toward her parents' hut, breathed through the fear in her throat that had to be nothing. Was nothing.

Her feet bumped into something and she tripped, fell over in the wet dirt. The breath whooshed from her lungs. It was dark. But she knew what that wet was. No. She *didn't* want to know. She struggled to her feet, hands reaching out, trembling, to touch what she had fallen over. She hissed in shock and a cry wrenched itself from her throat. A body, still warm. She squeezed her eyes shut, opened them and looked down.

"Nitu?"

Her brother. His face slack. A knife near his hand. Wet. Ny jumped up and ran toward her parents' hut. Dark. Wet under her feet. The door pulled shut as if they were sleeping. She shoved it open and tumbled inside. She screamed. A forced cry abruptly cut off by a hand over her mouth. She saw them. In the dark. Her parents. Their necks open and raw with cut flesh and blood. Eyes staring up at nothing.

Baba!

A numbing cold gripped her. She wanted to crawl to where her parents lay, gutted. But her body wouldn't let her. Her elbow slashed back and she spun, suddenly released, slamming her elbow up again to crack into a man's face. She ran for the knife at her father's waist. Tripped in the wet. Wanted to scream but bit her tongue. More wet. Hands grabbed her legs, dragged her across the floor, and flipped her over. But the knife was already in her hand. She slashed and felt the blade sink into flesh. Heard a gasp. More hands. An explosion of pain in her face. Dizziness. Voices hissing to each other in a language she barely knew. Her hands grasped and twisted behind her back. Tied.

Her head rocked with dizziness and pain, but she still fought. Her foot lashing out, the crack of her heel meeting flesh, the thud of a body falling. But someone twisted her wrist and wrenched the knife from her hand.

Scream. She should scream again.

But she barely opened her mouth before a cloth rammed into her mouth, rancid and smelling of old meat and sweat, the taste like dust. She scuttled backward on the floor, shoving aside the animal skins, skinning her elbows and the backs of her thighs on the stone floor.

"Hold her!"

"Get the sleeping sap!"

A body dropped on top of her, heavy and sweaty. It pinned her to the ground the same instant she bumped into something beside her. She twisted away from the foul breath of the man on top of her, still kicking and fighting to get away. Gasping around the cloth stuffed in her mouth, she yanked her head back, ready to head butt him when she froze.

"Iya..." She stared into her mother's unseeing eyes.

Another weight fell on her ankles, but she barely felt it.

Iya! She squeezed her eyes shut. *No. Please. Let this be a dream.*

But even as she felt her mind shutting down, her body bucked and heaved, animalistic noises growling from her throat. But she couldn't move. Three men. One sat on her ankles, another pressed his weight onto her chest, then another still appeared at her head holding a drinking gourd. The man from the market.

She shrank back when she recognized him. But she couldn't move. He gripped the hinges of her jaw until her mouth fell open then he wrenched the cloth from between her lips. She twisted her head, trying to get away, but he poured something into her mouth, milky and bitter, that dribbled down the sides of her face.

She gagged and tried to yank her head away, spit out the sap, but they clamped her nose and mouth shut, a musky hand tight over her face. She gasped, fighting for air, and swallowed because she had to. The cloth was stuffed back into her mouth.

Her vision blurred and she blinked, body growing slack in the men's grip.

No! No. No...

The men lifted her and her world tilted even more. Breath shoved from her when someone dropped her, belly-first, over his shoulder. With her hands tied behind her back, her mouth gagged, Ny twisted her body. But it was a weak version of what she intended. The screams were trapped in her throat as the men—those men who would die—carried her through the compound, past the trees she had climbed as a child, the dead fire pit, past Nitu cut open in the dirt. She blinked wildly as the rest of her started to lose sensation.

She couldn't move, she could only see. Ndewele's door crooked and a leg, bloodied and gray, limp in the doorway. Her brother's hut.

Kizo! He'd been there. Because of her.

All the huts were dark. Everything was silent.

Her brothers. Her iya. Her baba. The pain scraped through Nyandoro and she screamed and screamed. Jaws working behind the cloth, trying to push it out with her tongue. But she was weak. She was tired. She felt every ache in her body.

The man's shoulder dug into her belly with each step he took, taking her family farther and farther away from her. Their bodies. Their love. What she had known her entire life. Through drooping eyelids, she stared into the dark, watching her life fade away as the men took her into the bush, their footsteps quiet, their mouths silent.

Be strong. This is not how it ends.

Ny forced her eyes to stay open, tried to yank her body away from the murderer who carried her. But all she could do was move her head and look up.

Trees swam above her, their branches wide and frightening in the dark. The stars mocked her with their brightness. She blinked when a splatter of wet hit her eyes. Then another and another until she realized it was raining. Rain. After so long of praying for it, expecting it and hoping for it. But all the rain in all the villages couldn't wash her pain or the blood away. A sob unfurled from the back of her throat. She coughed on the dryness in her mouth. Heaved with the pain of her body.

Her neck hurt. It was exhausting to keep her eyes open. Giving in would only be a relief. She took a shuddering breath and gasped at the sharper pain, in her ribs, in her chest. Rain splashed on her cheek, dripping down over her mouth but, because of the cloth, she couldn't taste it. The rain and its relief were as far from her as the stars in the sky. As far as her parents. As far as Duni. She gasped again.

And everything went dark.

PART TWO

CHAPTER SEVEN

Pain yanked her out of the darkness.

A burning in her wrists and ankles woke her from a strange dream that she'd lost everything. Nyandoro opened her eyes that were gritty and swollen, her lashes matted together with...tears? She thought about rolling over on her sleeping mat and looking through the window to check the position of the sun. But she was still so tired. Was it time to go with her father to the council meeting?

But when she tried to turn, she couldn't. Her hands were tied. Her wrists were tied. Her legs. And her body was moving through the air. Strung up at the wrists and ankles to a long branch and carried like a carcass, the spoils of a successful hunt. Her body swayed with each step her captors took, the burning pain sharpened. She gasped, the breath scratching her raw throat, as everything came rushing back.

Blood.

Death.

Capture.

It hadn't been a dream. A man appeared above her, his features clear despite the darkness. He was tall, his bare chest and stomach ropey with muscle. A scar curved up the corner of his mouth in a permanent and frightening smile.

"She is awake."

"Fix it."

The men stopped, and she swung between them, the sky above her dizzying and dark. A hand yanked her jaw and she hissed at the pain, a lingering soreness from where one of them had done that to her before. The drinking gourd appeared above her head, open and pouring.

"No!" She tried to jerk away but the hand was strong, and she was too weak. The white sap dribbled into her mouth, bitter and thick. She choked and tried to spit, twisting against the hold on her face.

"Grab her!"

Hands gripped her everywhere. Someone caught her head in a vice.

"I will kill you!" She tongued out the sap, but the man just poured more into her mouth, she had to swallow it or drown. She could hear the scuffling of their feet on the forest floor, the harsh breathing of the ones who held her, her own gasping and choking breath. Otherwise, the forest was silent. The rain from her dreams, gone.

Her body sagged. She could barely feel the pain in her wrists and ankles anymore. The tall man slapped her face, and she felt the impact reverberate through her whole body, but not the sting. Her eyes dropped closed.

"Let us continue on."

Nyandoro woke up too many times still trapped in her nightmare. And each time they poured the sap down her throat, choking her with it until she swallowed enough to lose awareness of everything. The fifth or fifteenth time it was almost a relief. Sunlight came then darkness then sunlight again. Her body roasted in the heat before a rough blanket landed on her, scratching her skin, her face, making her sweat.

Darkness again.

The sound of chatter woke her, common rhythms of village life. It was night again. The noises were so soothing, so familiar, she could've almost fooled herself into thinking she was home and everything was fine. Almost.

The sound of the men's footsteps changed from dirt to grass then harder ground. Their footsteps thumped on what sounded like stone. They were indoors. She felt lowered swiftly to the floor, then blanket abruptly disappeared from her head.

Nyandoro blinked, trying to focus. Bright torches surrounded her in a large stone hall. A man sat on a chair, a throne, watching her. He was a big man with youthful muscle just turning to fat, a square face, and greedy eyes. The mane and skin of a lion, bushy and thick, hung from his shoulders and a necklace made from the teeth of another big animal gleamed at his neck. The warrior's skirt under his softening belly seemed just for show.

He said something in a familiar language. For a moment, it was all sound and the fierce glitter of his eyes, then the words resolved themselves into one of the languages her father had taught her. A language that was spoken nowhere close to her village.

"Are you sure this is her?" the man in the lion skin asked.

He stood up and walked close to Nyandoro but not close enough to touch. He wasn't as tall as the men who'd taken her, but he walked like he thought he was, an arrogant swagger that made his skirt sweep the air like peacock feathers. The knife sheathed at his waist was big, bone-handled, but looked purely decorative.

"This *puny* thing is the one they want?"

"Yes. We asked in the village. She is the only girl from a female worshipper of Yemaya. Five brothers were before her."

"Were?"

"We couldn't take the chance that they would alert the rest of the village. They did not make it easy."

The tears rushed down Nyandoro's face before she could stop them. *All dead? Every single one?* She tightened her body, tried to tighten her emotions like she'd seen her brothers do, but the pain was too much for her to keep inside her bruised body. The raw agony shredded her throat, and she screamed it out of her, jerking and flailing against the stick that held her prisoner. What had her brothers or her parents done to deserve this?

"Shut her up."

One of her kidnappers appeared in her sight, fist raised. He punched her, and she stumbled back, blinded by pain, and then she was falling.

Falling.

When she awoke again, the stick was gone, but her wrists and ankles were still tied. The stone floor scratched her side, her cheek. The chief, or whatever he was, was once again sitting on the high throne, watching her while her kidnappers stood nearby. She couldn't see them, but she felt them as surely as she felt the ache in her ribs. Pressing a hand to her side, Nyandoro carefully sat up.

"You decided to rejoin us," the chief said. "Good."

The light from the torches flickered and dipped from the breeze coming through the windows of the large room. It crawled across the chief's face and bare chest, his arrogance on display for anyone to see.

Nyandoro struggled to her feet. Dangling at her sides, her fingers curled around nothing. She longed for a knife to kill this man, to skin this man, and present his carcass for the jackals to choke on. She limped toward the throne, one shuffling step after another. The men behind her must have made a move to come closer because the chief lifted a hand, palm out, a command to stay back. His eyes were dark with power and the knowledge that she had none of her own.

"Be careful," one of the men behind her said. "She fights like a man."

"Do you?" The chief looked amused. He watched her with the eyes of someone used to looking down on people. "Do you fight like a man?"

"I fight like a woman," she said. Her voice was scratchy and rough from disuse, so low she barely heard herself. "But you are worse than a dog." It hurt to talk and her mouth was dry. But she worked up enough spit to splatter some at the chief's feet.

His expression didn't change, but she saw the disgust in him, the anger. With very purposeful steps, he left the throne and came closer, stepping over the puddle of spit in front of him.

The chief looked at the men behind her. "She has no respect." He was apparently finished talking to her. His eyes burned over her face, her body. Although he came closer, he stayed just far enough away, out of the range of a head-butt, a desperate lunge. "But she is beautiful, a worthy addition to my wives. I should teach her to bow before a great man."

"Great man?" she snarled at him. "More like a cowardly dog who would kill elders and pregnant women."

He slapped her, and her head snapped back. She growled and spit on him, the gob of spittle landing on his chest instead of his face like she'd intended. This time, he punched her in the stomach. Hard. Then her chest and face until she was gasping from the pain, blood in her mouth, a barrage of punches that dropped her back on the stone floor. The ropes cut into her wrists and her ankles with each jerk and flail of her body.

Wet pain dripped down her face, but the pain in that moment was such a relief from the ache of loss in her chest.

With the pain riding the surface of her skin, she couldn't think about what she'd left behind. She couldn't think about anything.

"Dog!" she panted between pained breaths. "You're nothing more than a coward." She used the only weapons at her disposal.

He slammed his fist into her belly. "You dare?"

Through the pain, she felt hands jerk at her, pulling her away from the chief. His men. They didn't touch him, only pulled her away, her back scraping against the floor, her chanting scream—"Dog! Dog! Dog!"—the only weapon at her disposal. The men pulled her to her feet and slammed her back against the wall, held her there, pinned like an insect. Their sandaled feet stomped on the tops of hers and shoved her heels into the back of the wall. She couldn't move.

The chief growled and grabbed his waist knife. "Give her to me!"

"My lord, stop!" Two men jumped in front of Nyandoro. "If you kill her, they will not pay and we will not get what we want."

Although she couldn't see the chief past the barrier of the two men, Nyandoro felt his stare. His breathing, thick and loud, huffed in the room and he stepped to the side of the men's thick bodies so she could see him. "This is not finished." The chief tucked his knife back into his belt. "Put her in the cell and watch her. At first light, pack her up and take her to the woman. Make sure we get what was bargained for."

Take her where?

She'd heard of foreign slavers in the area, the men from across the sea who took women who wandered too far away from their villages or bargained with the basest men to take entire tribes of people away from the continent. She would not be one of them. She would not.

Nyandoro snarled at the chief. She didn't care what else he did to her. He'd slaughtered her family, her parents, her brothers. What else did she have for him to take?

Kizo. She started to shake at the thought of her brother, her friend, who was dead because of her. A sob broke from between her clenched teeth.

"Now you cry." He bared his teeth at her. "There's much worse I can do to you. Remember that."

She sagged in the men's grip. The "much worse" was already done. Life was nothing, nothing more than waiting for death. And if that meant it would come by his hand, then she was ready.

"Go fuck the dog who bred you!" She straightened against the wall and tipped her head back, feeling the blood sluggishly run down her face, into her mouth. One of the men jumped in front of her an instant before the chief grabbed for his knife again. This time the men and their logic didn't stop him. He hacked at the man in front of her to get to her, tearing into his flesh with the knife and splashing blood on the floor. The man shouted in pain and tried to get away.

One of the kidnappers grabbed Nyandoro and dragged her away from the chief and out of the room.

"Stupid woman!"

He threw her in a cell. A small room ripe with the stink of old piss and shit, misery and grief sunk deep in the stone. From the ceiling, a hook dangled, suspended on a long iron chain. The man raked his eyes over her body, bound and helpless with the thin cloth hiking up to her thighs. He grabbed Nyandoro, shoved her into the stone floor. She landed on her bottom, her palms scraping against the floor, bringing fresh pain. Her heart thudded loudly in her ears, fear and fury rushing with equal strength through her. She didn't take her eyes off him.

She twisted her wrists in the ropes, a silent struggle while she met his narrowed eyes. Those eyes crawled down her face and over her body, the front of his loin cloth began to lift. Nyandoro shrank back into the floor and clenched her fists.

But footsteps sounded just outside the door and then another shadow leaned over her bringing with it the familiar drinking gourd. Relief warred with revulsion. Her eyes skittered to the first man, the one with rape on his mind, then to the water skin filled with the promise of oblivion. Would he...? Before she could finish the thought, the water skin lowered. With no choice, she opened her mouth and closed her eyes, welcoming the disappearance of pain.

❖

Nyandoro woke to her body emptying itself. On her stomach, she convulsed on the stone floor of the cell where they'd dumped her. Bile gushed from her mouth in a hot flood. Her belly cramped, clutching hard and tight at nothing. The vomit spread around her cheek pressed into the gritty floor.

After there was nothing left in her stomach to come up, she struggled to sit, wincing from the aches and hurts that stabbed her from face to foot. Her mouth and face were raw from the chief's fists, her belly was one massive bruise. She felt sick and achy, shivers wracked her body, and her forehead was damp with sweat. Nyandoro drew in a shallow breath and wiped her wet mouth with the back of her hand. She realized then that they'd freed her wrists. But not her ankles. Apparently, they didn't want her to drown in her vomit. How kind.

It was too dark in her cell to see anything clearly. Her own hands were only vague shadows in front of her face although, with each breath, the outlines of her prison became clearer. She slid back on her bottom until her back hit the wall, consciously not thinking about what else was on the floor aside from her own vomit. The cool stone felt good through the filthy and tattered remains of her breast cloth so she focused on that small mercy.

Nyandoro didn't know how long she'd been unconscious, she never did. It was only the position of the sun in the sky that gave her some clue how long she'd been under the influence of the sleep sap. Although she'd never taken it of her own free will, it was a drug she was familiar with.

Her father's sister was the village healer before she died, passing the responsibility to her youngest daughter. She knew about berries and herbs to prevent a baby, to make a man or woman fall in love, to ease a headache. And ones to kill. Always curious, Nyandoro had sat with her to learn and ask questions when she was very young. But since her aunt died, she lost interest. Being among the blood berries and high bushes of mint only made her sad.

She must be losing her mind to think now about mint leaves and her long dead aunt. Nyandoro's head dropped forward, stale breath huffing from between her lips that smelled like...yes, the sleeping sap.

Her body, ambushed by dose after dose of the sap, was rejecting it. The sap wasn't meant for prolonged use. If they fed her much more of it, she would die. She lifted her head, blinking into the darkness.

They didn't want to kill her. But she would force them to.

Her life was emptiness now.

But what about Duni? The question whispered at the back of her mind. With it came the last sight she'd had of Duni, her jewel eyes bright with love and anticipation of their future together.

"No, I can't..."

Nyandoro groaned out loud and pressed her face hard into the tops of her knees until it hurt, the self-inflicted pain bringing her back from the abyss of her thoughts. Slowly, she straightened, she rested her head back against the wall, and waited. It was a long time before she heard the distant sound of footsteps, then a scratch outside the door.

She tensed, steeling herself for hands to grab her and truss her up again. This time, she would fight harder—bite, kick, scream—and force one of them to snap her neck. They wanted to. She could see it in their faces.

Her palms pressed down into the gritty floor. She clenched her jaw and waited.

The heavy door pushed open. Bright light flooded in, blinding her, forcing her eyes shut, and she turned away from it, raising her arm. But she only heard the sound of wooden bowls clattering against the stone floor, then the door slammed shut.

One bowl had food, a thin cornmeal, but the other had water. She ignored the food and grabbed the water, forced herself to drink it slowly so her belly wouldn't cramp and force her to vomit it back up. Her throat was so dry, she was so thirsty. Water dribbling from the corners of her mouth and down her neck. Too quickly, it was all gone. She wiped a hand across her face. Too late, she realized the water was a little too thick, that it had a slightly bitter taste. She gasped, her head spinning, hands braced against the floor. Her stomach seized again and she cursed, sluggishly rolling her body in time to avoid falling flat on her face into the stone.

❖

When Nyandoro woke, it was still dark. She shifted her back against the floor, pain twisting in her belly. Her ribs ached and her face felt swollen, her mouth twice its normal size. But the pain wasn't as bad as before. Her thoughts felt clearer. Her body less sluggish. The bowl of meal was gone, as was the water. Instead there was a neatly folded hand cloth in a small, shallow bowl of water, a smaller bowl of soap. She levered herself upright and toward the soap and water, aware suddenly of how much she stank.

With the soapy rag and water, she cleaned her face, wiping away the traces of vomit on her throat and neck. Her stained and ripped clothes hung from her, rancid with the smell of vomit, sweat, and blood. But she couldn't do anything about that.

She wrinkled her nose at the now brown water and emptied most of it in the corner of her cell. Cleaning herself up left her panting and weak. She listened for signs of someone guarding the door but heard nothing. Were they all asleep?

Carefully, Nyandoro stood up and hovered by the door, quiet. She stretched her body, limb by limb, testing its limits with this new poison they were feeding her. She was sore all over. Legs, belly, wrists, even her neck from sleeping on the stone floor. But she could move without constant pain. Her body almost felt like hers again.

She ignored her mind, her thoughts, all the things that would make her fall to her knees and scream for her life to end. There was more than one way to get what she wanted. Nyandoro stood and waited.

Eventually, the key's rattle in the door came again, then the quiet sound of breathing, a flood of light, then a hand low to the floor where she'd been expecting it.

She gripped the hand and pulled. The man grunted and tried to pull back, but she braced her foot on the edge of the door and used her entire body weight to drag him into her cell, and before he could shout out to the others, she cracked the water bowl across his face with a jarring hit she felt all the way through her shoulder. She swung the bowl in the other direction and smashed it into his other cheek. He howled in pain and rage, and tried to grab her, but she jumped on his back, gripped his jaw, and twisted hard.

His neck cracked, broke. No harder than killing an animal. His brothers in arms were fast, tumbling inside the cell in twos and threes. But he was already dead.

They jumped over the dead man, one set of hands pulled his body through the open door as they shouted to each other, grabbed her, and flung her to the floor. Her back slammed into the ground. Pain. A screaming cry of her shoulder being dislocated, the stone scraping against her shoulders.

Kill me. She willed them to do it, begged them to without saying a word. *Kill me.*

"He's dead!"

Someone grabbed her wrists and tied them together, dragged her across the floor and lifted her, hung her on the hook by the rope around her wrists and pulled the hook higher into the air until only the tips of her toes touched the floor.

"We have to get her out of here before the chief kills her."

"Or before I do." One of her kidnappers stood in the cell doorway. The tall, scarred one. His eyes burned with anger and he looked ready to kill her. She growled at him.

Kill me.

She deliberately rattled the chains suspending her on the hook. "If you think you can, try it!"

Kill me.

His eyes cut into her and he growled low in his chest. "If we didn't have to turn you over to them in one piece…"

Nyandoro rattled the chains again. She'd made no one any such promise, and she would kill as many of them as it took for them to break and kill her too. Scar came closer, all threatening lines and angles. Despite the pain pulling at her body, the ropes tying her wrists and ankles, she shifted her weight, gripped the chain that held her up, getting ready to snap her legs up and break his neck, or whatever part of his body he dared to get close enough to her.

But he was smarter than he looked. He stopped. Too late, she noticed a flash of movement behind her. She twisted around to see what or who it was, but a fist smashed into her face. She hissed from the blow. More pain. Hands gripping her legs tight and holding them still. Scar clamped his hand around her jaw and lifted the drinking gourd she hadn't even noticed. He poured the sap down her throat. She roared at them, but that didn't stop the pain and choking and helplessness that flooded into her. Like sleep.

CHAPTER EIGHT

Nyandoro opened her eyes and knew she was dreaming. She was in a large stone room with white walls, and she was comfortable. Instead of the filthy clothes she'd been wearing the last time her eyes were open, a white cloth covered her body from throat to toes. Sunlight poured over the bed from a window near her feet and the ceiling above her was luxuriously high, its smooth stones shimmering as if lit from within.

It must have been a dream. The smell of green grass and wildflowers drifted through the window, and she heard children laughing. It felt like she was back at the village. Everything was clean. There was no smell of a long journey. No dust. No blood. Here, it seemed entirely possible that her mother would walk in the door at any moment, that she would touch her forehead and ask why she was still sleeping with the sun so high in the sky.

Nyandoro closed her eyes. But that would never happen. Her mother was gone. Dead. Her throat slit by the chief's men. Nyandoro whimpered, a sound like a dying animal. She clamped her mouth shut and sat up on the mat, bracing herself for pain. But she felt none. The cloth fell away to her waist, baring her breasts and stomach.

"She is awake."

She heard the voice, speaking in an unfamiliar language that she somehow understood, but didn't see anyone. For a moment, the cool comfort of the room and the strange female voice just outside the door soothed her. Then she remembered where she'd been the last time she opened her eyes.

No! She wouldn't let herself be fooled.

Panic jerked her to her feet on top of the sleeping mat. She slammed her back to the wall and looked frantically around for weapons, eyes jumping from the abnormally high and wide sleeping mat where she stood to the nearby stool and woven grass rug on the floor, the chest-high wooden shelf with folded *kangas* neatly stacked inside it.

There was nothing. All she had to defend herself was her own body. That would be enough.

Nyandoro crouched low, getting ready to strike.

"You should rest."

A woman came into the room. At least Nyandoro assumed it was a woman. She was beautiful and, with each step she took farther into the room, a warm and welcoming scent flooded over Nyandoro.

She was tall, taller than even Nyandoro's mother, and wore her hair in dozens of small plaits. The front plaits were pulled up to the top of her head to form a twisting crown, thick plaits of hair only a shade or two darker than her skin. She carried herself like one used to ruling, upright and regal, but her eyes were pulled tight at the corners like everything she did was a great effort. Despite that, those eyes seemed dark and wild, ever changing, like the skies in the midst of a storm. This woman was a stranger to her.

"I don't want to be in this dream anymore." Nyandoro turned her head away. She closed her eyes and willed herself to wake up. All this softness was a trap. She'd rather be in the walking nightmare of the chief's jail than this torment of a life that wasn't real, whose comforts were a tease and a way to take her off-guard.

"This is no dream, Nyandoro." The woman sat at the foot of the mat, and Nyandoro slid away from her along the wall. "May I call you that?"

"Since I'm going to wake up any moment now, you can call me anything you want."

"This is no dream," the woman said again. "The men came with you in the night and left you here. They are gone now."

At the mention of her jailors, the men who had killed her family, Nyandoro stiffened. Slowly, she straightened but did not let her guard down. "What are you talking about?"

"The men left. I told them they could go. Without them here, I can give you a proper welcome to my home."

Nyandoro pressed her back even more into the wall, and her heart beat even faster in her chest. "You did this? You sent them to bring me here?"

"Of course. You belong here."

The pulse thundered in her ears. "*You*? You did this?" Her hands started to shake. "You're the reason my family is dead?"

The woman's blank face grew even more so. "Dead? No one should be dead."

"Don't pretend like you don't know!" Nyandoro snarled. "You're the reason this happened!" She tensed, ready to jump on the woman and punch her face in until all the bones cracked and the white walls were splashed with her blood. But the crisp and calming scent pushed her back into the wall, soothed her muscles until she was vibrating against the wall, heavy with violent intent but helpless to do anything about it.

The woman stood up. "What did they do?"

Nyandoro panted through her clenched her teeth, tried to fight the odd effect of the woman's smell. Her muscles useless and hard, pressed to the wall and shaking.

What in the name of heaven is happening to me?

She wanted to curse at the woman, to do *something*, but instead the terror of the previous nights, of the night she found her family, came rushing to her in a flood. The nausea. Anger. Pain beyond pain.

"They came at night," she finally said. "I first saw one of them in the market when I was with my iya." The day rushed back, the heat of the morning, her mother's laugh that she would never hear again. Through trembling lips, she tortured herself with the story of what happened. Even as it all seemed like some terrible nightmare while she stood on soft sheets and the smell of sunlight and nearby rains flooding her senses. Those things, she thought to herself even as she told her story, her parents' death and the softness of the room she found herself in, should not exist in the same world. "The last thing I remember is being in a cell. They wanted to defile me. They wanted to kill me."

With each word Nyandoro spoke, the woman seemed to sag inside her skin, her glow diminishing to a sickly gray, the corners of her eyes pulling tight. When Nyandoro finished, looking up in a daze, she saw that the woman was again sitting on the sleeping mat, her palms flat against it as if only that kept her from falling over.

"No!" the woman said. "That is not what I told them to do."

"Well, that is what they did," Nyandoro hissed, fighting the effect of the woman's smell on her. She did not want to be calmed. "And I'd rather slit your throat than be welcomed here in your house."

The woman shook her head, eyes wide and white in her face, a flash of pale that obliterated all the brown. She beat her chest once, threw her head back to stare at the ceiling. Nyandoro thought she heard a crack of thunder in the distance. The woman stumbled to her feet and did not look at her. With a stuttering stride that made her look at once sick and uncertain, she left the room.

When she left, she took her calming scent with her. Nyandoro sagged back down into a crouch, finally able to move. What did that woman do to her?

She looked frantically around the room. *I need to leave. I have—*

A rustling in the doorway brought her head around and her fists up. A young woman hovered there, her eyes on Nyandoro. She was delicate and beautiful with wide eyes and a bud-like mouth. Her body was covered from throat to toes in a flowing, bright blue dress. The girl carried a tray with food and drink.

Something about her delicate looks, the halo of hair around her face, and her large eyes, made Nyandoro feel protective toward her, like the last thing she wanted to do was hurt someone like her. Was this more trickery and magic?

"My pardons, mistress." She put the tray on the small table near the bed and stepped back with her hands clasped at her belly. "The queen sends food for you and something to quench your thirst."

Still staring at the girl, Nyandoro shook her head. "I'm not hungry." But her belly chose that moment to rumble loudly. Her stomach might hunger for food, but she didn't want to take the chance of being drugged again. She'd rather walk toward the fires of hell with her eyes wide open than wake to find herself already in it.

The girl dipped her eyes. "As you wish. I will leave the tray here in case you change your mind. Also, if you chose not to eat, I am also here to help you with your bath."

It was on the tip of Nyandoro's tongue to refuse that as well. But she looked down at her naked body. Even though she no longer wore the clothes from her village—torn, bloodied, foul with her body's fluids—whatever cleaning had been done to her body was only superficial. Her mouth felt thick and sour, her skin was gritty with dirty in places, and under her fingernails was dark with blood.

"A bath," she said.

"Good. I will prepare one for you." The girl slipped from the room but was back within moments, followed by four women who carried a large bathing tub between them. Another two came with water gourds, filling up the tub before leaving behind a bathing cloth and soap near the tub. The whole thing happened within moments. The girl who'd brought the food approached Nyandoro.

"Come," she said. "I will bathe you now."

Nyandoro crouched on the edge of the sleeping mat and looked down at the girl. "No. I don't want you to touch me. I can bathe myself."

The girl froze, like she didn't know what to do with Nyandoro's refusal. "But the queen said—"

"Tell her that I insist on bathing myself. I will bathe and I will only eat with the queen if she shares a meal with me." She wasn't prideful enough to refuse food. She was hungry enough that her belly cramped with it. But she wasn't taking the chance of being drugged again.

The girl's face was tense. She chewed her bottom lip before making a small movement of resignation.

"Very well." She left the room and left Nyandoro alone.

It was disorienting. Coming from her living nightmare of captivity to this…this opulent kindness. Surely a trap. Nyandoro felt like she was suffocating under cloth, separated from the real world by nightmares and dreams she could not tell from reality.

She knew she should be more agitated, more ready to kill, looking for something to kill this woman with and escape to… to somewhere. But all she felt was weak and bereaved. Her family was dead and Duni, though alive, might as well be in another world. If she were a different person, not her mother's daughter, she would've cut her own throat and left this entire misery behind so she could join her family wherever they were.

But she was who she was.

Once, when she was just learning to hunt, Nyandoro had fallen in the grass and twisted her ankle. Her shout of pain had startled a nearby herd of ostriches. They ran over her, stampeded over her body curled protectively into itself on the ground. She felt every crush of their feet, bruises flaring up under her skin, each stomp of their feet on her curled body. Pulped. She's felt pulped like an orange flung hard into the ground while everything soft inside her rolled around loose under her bruised flesh. A hand grabbed her—Kizo's, she found out later—and yanked her from under the thunderous feet and into the cool protection of the underbrush. Like then, her entire body was a massive bruise, but Kizo was not here to save her now. Nyandoro bit into her clenched fist.

The young girl came back into the room, this time with a wash cloth and square of cake soap in her hands. At the look at Nyandoro, she faltered. Then continued into the room to put the cloth and soap on the edge of the tub. She pulled a stool closer to the window and sat down to continue weaving a small, unfinished straw basket.

Nyandoro climbed into the tub. The water, hot and scented with mint, slid over her flesh, over the bruises on her feet, legs, thighs. It lapped at her skin, a comfort and calm. She didn't trust those feelings. They didn't make sense to her. Not when she was in a stranger's house, in a stranger's tub, and a woman whose name she did not even know watched her bathe.

"What's your name?" she asked the girl.

Wide, long-lashed eyes flashed up from the basket. She blinked as if she wasn't sure Nyandoro was talking to her. "Um…I'm Anesa."

"It's good to meet you, Anesa." Nyandoro picked up the washcloth and soap and began to clean herself. "Can you tell me where I am?"

Anesa bit her lip, looking uncertain. "We are in the palace of the Rain Queen," she said with more than a little reluctance.

The Rain Queen who didn't exist? Did this girl take her for a fool? "But where is that? Are we still in the shadow of the great white mountain Kilimanjaro?"

The basket whispered between Anesa's hands as she wove the thick blades of grass together. "We are all in the shadow of the great white mountain," she said. "You, me, the queen. By the grace of Yemaya, we will remain."

"Yemaya?" She was surprised at the mention of the Orisha of her mother. "What does she have to do with this?"

Anesa looked at her almost in pity. "Your iya bargained with Yemaya. If—when she gave birth to a girl, she would keep her while she remained a child then give her to Yemaya once she became a woman."

"Why would she?" Nyandoro asked, though she remembered all too well the many, many times her mother poured libations and made offerings to Yemaya, especially in the days before her death. "My iya paid Yemaya every respect, even when Yemaya did nothing for her." Nyandoro didn't bother to explain her indifference where the Orishas were concerned. Most times, she doubted they even existed.

"The Orishas do not work in the most direct way," Anesa said. "There might have been honors Yemaya granted your family you are unaware of, favors that were made to look as if they came from another human."

"I've always preferred the direct approach, and want others to do the same."

"Not everything in the world can be as you like." Anesa shrugged and went back to her weaving.

She didn't look up for a long time. But when Nyandoro stepped out of the water, she was waiting next to the tub with a clean towel, oils for her skin, and a new dress. Nyandoro dried herself while Anesa went back to her weaving.

It was easy to imagine that all this was a true respite from everything she'd been through over the last few days. The kindness of the women. Her first hot bath in months. But Nyandoro was no one's fool.

"I'm ready," she said once she was dry, oiled, and dressed.

"You don't have to be ready. Just rest. You don't have to go anywhere." Anesa sat with the unfinished basket in her lap, her gaze soft and kind. But Nyandoro didn't want that kindness directed at her. She wanted to see their true faces. They didn't bring her all this way, kill her family, and take her away from her life just to be kind.

"No," Nyandoro said. "Take me to her or wherever you want me to go."

Anesa put aside her weaving. The chair creaked when she stood up. Frowning, she touched Nyandoro's shoulder, pushing her gently toward the bed. But she didn't allow herself to be moved.

Anesa was young, as young as her brother's wife had been. Nyandoro tensed to push her away, but she couldn't bring herself to harm the girl. She was just a servant in this place. She wasn't to blame for anything that happened. And Nyandoro *was* tired. The bath had washed away the dirt from her skin, but left exhaustion in its wake.

"Rest," Anesa said again. "It will be okay."

Nyandoro allowed herself to be pushed toward the mat this time. The bedding was soft and her eyes were closing. Her body relaxed.

"Thank you, Anesa," she said because she was weak.

"It is my honor to help care for you." The girl's words followed her down into sleep.

When the dream came, she was grateful for it. The woman was there.

"I missed you," Nyandoro said, surprising herself.

The woman looked pleased. "Did you really?"

Nyandoro didn't feel the need to repeat herself. She and the woman sat alone on a familiar high rock overlooking a familiar river. Down the path and through the bush, if she dared to follow, would she find her parents, her family alive and waiting for her to return?

"No, you won't." The woman tossed a handful of seeds into the river below their feet. "I'm sorry."

The anger rose in Nyandoro, bitter and dangerous even muffled beneath the softness of dreams. "Then why bring me here?"

"I did not. Your heart did."

Nyandoro grabbed at her chest, discovering then that she was naked. "My heart? My heart?" She sank her fingers into her skin, found it surprisingly easy to push them even deeper, below the flesh, through tissue and straight to the pulsing meat of her heart. It felt useless in her fist with its blood and thumping heat. What was it good for? With a hoarse scream, she yanked the heart out of her chest. It drummed, a red and wet sound, and dripped scarlet through the clench of her fingers and down her wrist.

"I have no heart," she said, and tossed the useless thing toward the river.

The woman cried out, a hand flinging out to reach for the useless heart as it sailed through the air. "No! It's mine."

But the muscle landed with a bloody splash in the water. Golden sunlight glimmered over the river's swirling surface and on the discarded heart that pulsed, once then twice, before sinking beneath rippling eddies.

"What have you done?" For the first time, true emotion showed on the woman's face, a sadness as deep as the river.

"Nothing that hasn't already been done in truth. I think you already know that."

The woman's chin quivered and her large eyes flashed with unshed tears. She called Nyandoro's name and reached out, but Nyandoro turned away from her and from the river. A flash of yellow on the path drew her eyes and she shot to her feet.

It was Duni. She was walking away in her wedding yellow, a basket balanced on her head and her hips swaying beneath the drape of waist beads. Nyandoro watched her, and wished she had kept that pulsing mess in her chest to give to its rightful owner.

"I'm sorry," she said to Duni's retreating back. And meant it.

She woke up to Anesa on the edge of her sleeping mat. The girl had her hand on Nyandoro's ankle, a hot and unpleasant weight. "Are you all right? You cried out in your sleep."

Nyandoro gently eased her foot away from Anesa's touch while pieces of the dream clung to her still. The despair of being back in her village and knowing her family was not there. The ache of seeing Duni alive, but with her back turned, as if she'd moved on from the promises she and Nyandoro had made to each other.

"I'm awake," Nyandoro said in response to Anise's question.

She sat up on the mat and shoved the last of sleep away. Despite the clinging pieces of the dream, she felt more clearheaded than she had in a long time. "I'd like to see the queen."

After looking at her for a long moment, Anesa nodded. "Very well."

When Nyandoro was dressed, Anesa led her down a long hallway, through a palace that glowed with wealth. Not just in the gold gleaming on the arms of the women they passed or the complex construction of the building or even the silk tapestries on the walls. It was in the happiness of the women, most of whom sat on wide chairs, talking. They mended spears, they wove baskets, they held children in their laps. And they all watched Nyandoro.

They found the queen on a terrace overlooking a large courtyard. Like most of the women in the palace, she wore bright blue, a color that well-suited her onyx skin.

"Thank you, Anesa." The queen touched the girl's arm.

Anesa blushed, a hand rushing out to squeeze the elbow of the woman who called herself queen. There was sadness there. Nyandoro looked away from their quick display of affection, because it was unmistakably affection.

She sat at the table set for two. In the center of the table lay a shallow bowl filled with water and sprinkled with tiny orchids. The purple flowers swam on the surface of the water as if carried along on some invisible tide. They smelled sweet.

"Thank you for joining me," the queen said once Anesa had gone back inside.

"Did I have a choice?"

A spasm of an emotion moved across her face, then a smile took its place. Not a real one, though. "Of course. If you didn't want to come out here, I would have come to you."

The queen leaned back in her chair and looked Nyandoro over, her changeable eyes touching every visible inch of her, obviously searching for something she hoped to find across the ble from her.

But Nyandoro was growing impatient with her stares. The terrace had a view of a massive, grassy courtyard with enough space to fit her own family compound ten times over. Scattered fruit trees of all kinds provided shade and food, and the wide wings of the palace spread out in a semi-circle whose open mouth yawned toward the arched stone gateway leading out into the larger valley. Everything about this place was familiar, like she'd seen it before but couldn't recall where. Frowning, Nyandoro turned her gaze back to the queen.

"Why am I here?" she asked.

"Because I want to show you what is mine." The queen glanced over Nyandoro's shoulder and signaled to someone with a lazy curl of her fingers, apparently done with her visual inventory.

"I don't care what belongs to you," Nyandoro said.

"You will."

Footsteps approached the table, and the queen moved back to allow two women to arrange food and drink before them. The two women were not young, but they moved like they were, setting out the meal with quick, spare motions. The food they left smelled tempting, like heat and spice. Bite-sized pieces of meat simmered in a creamy sauce flecked with pieces of red pepper and green onion. Pale slices of yam, still hot from the cook fire, made a pretty circle around meat on the platter.

The queen gestured to the platter and two serving plates. "Please, eat."

Outside the walls of the palace, the breeze was mild and cool, fluttering the edges of Nyandoro's dress. While they talked, a group of children had wandered into the courtyard. They played and danced in a wide circle, chattering in a different language. It took a moment for Nyandoro to realize they were all girls.

Had they been kidnapped by the queen too?

"I was told you wouldn't eat unless I did." The queen reached for the platter. Nyandoro's stomach rumbled. Impelled by her hunger, she took the food before the queen did, turning it around so that the pieces of meat the queen was reaching for were turned toward her instead.

"That's true. I won't." Nyandoro sat back in her chair without touching her food.

The burn of anger and sorrow and shame—*how could I have let this happen?*—held her locked to the chair. A terror that, after a bite of food, she would lose her awareness then wake to more blood, more pain, more loss. Duni's face, and the last time she saw its beloved curve, flashed behind her lowered eyelids and her belly clenched, the sadness rising with a sob. She swallowed it and smoothed her face.

The queen looked at her with that peculiar hurt expression again. She put some meat on her plate, then paused, allowing Nyandoro to do what she would with the other plate—she did nothing—and reached for a slice of yam. The yam was white with curling trails of steam rising from it. Nyandoro didn't flinch from its heat.

Reaching for her food, the queen accidentally bumped the small bowl holding the purple orchids. Her women could have easily removed it. If anything, it was in the way. But the queen moved reverently around the bowl as if it belonged at the table more than she did.

She poured herself a mug of fruit juice. "There are no words that can express my regret about what happened to your family."

Regret? Nyandoro snarled across the table at her. "You're right. So don't try to offer them." The queen winced again. But she deserved none of Nyandoro's mercy. "Because of you, I have no family. I have nothing."

"That's not what I sent them to do. They were—"

Nyandoro cut her off before she could go any further. "It doesn't matter what you intended."

The muscles along the queen's jaw tensed and released. She put a hand, palm down, on the table. "Eat," she said.

Only after the queen took bites of the food and drank from the fruit juice she poured from the gourd did Nyandoro reach for her own portion.

The meat was tender and flavorful. Its juices exploded on Nyandoro's tongue like a well-pleased woman. She swallowed thickly, banishing the thought of Duni before it could fully form. She had to focus on what was before her, not behind. This woman wanted something from her, something she wasn't afraid to resort to kidnapping for. Nyandoro couldn't afford to get distracted from thoughts of escape, and revenge, by good food and innocent-looking women. Those things she'd had in abundance in her village and could have anywhere. But she kept eating. She needed her body to be strong for whatever was to come.

Across from her, the Rain Queen ate in silence, only occasionally looking out at the children in the courtyard or up at the clear sky. Thin wisps of clouds floated across the sharp blue sky and over the entrance to the compound in a way that pricked at Nyandoro's memory. She'd never been to this place before, but something about it reminded her strongly of somewhere else.

"I am dying."

One of the little girls in the courtyard waved up at them. Nyandoro waved back.

"What does that have to do with me?" she asked.

The queen wiped her hands on a damp cloth and carefully put the cloth back on the table. "Yemaya has decided, after I die, you will take my place."

"No." Nyandoro flinched back in automatic revulsion. "What you and your spirits decide has nothing to do with me."

"She did not ask your opinion on the matter."

"Obviously. But I'm telling you and her both, I'm not a pawn and I'm not a toy. Whatever you have in mind for me, forget it."

You do not refuse an Orisha. The voice that had been so absent from her head for the past few weeks returned, weak but undeniable.

Nyandoro clenched her teeth. *I will tell anyone what I damn well please.*

"Don't refuse this honor just because of your pride."

"My pride?" The urge to do violence flared quickly inside Nyandoro, the only warning the hot flush across her cheekbones, the snap of her teeth. "You think this is about my fucking *pride*?" Nyandoro's hands clenched into fists, and she pushed herself back from the table to stop herself from leaping across it and pummeling this so-called dying woman to death. "I refuse you and your bitch because YOU. KILLED. MY. FAMILY." Her shout ricocheted around the terrace, down into the courtyard. Nyandoro felt the women watching her, the children's frightened faces, but didn't care.

She stood up, her knees trembling, her body flushed with anger.

"Do you think I'd trade their lives for your dirty power? All I want—" Tears burned Nyandoro from the inside, but she refused to let them fall. "All I want is my family back. My parents, my brothers, my wife."

Her eyes blurred. Her hands shook. She stared at the children in the courtyard, the green grass and high mountain, the swaying trees she could see beyond the circle of the palace grounds. All this belonged to the queen and could be hers. She remembered then, the night by the river when she told Duni she would one day have a big house, and a wife, wealth enough for a hundred chiefs. Nyandoro bit back a sob, swallowed it until it was nothing more than a sigh.

Had she brought all this on herself, wanting too soon to taste adult things, coveting what was not meant for her? Nyandoro easily remembered Duni in her wedding clothes, the black *kanga* unwinding from around her body and face to reveal her woman's body glowing from beneath the bright yellow of her wedding drapery, the brutal fist of lust that had curled in Nyandoro's belly, making her think *MINE*.

She shook her head and clenched her trembling hands. *No.*

Nyandoro couldn't keep living if that was so. She looked down at the queen. "That's all I want. My family. Not your disgusting house full of slave women."

She turned to walk away, but couldn't move. Her feet were stuck to the floor. "Let me go."

But the queen didn't seem to hear her.

"When Yemaya called me, I had no choice." The queen spoke softly, her voice low like she was remembering that long ago day, that hour. "I'd already reached my twentieth season. I was married and had a child growing in my belly. A life like this—," she waved her hand to indicate the women talking in the anteroom, their voices a rhythmic percussion in the warm afternoon, the massive courtyard, the palace, "—was so far from my reality that it might as well have been a dream." Her face hardened. "I had no choice."

"But *I*," Nyandoro thumped her chest, "have a choice." She had to. Or everything she trusted in—free will, her own personal power—was ashes.

A look of pity settled on the queen's face. Her eyes dropped to the bowl of water on the table with the sweet orchids. "You may think you can resist this, but you cannot. When Yemaya wants something, she gets it."

"She can't force me into this."

"It wouldn't be force, it would be a paradise. This life with Yemaya is more than you ever dreamed of in that little village of yours."

"You don't know anything about my life before this place, so don't presume." Nyandoro crossed her arms. She felt foolish standing while the queen sat before her meal, so she reclaimed her seat. But she was done with the food.

The queen made a motion, and a young woman came to take the remnants of their meal away, head bowed, her bow of a mouth turned down at the corners.

"I know you are in pain." The queen rested her elbows on the table and linked her fingers, rested her chin on them. "I know you want revenge, even if it is against me." Her mouth twitched in an unamused smile. "You can have your vengeance with the power you take from me."

Power. The woman spoke of power as if she could make her family's murderers fall dead with just one thought. Nyandoro knew that wasn't possible. Yemaya had sustained her mother's belief by providing small miracles, keeping her new family safe from the Portuguese invaders who had razed her entire home village. Provided her with a husband whose village was close to a river. Given her a girl child after five large and boisterous boys. But those were minor. Easily explained away with human persistence and her mother's own strength.

"You say you have power, but I see nothing." Nyandoro crossed her arms on the table.

The queen's smile was real this time. "You are truly a heathen. None of your mother's piety rubbed off on you, I see."

"My iya is dead." Nyandoro swallowed the hard lump in her throat. "So is her link to your Yemaya."

"For your sake, I wish that were true."

Distantly, Nyandoro heard the sound of thunder, but the skies stayed clear. The queen put a finger in the crystal bowl, stirring the water. The orchids swirled from the current she created but slid away from her finger to one side of the bowl, huddling together in a purple mass.

The queen tapped her finger and water splashed, but instead of falling back into the bowl, the drops of water hovered in the air then leapt onto the back of the queen's hand, formed the shape of a snake, silver and slick-bodied, to stare at Nyandoro. Its fangs flashed.

She gasped and jerked back in her chair, tried to jump to her feet, but the queen's hand clamped on to her thigh under the table and held her down. Nyandoro's breath whistled between her teeth as she fought against the hand, against the force, keeping her still. The snake wriggled across the table, leaving a wet trail.

Nyandoro tried to pull herself away from the thing that shouldn't exist, but it twisted toward her, tongue extended, a hissing sound like water falling from high rocks. The snake leapt onto her arm from the table, body cool and almost pleasant if it wasn't for the fear threatening to choke her. On her shoulder it curled, seeming to preen under her terrified stare.

Then it licked her face. Stroking her cheek with its cool and wet tongue. It turned to the queen, permission in every line of its body. The woman crooked her finger. The snake stretched its body as if it meant to leap away toward the bowl. But with a flick of the queen's fingers, it disintegrated in a splash. Water splattered Nyandoro's skin, wetting her dress, her face. She jerked in the chair, nearly falling back. That was when she realized she could move again. Nyandoro jumped to her feet, ready to slap the queen, her fear quickly turning into rage.

But at the table, the queen was shaking, her face no longer calm. Her breath came quickly from parted lips.

"Yemaya is mighty," she said despite her breathlessness. "She is not cruel. At least not very much." A smile twitched across her face. "It is not by her hand that your family died. Other forces are at work. She is not the only Orisha with power who still moves in this world."

"Is it the Orishas, or is it *you*?" Nyandoro injected as much scorn as she could into the last word.

At the edge of her awareness, the view of the world beyond the compound shifted, wavering like she looked at it through a wall of water. Then, as the queen's breathing smoothed, the image righted itself and gradually became what it was. Clear.

Nyandoro suddenly remembered. The dream of rain and The Woman she'd had on a night long ago while Duni slept at her side. She'd dreamt of the pale palace and its surrounding compound, of the power that kept them hidden. Looking at the queen now, Nyandoro knew the power that concealed the palace and its women was weak and getting weaker by the moment. It wouldn't keep them separate from the outside world for much longer.

The queen splashed her face with the water from the bowl of flowers then dried her skin with a cloth that appeared instantly from the hand of one of her women. Nyandoro flinched from the sight. Only moments before, a snake made of water had emerged from that bowl and done the woman's bidding. After her face was sufficiently dry, she put the cloth away.

"Come with me," the queen said. "There are things I must make you understand."

CHAPTER NINE

When they came in from the terrace, the women in the anteroom quieted and watched Nyandoro and their queen with collective concern in their eyes. They did not act like servants. Interesting.

"We are going for a walk," the queen told the gathering of women.

Two women unfolded themselves from the group, reaching for spears that Nyandoro hadn't noticed before. These women were neither tall nor strong. But the experience in their faces spoke of many battles, and not all of them won.

"No, stay here," the queen said. "We will not be long."

None of the women looked pleased. Nyandoro only waited with her hands clasped behind her back for the walk to begin. One of the women, who sat with a sleeping child in her lap, spoke up.

"My queen, your safety…"

"I will be perfectly safe with Nyandoro at my side. Yemaya has shown me she is very good with a spear. Her entire body is a weapon." She smiled grimly at that.

"This is what we are afraid of, my queen."

"Stop worrying." The queen dismissed their concern with a wave of her hand, not at all treating the women as if they were slaves or even servants. She gestured for Nyandoro to walk with her.

"Wives," she said with a faint smile. "They worry."

Wives? Nyandoro looked over her shoulder again at the women. A quick count told her there were eleven in all gathered in the room. Then she remembered where she was. Of course, someone who lived in an entire palace could afford to care for nearly a dozen wives. The thought of Duni tore at her. She bit the inside of her cheek until she tasted blood. That life didn't exist anymore.

She and the queen walked through the main hallway of the palace, a slow meandering past rooms and weapons and casually displayed riches. Art on the walls. Teenagers playing with well-made drums. Precious metals melted into bowls. The queen was showing off, showing Nyandoro what could be hers. She walked at her side with little to add about the compound's self-sustainability, the bargains that chiefs near and far had struck with her for rain. Despite her deliberate cultivation of disinterest, however, Nyandoro noticed everything.

The palace was beautiful. All the women—and Nyandoro noticed immediately that there were no men, no boys—were well dressed, healthy-looking, and happy. They glanced at her with curiosity, then at the queen with some version of love or respect then carried on with whatever they were doing.

The large hallway branched off into different rooms, all brightly lit. As she passed one room, its entranceway wide and arched, she smelled food, heard laughter and conversation, felt the faint heat from a hearth fire.

The courtyard held many shade trees. A few women. The children still playing in their circle. Under a wide fig tree, a woman dressed in a warrior's short tunic nursed a baby at her breast while she rested her head on the tree's thick trunk. Sunlight slid through the leaves and shifted over her face, over the baby, glimmering gold on their skin. A spear leaned near her. Nyandoro looked away from them, feeling as if she were disturbing their quiet.

The palace rested in a valley, but the path Nyandoro and the queen took on foot wound them through long fields of green grass, through tall trees swaying with the breeze, with the chattering of monkeys perched above, and the sound of the sea not far away.

It felt good to walk outside again. Her legs had been shaky with the first step, and the second. But she grew stronger with each long stride she took at the queen's side, her legs and feet moving with surprising power under the bright yellow dress that brushed the ground and caressed her thighs and legs. The dress felt too cumbersome to fight in but was a whisper of luxury against her skin.

They walked to the ocean, mimicking each other's footsteps across the sand. The queen's dress was shorter than hers. She moved across the beach more freely, her sandaled feet sinking into the white to contrast with her dark feet. They skirted the edge of the water, still in silence.

A flash of something caught Nyandoro's eyes. The curved side of one boat, then two. She blinked to see if it was an illusion, a trick of rain and water. But when her eyes opened, the boats were still there.

Nyandoro flickered her gaze between the boats and the forest and the route they had taken, noticing the limited avenues for escape, plotting how long it would take her to make her way through the trees after killing the queen. They had walked for what could have been two or more *maili*. The queen looked weak. Her show of power at the table had cost her. She wasn't strong enough to take Nyandoro in a fight.

A coconut tree had fallen across the sand, its long and dark body stretched from the forest to the water, leaves sweeping to and fro in the tide. The queen sat on the tree's trunk, straddling it like a young girl, and stared out to sea. A salt-laced breeze whispered around and over them.

The queen began to speak. "When I took the mantle of Rain Queen almost three hundred seasons ago"—Nyandoro drew in a shocked breath—"I took it willingly, despite the life I had to leave behind. As did my predecessor. We won't force you into this."

Nyandoro choked back a laugh of disbelief. "Your search for a new queen *killed* my family and dragged me halfway across the world. It made me give up the woman I love. All this feels like force to me."

"Except for *you* then, no one has come here by force." The wind dragged at her dress and flapped it against her thighs, bare and taut draped over the trunk of the coconut tree. "This place is a refuge," the queen said. She spoke like she was explaining things to a child. "Many of the women here came from other villages where they were cast off by their husbands and had no family or place else to turn."

Like Duni.

Nyandoro latched on to the thought of her would-be wife, something precious she'd kept for herself through the long journey from Jaguar Village to this place. The alternative to dying or giving in to the Rain Queen's demands was escaping and going back to Duni. But then what? Nyandoro couldn't imagine the rest. They had taken so much from her.

Sorrow rippled under her skin and pulled her face tight. She crossed her arms over her belly. "I thought you killed all the men here and got rid of all the boy children."

"No man has ever been welcomed into the palace," the queen said with a pleased smile. "Some of the women come already pregnant. The ones who stay and take other women as wives are blessed by Yemaya with baby girls."

"What?" The women had babies with each other?

"Yemaya makes many things possible. Especially such a small thing as having a family to call your own."

"So you have daughters here? Other than Anesa?"

"Of course. I've been here for a very long time and I enjoy taking my wives to bed." A wicked light flickered in the queen's eyes. "It is one of many joys that come with the throne."

She was pitifully transparent, trying to tempt Nyandoro with all she had. But it wasn't working.

"All that sounds very well and good, but I still won't accept it."

All humor fell from the queen's face. Her eyes flashed white. "You have to."

"I don't have to do anything but die."

"Then you will die without avenging the death of your family." The queen's words were like arrows slamming into Nyandoro's chest. She drew in a breath, and it *hurt*.

But that hurt quickly turned to anger. It lashed through her like a lightning storm and incinerated any sense of caution she might have had. She looked across the water. Kizo had wanted to wander the world and see all the beauty it had to offer. Now he never would.

Nyandoro clenched her trembling hand into a fist. And swung it at the queen. The woman didn't hesitate. She jerked back from Nyandoro's fist so fast her dress threshed the air with the sound of frightened birds, and she was returning the blow, leaping *into* Nyandoro instead of away. Hands shoved hard into Nyandoro's chest and she staggered back, eyes narrowing, her body readying itself for a real fight.

This was not the weak woman she expected. The queen slammed a fist into her belly. She gasped at the pain and leapt back, the sand sucking her feet deep. But she steadied herself, whirled back into the fray with her body feeling even stronger than before, the blood rushing through her fast and sweet.

Yes. This was more like it. An equal fight where she could defend herself or at least die with the enemy's blood on her lips. She flipped to the other side of the tree, using precious moments to rip the hem of her dress so she could free her legs from their betraying softness. The queen came at her in a graceful somersault, blue dress flapping around her slender body, the sun glinting off her skin. Her foot kicked high and Nyandoro ducked, catching the blow on her shoulder instead of her head. It hurt. But she twisted into the queen with a hard thrust of her palm and she staggered back. And came for Nyandoro as if the blow never happened. She was definitely strong. And Nyandoro realized, her breath coming faster, sweat gathering in the small of her back and on her forehead, they were evenly matched.

The queen came at her, blow after blow, pushing her into the sea. The salt water splashed up around their legs, into her face, her mouth. The thumping rhythm, the sting of their blows took her back to another place, sparring with her brothers, feeling the bite of their fists or feet on her body, the satisfaction of landing a hit of her own. And because that memory came to her, she fought the queen harder. Spinning and kicking.

She could feel her lips skinning back from her teeth, the rage from earlier at the table take her over, make her want to see red blood spilled on the white sand. Because of this woman, her family was gone. Because of this woman, she had no one. Because of this woman, she was forced to wander the continent like a clan-less person. She roared and came at the bitch again.

The queen's skin glowed with sweat, but she was almost smiling. There was no bloodlust in her. Her movements were graceful and practiced, like she was doing work that was necessary, not something she enjoyed or even whose outcome she was invested in seeing. That made Nyandoro even angrier.

"I'll gut you, bitch!"

The queen had the nerve to laugh in her face. "You can try." She wasn't even breathing hard.

The queen's hand flashed out and caught Nyandoro in the face. She felt her lip split, felt blood gush, tasted it. But she didn't dwell on it. She kicked out, snarled in triumph when the blow connected and the queen dropped back into the sand. But before Nyandoro could take advantage, the queen was back on her feet and darting away. She followed to grab her but felt the slam of a fist instead. She lashed out through the pain and caught the queen high up on her cheekbone. She could feel the skin split under her knuckle and growled in triumph, ready to take her down.

A piercing cry froze her next movement. In that split second, she cursed herself for freezing up at some strange sound but realized a movement later that the queen had done the same and was looking over her shoulder toward the palace. It was an alarm. Nyandoro sensed it in the sudden fear and resolution on the queen's face, her abrupt dismissal of Nyandoro as a threat. She turned from Nyandoro and ran toward the palace.

She felt a pull toward the queen, a stretching of time and a disorientation and then they were, impossibly, in the courtyard of the palace and the queen was staggering where she stood as if she had been pulled by a sudden and strong breeze. She had used her power to get them back from the beach. It was using this power, Nyandoro realized, that made her weak, not using her physical body. Anesa slipped from a nearby corridor, her eyes wide with fear.

"The watchers on the mountain see men approaching."

The queen took a moment to catch her breath. "Do we know who they are?"

"They wear the familiar markings of the men who left Nyandoro eight days ago."

Eight days?

The queen nodded as if she had been expecting the news. "Send three guards. Have them go to the men and ask what they want."

"Iya, you know what they want. You saw it in your dream."

This was her daughter? Nyandoro narrowed her eyes at Anesa, trying to find traces of the queen in her face. But she found a delicate sweetness in Anesa that was absent from the queen's beautiful but unyielding face.

"This may not be the moment I dreamt," the queen said.

But even Nyandoro sensed the lie. The queen knew what the men had come for. Did they want to take her back? Her hands turned into fists. They wouldn't get her alive again.

The previously peaceful palace was now a blur of motion and worry percolated like a bad smell in the air. Nyandoro could taste its bitter tang with each breath. After sparing another desperate look at her mother, Anesa ran back where she came from.

"What's happening?" Nyandoro demanded. "What are those men here for?"

The queen turned away, or at least tried to, but Nyandoro grabbed her hand. "Tell me!"

Under her hand, she felt the power in the woman, a flicker of electricity under her skin, lightning sparking up into her arm, painful and hot. But Nyandoro did not let go. "Tell me," she insisted again.

The queen snarled. "You want to know what they want?" Her teeth were a ferocious white against her skin. She grabbed Nyandoro's other hand in a vice grip.

A tingling buzzed through Nyandoro's hands, running up her arms and into her chest. Images flooded her mind.

Men at the farthest entrance to their oddly placed valley, hills on both sides, the mouth of their valley leading out to the sea. Running in controlled formation and carrying spears. Hundreds of men. Then another image, more like a thought or an order. A wish. The palace burning, white under dark smoke and yellow flames. Men pushing women into the ground and burrowing furiously between their thighs. Dead warrior women everywhere and, in the back of the palace near the beach, in relief against the burning house, a rising pile of valuables—gold and jewelry, goats and cows, women tied together with rope to be taken away in slavery, the queen dead and a man standing at the center of it all with his hands raised to the heavens while lightning pulsed overhead in the sky.

The queen pulled her hand away and the visions dropped from Nyandoro's mind. She gasped, eyes blinking frantically as fear bathed her body in stink. Even though it was all in her head, she could still smell the charred bodies from the vision, feel the smoke from the palace burning into her eyes.

Nyandoro couldn't catch her breath. "Can they do that?"

"They think they can," the queen said. "Whenever we have a transition between queens, there is always a risk. Our power is at its lowest, and some try to take advantage. The outside world thinks we have great wealth here. Jewels and power that ordinary men can use. Every three hundred seasons they forget that even at our weakest, we are still strong. They must be made to remember again." Something dangerous flashed in her eyes, but it quickly flickered out. She didn't have enough strength for even a threat.

She reached out a hand to Nyandoro. "Become the new Rain Queen and stop them."

That couldn't be the only solution. "No. I can't." Nyandoro shook her head and stepped away, physically separating herself from the queen and her problems. Their fight was not hers.

The queen's expression shuttered and became hard. "Then stay out of our way."

She rushed from the room in a sweep of blue cloth. Nyandoro stood frozen in the chaos, panic racing down her spine while women raced through the hallways, some carrying weapons, others cradling children.

A pair of warriors, armored in thick animal skins and carrying blades at their blue-sashed waists, bumped into Nyandoro's shoulder as they ran past. Her heart drummed between her ribs. The blood rushed through her, a swift and dizzying flood. She didn't want to go back with the men. This time, they wouldn't worry about keeping her whole, or even alive. They would use her like the women in the vision, then they would sell her to anyone who had enough cowrie to pay. The quim of the would-be Rain Queen to the highest bidder. Fear gripped her belly.

She couldn't stay here.

She couldn't allow herself to be taken by those men again.

She wouldn't let them rape and torture her.

She had no choice but to fight. For herself.

A deep breath of resolve and Nyandoro turned to follow the queen. She'd only taken a few steps before Anesa appeared at her side. The young girl's face was frightened, her large eyes on the verge of spilling over with tears. She fell into step with Nyandoro, easily keeping up with her near run against the stream of women rushing the other way.

"Why won't you take the queen's power?" Anesa asked, breathless and sad. "We waited so long for you to come to us. We allowed you to have a life. Is this how you will allow all of our waiting to end?" She jerked her arm toward the upheaval around them. "Those men will not be merciful with us."

Apparently, she hadn't believed her mother's words about not knowing what the men wanted either. Not that she had to be an oracle to know what a group of armed men bearing down on a houseful of women wanted. The specifics were unclear, but the broader picture was not. They would all die, be tortured for sport, or end up enslaved.

"This has nothing to do with me. You brought me here. You caused this. Your fight with those animals has nothing to do with me."

"But those animals are the ones that killed your family. Don't you want to take revenge on them?" Anesa was very much her mother's child.

Revenge? No, this was suicide. Nyandoro started to tell the girl as much, but Anesa dragged her to a stop, pulled her from the path of the women rushing past. Her hands gripped the front of Nyandoro's dress.

"Don't make us lose everything," she said, her voice breathless with desperation. "You can stop all this."

The panic in her face, the way her body trembled like a bird caught in a windstorm, almost broke Nyandoro's resolve. But she steeled her spine. There was only one person she would fight for now, and that was herself.

She needed to find a spear, a *tapanga*. And she needed to leave this place. Nyandoro untangled Anesa fingers from the front her dress. "Where are your weapons?"

A look of triumph and gladness transformed the girl's face, then she frowned. "You cannot fight them when your body vulnerable like this. You need my iya's power."

Nyandoro thought briefly of lying, telling the girl what she wanted to hear so she'd show her the weapons room. But it seemed too cruel. "I'm sorry, but your iya will die queen of this place."

"Please! No." Anesa grabbed her arm.

But Nyandoro didn't have time for any of this. These women had destroyed everything she had. She wasn't going to reward them by giving them what they wanted. But she *would* take what she needed from them. A quickly drawn breath and she slammed her elbow into Anise's head.

With a sharp cry, the girl collapsed. Nyandoro cradled her light form, leaned her against a nearby wall and out of sight behind a large potted palm. Then she turned and ran with the other women. She pushed through the confusion of female bodies, women running to the safer parts of the palace, deeper rooms with no windows and trapdoors to prevent invaders from finding them. Nyandoro remembered her vision and how the palace had burned. The women didn't stand a chance. But she didn't want to pity them. Nyandoro ran faster, pushing her way through the sharp stink of fear clogging the hallways, and focused on the direction where the armed warrior women came from. Where they came from, she was sure to find weapons.

Her instincts were right. In the weapons room at the end of a twisting hallway, she grabbed a long blade from its place beside dozens of others on the wall. Feeling eyes on her, she twisted around with the blade in hand. A passing group of women peered into the room at her then, ignoring Nyandoro, moved on as if there was nothing to see. They looked like guards, these women who wore short blue tunics and carried long *tapangas* and short daggers strapped to their waists. One of the women even carried an axe.

How far away were the invaders? The women acted as if they would appear at their doorstep at any moment. Nyandoro grabbed a belt and bucked it around her waist, slid a *tapanga* and a short dagger into the loops designed to carry them. Then she left the palace.

Even in the growing darkness, it was easy to find the path she and the queen had taken down to the sea. She walked quickly away from the palace. It wasn't her responsibility. It *wasn't*. She could do nothing for these women short of giving away what was left of her life. Those assurances didn't stop the guilt from following her down to the sand and to the small flotilla of boats she'd seen when she and the queen had had their "talk."

The boat she wanted was one of half a dozen tethered to the shore. It floated placidly in the blue-green water between larger boats, small enough to carry her alone to anyplace she wanted. The vessel's very presence on the shore, quiet and unbothered, screamed in sharp contrast to the chaos Nyandoro had left behind at the palace. Her guilt screamed even louder.

It's not your problem.

It's not your problem.

Chanting the words under her breath, she ran toward the small boat, her sandaled feet sinking into the sand with each step. The sound of the sea whispered at her, tugging at her the closer she drew to the dark wooden boat with a foreign word scrawled across its side.

Liberdade.

Nyandoro tugged at the rope holding the boat prisoner to the land, her fingers fumbling with the rough twine, slipping over and over again, unable to disconnect the line.

"Fuck!"

She yanked at the rope and it cut into her skin, burning with each frustrated tug. The wet sand squelched between her toes and gently pulled her farther toward the water. She should go. She *wanted* to go. Duni and a peaceful life waited for her on the other side of this journey. But still, Nyandoro didn't do what would've been the simplest thing: cut the boat's tether with the blade at her waist. Instead, her hands stopped moving on the rope. She cursed again.

The sea was dark, and growing darker. Stars peered down from the sky and the moon was fat and white, giving off the perfect amount of light to sail by. A sharp scream cut through the trees. Nyandoro gripped the edge of the boat and dropped her head in defeat. She turned and ran back up the path.

In the valley, the palace was already on fire.

A small blaze raging under the lower window of one of the palace rooms, the invaders' first attempts to smoke out the women. The queen's women fought the invaders in the courtyard, on the rise of the hill. But it wasn't enough. They needed help.

Nyandoro drew her *tapanga* with the sound of steel against leather and ran toward the men who swarmed like ants down from the mountain on both sides of the palace. The men numbered in the hundreds. Their feet drummed into the dirt and their necklaces made of animal teeth and bone looked wet in the dark, frightening symbols of what they could do to these women and girls once—if—they took the palace. Nyandoro ran faster, dimly aware of the wet grass under her feet, blood, not water. Like in her village.

Nyandoro slashed the throat of the first man she reached.

His gurgling scream drew the attention of men nearby, and her presence on the field of blood was no longer a secret.

With every man that came at her, she imagined the men who had taken her family, their gloating faces, and their chief. She slashed with the sharp blade, dancing between thrusting spears and slashing knives before they could touch her, pushing into the never-ending surge of men that rushed toward the palace.

These men were strong, well-rested and well-armed. But she didn't stop. She kept slashing until her shoulder ached from the thud of her *tapanga* into flesh and bone, kicking the dead men from the end of her blade with her foot, moving silently through the chaos and using her size and agility to her advantage.

Flesh pounded flesh. Men and women screamed in pain. Blood splashed her hands, her face. In the madness of the fight, Nyandoro imagined the white walls of the palace splashed with red. She gasped when a punch landed on her face and split her lip, exploding the taste of blood in her mouth. The blow brought her firmly back into the fight, and she howled at the soldier who came at her throat with his blade. Nyandoro split his belly and darted away.

But there were so many of them.

The grunts and screams of men, of women, echoed through the valley. Both sides were losing. Nyandoro imagined the frightened faces of the children, the women hiding in those rooms vulnerable to fire and death. She slashed through the men, gasping. The breath whooshing from her mouth, her chest heaving, her arms stinging from minor cuts.

How would the queen win this? It looked impossible. It looked like she would get her chance to die after all. She was ready.

To her left, another woman went down under a spear, but she took her killer with her, ramming her blade up into an invader's body and twisting just before the light leached out of her eyes. The men hadn't made it into the palace, but it was only a matter of time. Panting, she ran toward the building, dodging men and bodies and spears, keeping low to the ground and constantly moving, her eyes already adjusted to the moonlit night.

She leapt over a rangy man, slashing through the meat of his neck before he could make it farther toward the palace. She ran up the steps. Then gasped at a punching pain at her back. She fell down to one knee, reached back to feel the steel lance buried in her back. Shelter. She needed to find shelter.

Nyandoro spun and hid behind a column, hissing from the pain when the spear jolted in her flesh. It *burned*. She twisted and reached back, wrenched the spear with a liquid squelch from between her shoulder blades. Agony. Her throat raw, she screamed and hurled the spear. It rammed into a man leaping toward her, slashing into his neck. But the move cost her and she slipped down the white steps and into the grass, leaving a bloody trail. Blood filled her gasping mouth, coppery and strong. Swaying only a little, she jumped to her feet.

Up ahead, a pair of men jumped over an unguarded terrace. *Isn't that where—?*

Nyandoro's eyes narrowed when she saw Anesa, slashing and fierce, attack the men with a spear. Her movements were tight and graceful, admirable on a practice field, but not enough against men actually trying to kill her. Nyandoro grabbed a spear sticking from a dead invader's chest and threw it as hard as she could. It caught one of the men in the throat and he fell on top of Anesa. She screamed.

Nyandoro dodged a slashing *tapanga*, ran, and sprang onto the bent back of a woman warrior, landing on the thick stone railing with her short knife gripped in her hand. But both men were already dead. Anesa looked both feral and frightened, her face stained with blood.

Nyandoro dragged her to her feet.

"Come with me!"

Their feet pounded against the stone floors as they ran into the palace, Nyandoro pushing the girl ahead of her, heading where her instincts told her the queen was. From deep in the palace, she felt a thrum of power, followed it through the corridors to a small room with a door hidden by a false wall.

Nyandoro shoved Anesa into the room, panting. And stared at what she saw. The queen sat on the floor surrounded by children and young women, girls who had yet to pass five seasons. She was singing softly to them. A child sat in the queen's lap, bewildered eyes flickering around the room while she sucked her thumb. The child reminded Nyandoro of the baby girl her brother's wife would've had. A child who never got the chance to be born. She staggered where she stood.

The room stank of fear and resignation, women clutched each other, crying, and children sobbed into their mothers' breasts. Although a fight to the death raged outside their hidden door, it was just a matter of time before the invaders found them. Nyandoro stared at the child in the queen's lap, her wide-eyed vulnerability, her innocence. She drew in a hitching breath when the inevitable realization settled in her. These women and their children had nothing to do with what happened to her family. They were victims too.

"I'll do it." Nyandoro fell to her knees at the queen's feet. "I'll accept the power."

Anesa cried out, her voice jarring and loud over her mother's singing. She stared at Nyandoro in shock before rushing to the queen's side, gently pushing her way through the barrier of children to hang on to her mother's arm. She looked terrified.

The queen huffed out a sound that was very much like relief.

"There is no need to kneel for me, Nyandoro," she said. "You and I are the same." Her voice was low, rough.

The children, seeming to sense a change in the room all began to move away from the queen, throwing frightened glances at Nyandoro's face, the bloodied dagger in her hand, her torn dress. She shoved the dagger into her belt.

"It was them." Nyandoro jerked her head toward the children, the pregnant women, and the delicate looking ones who looked like they'd never so much as slaughtered a chicken in their lives. "I can't let those men in here with them."

"Whatever the reason, it is the right one."

"Iya..." Anesa clung to the queen's arm, tears running down her face. "Is it really time?"

Nyandoro frowned at her through the thundering of her heart, the mixed feelings twisting her stomach to shreds. She thought this was what Anesa wanted all along.

"You know this is what we have been expecting, my Anesa. Nothing is forever."

A sob twisted the young girl's face, and even the quiet children began to sniffle.

The queen pressed a kiss to Anesa's forehead then gently pulled away. "I've always loved you best," she said to her daughter.

Anesa's smile was watery and unconvincing. "I know you say that to all the others."

Nyandoro's fingers twitched with impatience. The blood was beginning to dry on her skin. More and more women were losing their lives the longer they continued with...whatever was going on here. Her mouth twisted with impatience.

"First you wanted none of this, now you're pushing for it to happen!" Anesa snapped. "You're an animal!"

Nyandoro didn't have time to decipher what was going on with her. "Either let me have the power or don't," she said. "But whatever the decision, we have to do something."

The queen put a hand on her daughter's head. "Shh, Anesa. She only wants to help."

"Now when it is almost too late and we've lost so many."

"Anesa!" The queen snapped her daughter's name, her patience apparently at an end. The girl shut her mouth. "Come, Nyandoro."

Anesa reluctantly moved away from her mother, and Nyandoro came to sit next to the Rain Queen, their thighs pressed together, knees raised. The queen twisted slightly so their foreheads were pressed together, their fingers laced. Her breath puffed against Nyandoro's mouth, warm and faintly sour. She felt cool. But with each passing moment, the places where they were pressed together grew warm.

"Yemaya, grant me the power," the Rain Queen said softly, the words low and ceremonial, "to give up what you have bestowed upon me for these many seasons."

For a moment, Nyandoro wondered what she should say, what she should do, then the words appeared in her mind and spilled from her mouth. "Yemaya grant me the power to accept what you so freely give."

Thunder rumbled in the distance, and the room crackled with power around them. From the contact point between their foreheads, Nyandoro felt a nearly unpleasant heat, as if she'd been lying in the noonday sun too long. Voices whispered. Wind rustled through trees in a place she could not see. Knowledge rushed into her in a dizzying swirl. She tilted her head by instinct, just as she felt the Rain Queen do the same.

Their mouths touched. Power flared between their bodies, a flash of pale lightning. Nyandoro opened her mouth to the liquid press of the queen's tongue, a blood-quickening suck and release of lips and breath that made her lashes flutter down in embarrassed arousal. Electricity danced between their mouths, slid down her throat and settled in wild heat in her belly. Power. The firm snare of the queen's teeth on her lower lip quickened desire between her legs, and she squirmed, pressed her thighs together, and, unable to help it, sighed into the hot mouth stroking hers. When the queen pulled back she was smiling.

Nyandoro flushed hot, aware of the children and Anesa nearby. A squeeze of her hand brought her attention back to the purpose of their union.

"We are rain," the queen said.

"Moonlight." Nyandoro trembled as she said the word.

"The fecundity of the valleys."

They spoke as one. "Until we are no more."

The room seemed to vibrate with each word they spoke, the air crackling, a sharp and bright smell of lighting and the sound of thunder filled the room.

Then Nyandoro couldn't breathe. Memories, not hers, pressed down on her. This Rain Queen on her first night at the palace, standing naked and in shock as her new wives bathed her. Another queen, long turned to dust, gasping in the throes of childbirth as her first and last daughter slid from between her thighs. Still another queen crouching in the middle of a charred battlefield with lightning exploding from her outspread hands to kill every man in her sight. And more and more.

Stupidly, Nyandoro tried to fight it. Pushing back against the heavy weight of the other queens' memories, of their lives.

"Breathe. It will be okay," the Rain Queen said against her cheek, her breath soothing and warm. "Don't fight. If you fight, it will take longer and it will hurt. Let her in. Allow yourself to be hers."

Nyandoro unclenched her fists slowly and let go of her fear. Her breathing calmed.

"Àṣẹ."

Then the lightning and thunder flashed out of existence, and the room was just like any other once again. A wavering moan left the Rain Queen's throat. She sagged toward the floor, but Nyandoro caught her before she fell. "My queen!"

But the Rain Queen raised a hand that was thinner than it had been just moments before. "I am called Aminifu once again," she said. "Now, you are as what I once was." Slowly, the youth began to disappear from Aminifu's features. Her skin grew papery and thin, age spots peppered the sides of her face, her hands. Aminifu sighed as if releasing a great weight. "Take care of the women here. Take care of Anesa and my other daughters."

"Iya!" As if the sound of her name had been her signal that the ceremony was over, Anesa rushed to Aminifu's side, sobs overtaking her. "Please, not yet! I need more time with you. Just a little more."

"You've had three hundred seasons with me, my little one. It is time to let go now."

Her thin palm brushed across Anesa's cheek with a sound like paper. Tears rolled down the young girl's face.

"My queen," Aminifu said, her voice barely above a whisper. "You must do it now."

"Yes." And Nyandoro did know what it was she should do.

She gathered all her will. Then blasted it into the world. Lightning flashed behind her eyelids and her entire world went white.

The power flashed through her like a cleansing fire. She felt everything—the minute growth of her fingernails, the desperation of the women in the palace, the life flowing out of Aminifu.

"She is well taken care of," a familiar voice whispered in her ear.

It was the same voice that had threaded through her thoughts since she was a small child, the woman who...

"You are *her*."

The woman, the being, bowed at the waist and the cowrie collar that hid her breasts shifted, revealing then concealing her brown nipples. "I am." The long *kanga* around her waist also moved, drifting around her legs like the waves of the sea.

With her rain washed eyes, she saw the Orisha for who she was. Not the beautiful woman who appeared to her in dreams. But the mother, the mermaid, the warrior woman, all aspects of her that her mind could not grasp before, all shifting from one to the next, never-ending. With Nyandoro in the half dream state where she was aware of the things happening in the world— Anesa crying, Aminifu feeling disoriented by the loss of power, the loss of her intimate conversations with Yemaya.

"I should be angry with you," Nyandoro said.

"You *are* angry with me." Yemaya curled her legs under her, although she had no legs and she wasn't in fact even resting on the floor with her but floating on a piece of the sea, rippling and bright. Nyandoro absently wondered if she touched it, would it be wet.

"Why don't you touch and see?" Yemaya's smiles were unlike any she had ever known. Sharp, sweet, dangerous, warm, devilish, mocking, filled with the best intent.

"I am not a child." Nyandoro didn't know where that comment came from. As soon as Nyandoro said the words, she knew they were wrong. Only Duni had looked at her like a child, though not for long.

"I know." Yemaya's finger trailed down her arm, a cool and shivery sensation that rippled all the way through her. "When you have adjusted to being mine, I will claim you in all the ways one being can claim another. I look forward to tasting you outside of dreams."

A hint of that promised pleasure snaked down Nyandoro's spine and made her think again of Duni.

"Am I dreaming now?" she asked with only a hint of the grief she was feeling.

Yemaya smiled again and flicked water over Nyandoro's face. "You tell me."

She closed her eyes against the cool spray. When she opened them, her face was wet and her enemies were dead.

CHAPTER TEN

The outer rooms of the palace, the courtyard, and the grassy stretch of land around the palace were filled with dead men. Nyandoro stood on the wide stone terrace and stared out at the fertile valley grass that was black from the hundreds of bodies that had simply dropped where they stood. Hearts stopped. Although she'd known they were there and dead because of her, seeing them made her gasp in shock. She swayed into the high railing of the terrace. The moonlight felt too bright on her face.

This power, she thought with bile rising in her throat, could easily turn me into a devil.

"My queen."

It took her a long time to realize the guard, hovering behind her on the terrace, was talking to her. She turned.

"What shall we do with the bodies?" A gash bled sluggishly high on the woman's cheekbones, but she didn't seem bothered by it. She stood with a hand gripping the handle of the *tapanga* sheathed at her waist.

What should we...? Oh, right. "Bury our sisters," Nyandoro said. She closed her eyes, and every dead invader around and inside the palace disintegrated into dust.

A ripple of approval came from that place inside her where Yemaya now lived.

But she only felt her own fear. Power pulsed through her hands like a new wound. Her entire body felt lit afire from the inside out, senses on high alert, aware of everything from the touch of the cloth on her skin to the strength of the tides on the nearby sea. It all frightened her. And it made her want safety. It made her want to take back her decision and say "no" to Aminifu, to tell her she'd made some terrible mistake.

But Aminifu was no longer the Rain Queen.

Nyandoro was, and she had things to do.

A warrior in blue armor appeared high on the rise with a bow and empty quiver. Even from there, Nyandoro could see the warrior was exhausted and at the end of her endurance. Smaller figures trailed from behind her, and they began their slow, winding way down into the valley. Nyandoro felt their loss. She could see the blood splashed on their faces, on their hands, and not all of it belonging to their enemies. They'd lost just as she had. Nyandoro was tired of losing.

The pulse hammered in her throat and her hands clenched into fists, driving short nails into her palms. She trembled all over. Was this fear? She'd experienced it enough in her lifetime and learned to mask it with jokes and false bravery. Only when she felt the growl rise in the back of her throat did she realize what she was feeling.

Rage. Mindless and all-consuming rage.

Aminifu and Anesa had what they wanted. The palace was safe from invaders.

She was the one left with nothing. Her life from now on would be empty. She only had a throne she never wanted. A broken marriage promise. Nightmares of dead bodies scattered around a cold hearth. And the men who had done this to her still walked the earth whole and unchanged.

Her anger burned. The heat of it rolled through her and pushed her forward through distance.

She emerged on a rock-paved road just outside the walls of a village. The wall was as tall as four men, the top jagged with sharp blades. Its gates were closed, but with a light push from her mind, Nyandoro opened them. The squeal and clatter of the massive gates yawning brought tall men with spears and *tapangas* running.

Nyandoro waved a hand infused with power and they fell back, looking confused, before turning back to their posts. The village, like the first time she'd seen it, appeared like any other. A main square and houses with vegetable gardens. Kanga cloths hanging to dry on lines strung between trees.

The streets were wider than Jaguar Village, and quiet. Nighttime left the village nearly deserted, but the strong glow of torchlights high on a hill and surrounding a large stone house, larger than the simple dwellings that spread out in a circle along the village walls, guided her to where she needed to be. The chief was there with advisors, she knew, waiting on news from his men sent to attack the queen.

He wasn't going to like the news she brought him.

Nyandoro pressed forward. She didn't hide herself, instead gave the guards a long look at her as she made her way down a narrow hallway toward the room where she sensed the chief's presence.

Feminine and soft. That's how she knew she looked to them. Her face was round and pretty in the torchlights, her tunic soft and loose around her body as it brushed the floor with each step. Her small knife, traded out for the more obvious *tapanga*, seemed a negligible presence at her waist.

But as Nyandoro came closer, one of the guards stared at her with growing suspicion. He recognizing her from when she'd been there before. A prisoner. He pointed his spear and opened his mouth to say something to her, but she waved her hand and put him to sleep along with the others.

Nyandoro opened the door. She saw the chief sitting high and tall on an ornate chair and talking with three of his men. The room was bright with torchlights. Two of the men stood near a table spread with maps, while the third leaned against a nearby wall with his spear propped up beside him, his arms crossed over his chest and his chin dropped low like he was taking a nap.

"We will win," one of the men was saying. He stood with his scarred fists braced against the wooden surface of the table. "The men were right behind the messengers carrying the girl. They were far enough behind that the women couldn't detect them, but close enough to have already started the fight."

"It won't be a fight," the chief said with a dismissive shrug. "You only fight with an equal." His eyes swept over the map. "We sent every available man. Their queen" he spat the word with contempt, "should be dead by now and her women rounded up for the foreign slavers."

"You're almost half right," Nyandoro said as she stepped fully into the room.

Their shock almost made her smile. She floated across the room, showing off now, her feet not touching the floor.

"Who are you?" One of the men near the table confronted her the same time the chief jumped to his feet, reaching for the *tapanga* at his waist.

"Grab her!" the chief growled.

Nyandoro did smile then. "I'd love to see you try. I'm not as weak as the last time I was here."

The last time had been tears and vomit and blood. All hers. This time would be a different story.

The one who had been napping against the wall moved the fastest. He had his spear in hand and was shooting toward Nyandoro before the other men properly registered the order from their chief. And the napping man looked familiar. He was one of the men who had touched her before and held her down. She remembered his smell, could almost feel the imprint of his hands on her skin.

It wasn't a good memory.

She grabbed him from mid-air and threw him into the wall. A hoarse shout and he splattered open, slid down the wall in red and brain streaks then was still. The other men didn't waste any more time. They rushed at her with their raised blades and the ring of the chief's orders in the air. Nyandoro didn't prolong it. She wasn't there for them. She dodged the first one, darting past his slashing *tapanga* and kicking him in the back. He grunted as he tripped forward and crashed into the table. Quickly, he righted himself and swung back to Nyandoro with his blade. But she'd already yanked the second one close and snapped his neck. Snarling, she grabbed the dead man by his feet and swung the limp body around in a wide circle, using it like a club to beat the other one back down. His big body slammed into the table again, this time breaking it in two with a sharp crack. A shard of wood from the table lanced through his chest the same time his agonized shriek filled the room. She dropped his friend's body in disgust.

Then it was just Nyandoro and the chief in the wrecked room. He stood only a few steps from her, his breath harsh and steady like a bull's, stance wide and the *tapanga* gripped tightly in a gray-knuckled hand.

"What do you want?" he spat.

"What would you want if someone killed everything you loved and took you prisoner?"

She asked the question casually, barely breathing hard after getting his men out of the way. A discarded spear clattered to the floor from the inclined surface of the broken table. Nyandoro picked it up. She snapped the wood from the metal blade and tested the sharpness of the blade with her thumb. She smiled in satisfaction when a line of blood appeared in its wake. A sharp movement of her hand flicked the blood away.

She looked up at the chief. "Hmm? What would you do if you were in my place?"

But he was looking down at her thumb where the blade had cut. She wasn't bleeding anymore, and the cut healed as she watched.

"You still bleed," he growled and rushed her.

She grinned. "So do you."

Nyandoro easily sidestepped his fist and the sharp thrust of the *tapanga*, dancing back and out of his way. Her robes fluttered around her as she moved.

Stop playing with him.

The familiar voice was gentle reason in her head. But she didn't want reason. She wanted blood. Nyandoro jumped over the broken table, a foot landing on the back of a dead man, and she used the body to push herself off and up high in the air, coming down with the blade raised high and slashing. The chief darted out of her way and kicked out, landing a hit to her ribs. She grunted and fell back, sighed when the pain only briefly registered before disappearing altogether.

"I'm going to kill you!" he gasped. "I don't know what they did to you in that godless place, but I'll slash you into pieces and bathe in your blood."

Nyandoro bared her teeth at him. "Come."

He came at her with a loud roar, careless and angry, leaving his belly wide open. Nyandoro took the gift he gave. She jabbed her knife into his stomach then yanked the small blade up, sharply twisting. He gasped and jerked against her, his body heaving and gushing blood. His *tapanga* clattered to the floor. Nyandoro shoved him away from her, her fist still gripping her knife and coated with his hot blood. He dropped to his back with a thud, landing in a sprawl with his belly raw red and puckered open, dripping out the ropes of his intestines. His chest heaved with his labored breath. The pulse shivered in his throat. Sweat coated his skin and his flickering lashes drooped low over burst blood vessels in his eye.

"You daughter of a goat!" he panted, his body bloody and twitching on the scattered maps of his planned conquest.

"I am no one's daughter," Nyandoro said. "You saw to that."

She slit his throat.

❖

When Aminifu's last breath left her body, her daughter was by her side. Nyandoro was not, but she was there to take care of the physical body she had left behind. She draped Aminifu's shell on the traditional funeral bed on the beach. On the white sand, a large stone slab that could have been a bed or even the rock next to the river in Nyandoro's village, the women of the palace surrounded Aminifu's body with flowers. Purple orchids, yellow poppies, white lilies still tight in their buds that would open in the afterlife and perfume her journey into Yemaya's arms. Clad in white, to mourn the death of an elder, sashes of red around their waists to signify the death of the queen, the entire palace of women fanned out on the beach around Aminifu's silent body.

Nyandoro stood at the head of the funeral slab in her white tunic and lifted her hands toward the ocean and Yemaya's dwelling place. There were no words needed, only the mournful rhythm of the drums lined along the beach, pounding out a hard beat, a heartbeat, that Aminifu no longer had. It began to rain, small droplets, then larger ones, pattering over their clothes, their heads, while the waves came closer and closer in. The seawater swirled around their feet, eddying around the slab while the rain fell.

With each drop of rain on her skin, Nyandoro felt both renewed and exposed, and tears she hadn't known were there spilled down her cheeks. She tried to imagine Duni standing by her side, but could not. Why would such a good woman allow herself to be near a murderer, someone who would kill another human and take pleasure from it? Nyandoro had no regrets about killing the lion-skin chief, but she knew that his death more than any other, forever separated her from the person she had been in Jaguar Village, and from the person she wanted.

The rain fell harder and so did her tears. The women began to hum, a rising and falling chorus as the rain fell harder and harder. Patting the petals of the flowers, the leaves growing around the dark lilies, on Aminifu's white funeral clothes. Nyandoro didn't notice it at first. The disintegration.

It was so gradual that it seemed just a trick of the late evening light. But then she saw it was true. The raindrops were disintegrating Aminifu's flesh, turning it to glittering black sand. Her face melted away, slowly, feature by feature, then her throat, her body, becoming nearly liquid and rushing from the funerary slab, slithering down with the heavy wet of the rain down to the sand where it writhed over the white sand, rushing into the ocean.

She didn't know how long she stood watching Yemaya reclaim her queen, feeling the cool rains on her face and shoulders, but when she looked up, most of the women were gone. A line of their beautiful bodies walked away from the beach and back up to the palace. Only she and Anesa stood with Aminifu's empty funeral dress and the flowers that had surrounded her.

"I don't know what I'm going to do without her," Anesa said, sounding lost and far away.

Nyandoro knew the feeling. Losing a parent, no matter how anticipated the loss, was one of the worst hurts under heaven. She put a hand on Anesa's shoulder. "You'll do what you have to," she said. "You'll survive."

❖

Much later that evening, after most of the women had gone to sleep, Yemaya appeared in her solid form, shimmering, her long skirts the color of abalone shells, her breasts bare, her smile tamed.

"And, you, Nyandoro?" she asked, settling into Nyandoro's lap. Her skin flickered from warm to cool where they touched. "Will you do what you must?"

Even knowing the limitless nature of Yemaya's power, Nyandoro couldn't stop the start of shock at her presence outside the world of dreams. Still, she wound her arms around Yemaya's waist and better arranged her slight weight so they could both be comfortable on the wooden chair. They sat on the terrace where Aminifu and Nyandoro once shared a meal.

Before Yemaya appeared, she'd been feeling her new power as Rain Queen settle more firmly around her bones, winding through her like smoke then solidifying, becoming part of the very essence of who she was. The memories of the previous queens were a constant litany of whispers just behind her ear, telling her and showing her what her life would be from now on. Being the seemingly non-threatening human emissary of one of the most powerful Orishas ever created. Bringing rains to dry regions that observed the ways of Yemaya. Serving as the seed-mother for women who could not accept the sperm of men to bring children into the world. Nyandoro was now these things and so much more. The responsibility of it all made her belly clench with anxiety. But the combined experiences of the rain queens who'd come before her already provided the strength she'd need in coming centuries.

Nyandoro breathed in acceptance and breathed out a sigh. Beyond where she sat, the courtyard was empty, silent, and the night sky too beautiful for words. Only one thing could make it better.

"What are you asking me?" Nyandoro asked Yemaya finally, although she already knew the answer to her own question.

The death of her family had taken away more than her connection to close blood. It had taken away her will to live. And even with the grace of Yemaya flooding through her invigorated body, in moments, she stood still, flushed with fury, her insides crawling with despair. It was because of Yemaya that she had lost her parents, Nitu, Andwele, Hakim, Adli, and Kizo. Duni. How could she reconcile that with her living in the Orisha's palace and doing everything she commanded?

Breath that smelled of sea salt wound through the air along with a sigh. "I have no command for you but to be happy," Yemaya said.

"That's the only command I cannot follow."

"Always so stubborn." Yemaya wound her arms around Nyandoro's shoulders, slathered a clumsy kiss on her cheek. Despite everything, Nyandoro felt a warm spark of affection for her. "I'll only ask one thing of you for the moment." Nyandoro stiffened, then consciously tried to relax when Yemaya trailed cool fingers down the side of her neck. "Only this," she continued. "Go to the place where this all started. There, you will find some relief from the pain you feel."

Nyandoro tilted her head to look at the sky. Clouds veiled the moon. The stars were still the same, pinpricks of light in the otherwise opaque and impenetrable fabric of night. The hills of their valley gleamed darkly with the memory of blood and of the men who had flooded down toward the palace at their peril.

A night bird shrieked. Relief from her pain, even the smallest measure, seemed then like the most elusive thing in the world.

❖

But in the end, Nyandoro did what Yemaya asked. Covered from head to foot in dark robes, she walked into Jaguar Village one late night. Along the path to her parents' compound, she smelled the familiar honey blossom tree, sweet and most potent, heard the full hum of the river through the trees, the sound of families settling in for the night. The moon was just bright enough to see by.

It was late, nearly the crossover to a new day. She wanted to make sure she had privacy to mourn in peace, to look at the last place she'd seen her family, alive and then dead.

At the entrance to her family compound, she paused with her hand on the trunk of the plum tree her mother planted the day Ndewele, her first, was born. Its leaves brushed her face, a rough caress, leaving behind its particular green smell.

Ndewele. Gone.

Her hand trembled and fell away from the tree that would no longer mark a life, only honor a death. The tremors took over her whole body, and she felt as helpless as the screaming newborn her dead brother had been. All this power at her fingertips, but for what?

Nyandoro forced herself to walk farther into the compound.

How long had it been since she'd been taken? Weeks? Months? Her sense of time was splintered. The compound was empty, ground neatly swept, the torches dark. No blood soaking into the dirt. No chopped foot stuck in an open door. It was like her family had never died here, or had never lived.

The fires of her mother's cookhouse would never again burn. Kizo would never clasp her shoulder, never share a drink with her. Nyandoro clenched her fingers into her thigh and willed the tears away. They burned to be released, but she was no longer that girl who indulged so easily in her emotions.

"Ny?"

She turned sharply at the sound of her childhood name, the thick drapes of cloth she wore fluttering up around her and flying up dust. Her throat tightened around a cry.

Duni stood beneath Ndewele's plum tree, hands clutching the trunk of the tree as if, without its support, she would fall. In the moonlight, sharp and unforgiving, she looked tired and worn out. The cloth around her body was frayed, her feet dusty, and her sandals on the verge of falling off. But her hair.

She had always been vain about her hair. Making the time, above anything else, to make sure her hair was oiled and combed, the twists of her hair glistened in the light. But now her hair was uncombed and dry, loose around her face and matted against her head in places. Nyandoro wanted to touch her. Was she real?

Duni jerked away with a gasp. Only then did Nyandoro realize she had come close, too quickly, and hovered there, a cowled stranger. She pushed the cloth away from her head and face. Duni choked on another gasp.

"It is you!" She stumbled back against the tree and slid down the rough bark to drop into the dirt. "Or am I dreaming again?" Tears spilled down her face and carved twin paths through the dust on her cheeks.

Duni's tears broke the paralysis that held Nyandoro back. She dropped to her knees and took Duni's hands. They were rough and work-worn, but she'd never felt anything so wonderful in her life. "No. I'm really here."

Duni stared at her, unblinking, her mouth opening and closing though no words came. Nyandoro squeezed her hands and tried to send her calm, but her own heart was fluttering in her chest. Misery and happiness coiled together inside her, painfully twisting her insides. The battle raged even more when Duni threw her arms around her and held on tight.

And as tightly as Duni held on, Nyandoro felt herself hold on tighter. The days trapped in alternate moments of unconsciousness and terror had kept her from this woman and from the love that could have been even greater if those men hadn't come bringing death. Nyandoro clamped her lips together to stop the desperate noises that throbbed in her throat, wanting to be set free. Cries she wanted to make because she had the woman in her arms who she could not keep. Trembling, she savored Duni's warmth against her body, the desperate clutch of fingernails into her waist through the thin cloth of her robe.

"You're here!" Duni whispered over and over again through her tears. After a long moment, she drew back, trembling. "Where have you been?" The tears had spiked her lashes and she looked vulnerable, delicate.

"I've been far away."

Her eyes pecked over Nyandoro from her uncovered head, faintly damp with rain, to her bare feet with the rings on her toes, gleaming faintly gold in the darkness. She pressed closer to Nyandoro, nearly sitting in her lap.

"Your family...everyone. They're gone."

"I know." Nyandoro breathed through the sharp and sudden pain that lanced under her ribs. "I came here right after it happened. The men who killed them took me."

"No!" Duni gripped her waist again, her eyes wide. "Are you well?"

"Yes..." Was she?

Her body was unharmed and felt even better than before the men had taken her. She was strong again, nearly invincible, all of her smooth and unscarred. But inside, she felt like a throbbing wound.

Yemaya had sent her back to the village to ease some of her pain. More pain, though, was what she'd found instead. Duni, crying and defeated, her tear-stained face only making Nyandoro question the decision she'd made to leave her in peace and not sully her with bloodied hands.

At the palace, that decision had made sense. But here in the courtyard, she could almost smell Kizo's blood and see her mother's dead eyes. Every place she looked was a reminder of what she had lost. These things made her want to hold tight to Duni and never let her go. She was all Nyandoro had left.

But that would be selfish.

"I…" I have to go. The words hovered on Nyandoro's lips. She knew she had to say them. But this was Duni, the only family she had left. Despite the warmth of the night, she shivered.

"What's wrong?" Duni asked.

"I have to leave."

"All right." Duni braced herself against Nyandoro's shoulder to stand up. "Just let me get my things."

Just tell her. "You can't…"

"I can't what?" Behind Duni, the stars were a sprinkling of light in the bleakness of the sky.

"You can't come with me," Nyandoro said. "I'm not the same person you knew before."

"And do I look the same to you?" Duni gestured to herself, and Nyandoro couldn't help but notice again how thin she was, the ashiness of her elbows and knees, the faded color of her kanga.

No, Duni was not the same. Even with the worry of sharing the same house with Ibada, she had kept herself shimmering and beautiful. And although Nyandoro still loved Duni, she could see that it was not only the kanga that was faded. Some of the life and passion and been drained from her too.

"You told me we had forever," Duni said.

It was an accusation and it stung Nyandoro, but the truth was more important than her hurt feelings. "Ny promised you forever," she said, feeling as separate from that carefree girl as night was from day. "She died here with her family."

"A change in your circumstances does not absolve you of your responsibilities, Nyandoro."

Responsibilities? No. Loving Duni had never been a responsibility, and promising to join their lives together was simply an extension of their love. How could she make Duni understand?

She drew in a long breath and released it. But could find no words to fill the silence.

"Take me with you," Duni said, frowning as Nyandoro's silence grew. "We can still be together."

Crickets shrilled and the darkness of the evening suddenly seemed oppressive, weighing Nyandoro down.

Duni drew a hissing breath, the hope draining from her face. "If you have to think that hard about whether or not to take me with you, then go. I won't beg." Duni raised herself to her full height, taller than Nyandoro, and stared down at her in scorn. "Have a good life." She paused. "Wife."

Nyandoro winced. Yes, that was what she once wanted. To be a wife to one woman, for one woman to be a wife to her. But that was before they took everything away from her.

But now you're the one throwing her away.

Nyandoro startled at the voice threading through her mind.

"Stay out of my thoughts!" She snapped out before she could think.

A breeze rose up suddenly and hissed through the trees. Fat raindrops spat from the sky, a quick burst that wet Nyandoro's hair and clothes, wet Duni. But the voice said nothing else.

"Who are you talking to?" Duni asked, staring up at the sky that was once again dry. "What's going—? You know what?

Never mind." She wiped the water from her face with hands that trembled. "Whatever you have going on is no concern of mine." She walked away.

And Nyandoro allowed it. She felt that pain again under her ribs, sharper, a knife splitting her open and laying her entrails out in the dirt. She opened her mouth to call Duni back. But nothing came out. Nothing.

Duni walked farther and farther away, past the place where Kizo had died, past Ndewele's tree, then—

Yemaya appeared in Duni's path. Her face beautiful and human, the ends of her braided hair brushing her shoulders, her peacock skirts fluttering around her hips and floating down to the ground. Her breasts were bare under the trailing ends of the beaded collar flowing from her slender throat. Light pulsed around her, a subtle and hypnotic glowing.

Duni stopped when she saw her, footsteps hesitating. "Do I know you? You seem…familiar."

Worried, Nyandoro took a step to come between them, but a step was the farthest she moved before an invisible and immovable force stopped her short.

"You don't have to stay in this village, Duni," Yemaya said, lulling and soft. Her skirts moved with the breeze and the salt sweetness of the ocean filled the air.

Duni backed away, her hands extended blindly behind her. "Who are you?"

"I'm who Nyandoro has been with all this time."

Duni looked sharply back at Nyandoro and clenched her arms tight around her stomach. Nyandoro didn't think it was possible, but she looked even worse than before. Not just hurt, but betrayed and confused.

"You can come with me too," Yemaya said.

But Duni shook her head, paying attention only to Nyandoro. Her eyes were wide and bleak. "This is what you've been doing while I've been dying here without you?" Duni's shout was pain itself.

"She and I weren't together in that way," Nyandoro said.

But Duni wasn't listening to her. She gathered the loose ends of her kanga around her shoulders and neck, huddling inside the cloth like she was trying to hide. "The least you could have done was tell me the truth, say you don't want me anymore. I've been mourning you." Tears cut into her cheeks. Her chin wobbled.

"Stop this!" Nyandoro snapped at Yemaya.

The Orisha merely raised an eyebrow at her. "If you won't handle your business, I will." She moved closer to Duni, a crying misery, who backed steadily away from her.

"You are her new wife?" she asked Yemaya.

"No, I am not." A flicker of cruel amusement crossed the Orisha's face. "Leave this place and come with me. There's nothing else for you here. Your parents are dead. Your husband has abandoned you."

"She told you about me?" Duni looked even more betrayed.

"She knows everything," Nyandoro snapped. Her patience was near its end with Yemaya's meddling in her life. "I didn't need to tell her."

"But you did! I never thought you were this cruel." Trembling like her body was caught in a storm, Duni turned and darted away from Nyandoro and Yemaya both. But Yemaya made a sound of impatience and grabbed Duni. She touched her forehead and Duni collapsed at her feet, sprawled in the dirt.

"No!" Not like this. The terror of losing consciousness then waking in a new and dangerous place was something Nyandoro knew well. She didn't want that for Duni. She ran to her, but Yemaya already held her limp body in her arms.

"You know where we'll be," Yemaya said. Then she disappeared with Duni.

Nyandoro spent valuable moments gaping after them like a landed fish before she rushed after them, using her new power to travel across hundreds of maili in the blink of an eye.

The palace. She appeared inside its main hallway with a flutter of her robes. The torchlights were bright and she winced against their glare. Anesa, already walking through the hallway ahead of her, turned with a sleeping child in her arms. She looked over Nyandoro's tumbled appearance, the cowl falling down around her shoulders, her breathlessness. Nyandoro calmed herself and wished the girl a happy evening. Then she left for the guest quarters, sure that was where Yemaya took Duni.

In the wide east wing of the palace, she searched room after empty room, then rechecked their collective memory. Yes, she was in the right place. But Duni wasn't here.

Nyandoro forced herself to breathe evenly, deeply. She pressed her back to the cool stone wall of the last empty sleeping room. Why would Yemaya do this thing after Nyandoro had given her everything she wanted? Her life. Her family. Her loyalty. She slid down the wall, then used her power to quietly shut the door so none of the passing women could see her. Tears burned behind her eyes. Her face grew hot.

The last time she'd cried was...

No. She did not have time to cry. There were women in peril and droughts and...

Shit.

Wet salt dripped into her mouth. Her head thudded back against the wall and she simply sat there.

Waiting. For the next time they needed her. For her next chance to give up everything else she had.

"Don't be such a baby."

It took her a moment to realize there was another voice in the room. A familiar voice. Because she didn't want to move too quickly and push the illusion away, she opened her eyes and slowly turned.

The room's largest window looked onto the valley's winding path leading down through the trees and to the water. Kizo sat perched on the ledge of this window. His feet dangled outside, but he was looking over his shoulder at Nyandoro. The last time she'd seen him, his head had nearly been cut from his body and he lay in a pool of blood big enough to drown in. He shouldn't be here.

"You shouldn't be here," she said.

He laughed, his teeth white and cheeks plumping in humor. "Neither should you." Then he shook his head, the snaking vines of his long hair moving over his bare shoulders and back.

Longing, heavy beyond measure, pressed into Nyandoro's chest. She wanted to go to him. She wanted to touch him to see if he was real.

But she stayed still, her back pressed to the wall, only her eyes devouring her brother. He wore one of his favorite outfits, which was to say he was nearly naked, only a short kanga around his waist. His chest gleamed in the moonlight pouring in through the window.

Part of her knew why she was seeing him. Being the Rain Queen, Yemaya's consort and the embodiment of her power on the earth, Nyandoro was now able to see into realms normal human eyes could not. But it didn't make seeing her brother any less frightening. The loss of him hit her again, like a punch to the chest, and left her breathless. Truly, she was alone now. Nyandoro breathed through her mouth, slowly, blinking at him, missing him, then she swallowed her pain. It had no place in the Rain Queen's palace.

"They slaughtered all of you like animals."

Kizo made a dismissive sound. "That's in the past, and our family is in another world now." He gestured to himself.

"This body does not exist." Kizo pointed to the valley beyond the window, the world outside out. "This is what you have now, and this is what you can change."

"This is nothing."

"Stop being such a baby. It doesn't suit you. Not now." He hopped down from the window and crept toward Nyandoro on soundless feet. Silver light poured through the window and followed him. "Think about Duni," he said. "Don't make me claw my way from heaven to throw her on top of you. That's not very celestial."

Nyandoro drew in a breath that actually hurt. She didn't realize she was sobbing until her brother's hand squeezed her shoulder hard enough for her to feel it. "I don't think I can do this," she said.

"This queen stuff is no big deal." He shrugged. "I'd do it for you, but I'm a bit indisposed at the moment." He nudged her with a smile. "The hardest thing for you to do now is forgive yourself and love Duni again. Allow her to love you."

"I never stopped loving her," Nyandoro croaked. Her tears fell harder and she felt on the verge of falling over onto her dead brother's knees.

"I know." Kizo squeezed her shoulder again and rose to his feet, a graceful line of beautiful dark. "Now get up. Iya didn't raise any of us to live on our knees, queen or not." The teasing familiarity of his tone pressed against her face like a cool cloth.

She drew in a breath, then two. "Okay." She stood up and wiped her face. "Okay."

"That's the sister I know." His face brightened with laughter. "I'd say give Duni a kiss for me, but that would be a little strange." He was leaving. His body language said as much.

Nyandoro panicked but stopped herself from begging him to stay. "Will I see you again?"

"Maybe. Maybe not. We'll just see how this goes. This spirit of the other world thing is new for me. And I suspect that your new…" He looked deliberately around the luxurious room. "…status has something to do with my access to this world."

"At least this Rain Queen business is good for something."

"It's good for a lot," Kizo said. "Did you see all the wives you have now?"

She drew back. "I won't share a sleeping mat with them!"

Kizo shook his head, looking genuinely sad. "Yeah, I would have made a much better Rain Queen than you." He glided to the window and looked out. "Fix your life, sister." Then he was gone.

She sat on the window ledge for a long time after he disappeared, turning over the words he'd left her with. Thinking about what it meant that sometime in the future, if she was very lucky, she would see him again. Eventually, she climbed down from the window, feeling an ache all through her body that was more emotional than physical. She knew this body of hers was strong, and that Yemaya protected what was hers from the ravages of time. She knew she was young. But already, it felt like a hundred seasons since she'd been pulled from everything she knew as familiar, even though it had only been two or three moons. At the door, Nyandoro drew a deep breath and then opened it.

The hallway was empty except for the fluttering hem of a bright blue robe disappearing around a corner. From a nearby room, she heard the sibilant sounds of a whispered conversation. Her sandals tapped softly against the painted tiles and torchlight flickered above her head, lighting her way down the corridor. Air flowed freely through the stone archways and high windows, bringing the scent of the sea. This was her life now. Quiet and lonely.

At the entrance to her rooms, something made Nyandoro pause. A sound. Quiet breathing. She looked around but saw nothing except for the long stretch of empty hallway behind her. She shoved open the thick blue door.

Duni lay on her sleeping mat. Draped in a long blue tunic of the style favored by the wives, she had her eyes wide open and watched Nyandoro's every step into the room. She'd been bathed and her hair combed, oiled to a fine sheen and puffed around her head like a dandelion. The bath and grooming had resurrected the beauty in her that Nyandoro was familiar with. But the sadness on Duni's face, worse even than when Ibada had thrown her out, wasn't something Nyandoro wanted to get used to. Duni sat up in a rustle of cloth and drew her knees to her chest. Although her posture was one of vulnerability and dread, the look she gave Nyandoro was pure venom.

"Why did your woman bring me here?" she asked.

Nyandoro shut the door and thought about telling Duni she was free to go, and to forget everything that happened that evening. She even opened her mouth with the words resting on her tongue.

But.

"I've killed men."

Duni jerked back, as if from a slap, her face settling into lines of shock.

"A man's blood dripped through my fingers like water, and the feel of it made me glad." Nyandoro skirted the high and wide sleeping mat to sit on the low stool she'd seen some of the servants use. Duni was beautiful there. So impossibly out of her reach. She might as well have been ripped open in the dirt like Kizo, like her iya, and all the others. Duni rested her chin on her upraised knees and stared at her.

"Well, don't you have anything to say?" Nyandoro asked after the silence threatened to choke her.

"Were these bad people?"

The childish question almost made Nyandoro laugh. "Does it matter?"

"Yes, it does." Duni pressed her back into the wall and shivered. The stone must have been cold. She pulled a large pillow from the end of the sleeping mat and put it between her skin and the wall. When she moved, Nyandoro saw there was no back to her tunic. The cloth draped low just below her spine, leaving her back bare and a warm mahogany in the torchlights. Duni would be soft if she touched her.

But Nyandoro jerked her thoughts back from such dangerous territory. "I've done things since I've been here that changed me from the girl you knew. I cannot be a wife to anyone. Especially not to you. You are…" good. Nyandoro didn't deserve her.

"You're right," Duni said, and Nyandoro winced. "You have become someone different since you've been away. You're making decisions for me like my no-longer-husband used to. The girl I knew would never do that."

"No!" Nyandoro refused to accept the comparison to Duni's old husband. He had acted selfishly, taking wife after wife without consideration for the women. He'd thrown Duni away like she was nothing. She stood up, suddenly agitated, her robes swishing around her feet. From outside came the faint crack of thunder. Lightning illuminated the dark sky. "I am not Ibada."

Duni squeezed her arms around her knees and stared back at her. "True. At least he had the courage to take me for a wife."

Thunder exploded nearby, shaking the room. "Are you trying to make me angry?"

"Only if the truth angers you." Duni rocked back against the wall, her hands braced flat on the sleeping met. Nyandoro realized then that Duni was shaking. She was afraid. The anger left her body in an explosive breath. The thunder outside died away, and the lightning flickered weakly before leaving the sky dark again. Moonlight burned at the edges of the windows, silently accusing as they reminded Nyandoro of Kizo and their earlier conversation.

"Duni...I would never hurt you." She sat carefully on the edge of the sleeping mat.

"Liar." Duni's voice shook. A tear slid from the corner of her eye and down her nose. "You hurt me when you didn't come back. You're hurting me now."

"That's not what I want," Nyandoro said. "You're my family. The only one I have left." Despite her ambivalence about Duni's presence at the palace, she was desperate to make her understand. She reached out, but Duni jerked her hand away. "After everything that happened, I was only doing what I could to protect you."

"You do not abandon family to the jackals and come back to look over the carcass." More tears fell. Duni angrily wiped them away. "That's what you've done to me, Nyandoro. You didn't protect—" Duni broke off with a gasp. She pressed back into the wall, terror distorting her face. Nyandoro whirled around.

Yemaya stood in the center of the room as herself. The blue and white of her seven-layered skirts moved in their own breeze, and her face shifting through all its aspects. Old woman. Virgin. Sea sorceress. "Must I do everything for you, beloved?" Her voice was like thundering waves crashing around Nyandoro's ears, strong and fearsome.

"What are you?" Duni asked, her eyes wide.

"No one you need to be jealous of," Yemaya said. "Nyandoro is mine, but she is also yours in the way that matters most to you." Her voice lowered and become kinder, more human. "She loves you. She did not come to this place of her own free will.

But she went to find you because she couldn't imagine a life here without you."

Nyandoro narrowed her eyes at Yemaya. She had no right to tell Duni what Nyandoro hadn't even allowed herself to admit.

"Yes, beloved?" Her tone was amused now, a playful breeze over calm waters.

It made Nyandoro feel anything but calm. "Stop!" she snapped. "I can tell Duni what she needs to know."

"I'm getting more information from this woman than you've given me." Duni moved away from the wall, her eyes trained on Yemaya. "Let her talk."

"She is no woman," Nyandoro said.

Yemaya laughed, but not unkindly, and the scales over her bare shoulders and breasts glimmered under the torchlights. Her eyes flickered to a lightning white then back to brown. "True." She drifted toward Duni with a liquid brush of her skirts over the tiles. Duni trembled, obviously frightened, but did not move. "Nyandoro is right. She is not the same woman you knew before. But that just means she needs you and your love more than ever. She just won't ask."

"I didn't ask for your meddling either."

"You don't have to ask me for the things you need." Yemaya's eyes glittered dangerously, letting Nyandoro know she was walking on a fine edge. Then she waved a hand through the air as if brushing aside her irritation. "Being my queen is not something to be endured until the next woman rises to take your place. Happiness is within your reach. Take it before it vanishes with the tide."

Happiness? How was that even possible with all she'd lost?

The Orisha shrugged her glittering shoulders as if to say, that's up to you to figure out. "Now that I've gotten the conversation started, I'll leave you two alone." The aspect of the wise woman took over her features, lined her face and whitened her hair. Her breasts sagged beneath the long string of beads making up her necklace. "Just do not forget, Nyandoro, Duni has lost everything too." Then she vanished.

The sound of the sea, deep and lulling, lingered after her. Nyandoro breathed in the salt scent she left behind and released a sigh. Before she could speak, Duni moved from protective huddle against the wall and slid to the edge of the sleeping mat with her feet on the floor. She kept at least five hand widths of space between her and Nyandoro.

"Don't let your...whatever guilt you into letting me stay," she said. "You don't want me here. I'll leave."

If only it were that simple.

Nyandoro considered her options, looking ahead to the hundreds of seasons she had yawning before her, all spent alone. She held out her hand. "Come," she said.

Duni watched her with suspicious eyes, her own hands clasped in her lap. Nyandoro held her hand steady, palm up. This wasn't the time for her to close herself off in a protective shell. She was no longer responsible just for herself. Not anymore. Like she'd told Duni, the child who ran through the streets of Jaguar Village didn't exist anymore. Ny had had the luxury of thinking only of herself, of her own desires and the most expedient ways of fulfilling them. That child was dead. Long live the queen. The queen had responsibilities and one of those responsibilities was Duni.

But there was another truth Nyandoro couldn't hide from herself.

"Please," she said. "I...I need you."

Surprise tugged Duni's eyes to hers, her eyelashes a fluttering of wingbeats against her cheeks. The silence deepened. Then finally, finally, she took Nyandoro's hand. Relief made Nyandoro pull her close, drawing in the scent of the mint oils the wives had rubbed into her skin and hair, the womanly essence that was uniquely Duni's. Her skin was soft, and Nyandoro missed softness. She'd missed her.

"Many things have happened since we saw each other last," Nyandoro said. She pulled her hands away from Duni, fingertips lingering briefly because she wanted so very much to keep touching her. "Let me show you."

The darkness in the palace, in the valley where it nestled, seemed more complete than anywhere Nyandoro had ever been. But the dark, like in Jaguar Village, was nothing to be feared. Instead, it was a soft cocoon of comfort that held them all until the sun rose, bringing an equally complete and all-encompassing light.

Since all the torchlights in the hall had been extinguished after Nyandoro walked through the door of her rooms, she and Duni stepped out into such a darkness. Nyandoro saw easily in the dark, but Duni stumbled and gripped her arm. She savored the startled hitch of Duni's breath against her cheek, the luxurious press of her body, the lush breasts and thighs whose taste she vividly remembered. Then, hesitating for longer than was strictly necessary, she turned the torchlights back on with a wave of her hand.

The lights rose on the flicker of Duni's tongue as she wet her lips, her lashes fluttering down as she looked away and took a step back. Nyandoro calmed her skittishness with a touch although her own blood beat loudly enough in her ears to drown out most of her old fears. They walked through the illuminated hallways together.

With each step she and Duni took, Nyandoro unearthed from beneath the burden of being Rain Queen all the love and desire she'd harbored for Duni over the seasons. The passion she'd felt for her the night they made love and the wildness inside her that had claimed Duni when she was about to marry another. Nyandoro's heart began a fast, lustful beat. How could she have fooled herself into thinking she could do without Duni?

Nyandoro linked her hands behind her back. "So, this is where I live now."

Unlike when she'd passed this way before, women ghosted through the hallways, slim and soft, full and hard, their gazes curious as they bent their heads together, their soft whispers making it no secret that they wandered the halls now in curiosity about who Duni was and why she was there. Duni met their gazes with a stiffened spine, and Nyandoro was proud of her.

"This palace is yours?" Duni asked as she straightened the drape of the tunic over her shoulders.

"No. If anything, I belong to it." Nyandoro's robes whispered against the tiled floors as she walked. "This is the palace of the Rain Queen and, for now, I am the queen."

"What?" Duni stumbled to a halt. "But that's not possible. The elders said she doesn't exist."

Nyandoro gently guided her forward with a hand on the small of her back, out to the terrace where she'd had her first, and last, meal with Aminifu. The sky's darkness was pierced with stars and the moon was a pale, waning disc among them. The brightest of the stars seemed to wink down at them. She braced her arms against the stone railing of the balcony and leaned out into the night. Without the dead men on the hill, or the urgency of committing her life to an entity she'd never previously believed in, the valley where she now lived was actually beautiful. Duni's shoulder brushed against hers.

"The elders didn't want to pay the price, and some just didn't want to pay it to a woman." Nyandoro sifted through Aminifu's memories of the talks she'd had with the village elders. She gripped the balcony when she realized one of those elders had been her father. A thick clot of grief rose up, but she quickly swallowed it.

"The rains did come, though," Duni said. "It was the night you…" Her voice stopped with a hiss and Nyandoro felt her stiffen where they touched. "The elders sacrificed you as the virgin?"

"They did not. It was my mother."

As Nyandoro said the words, she felt Yemaya's objection in her mind like a too-cold touch. She drew a steadying breath and pushed aside the familiar anger and resentment she felt toward her mother. But would she have done the same thing to get a girl child of her own?

Duni was shaking her head. "She would never—!"

"She did," Nyandoro said. "Iya wanted a girl and bargained with Yemaya for one. The catch was that she had to give the child back to Yemaya once she…I became an adult."

It had been a bargain made out of desperation, Nyandoro realized now. Her mother's whole life before Jaguar Village was made of women. Powerful women who ruled the village, loved their daughters, and raised them to be leaders. For a woman born into a society like that to have only sons, and five of them at that, it must have seemed the cruelest of jokes.

"Your poor iya," Duni said softly. Her warm shoulder pressed once into Nyandoro's again before she stepped away and back.

"Yes. I think toward the end of things, as I grew older, Iya regretted what she'd done. But only because she soon had to give me up." Nyandoro remembered the last time she'd seen her mother alive, the pride in her eyes warring with shadows Nyandoro had not been able to name. "I…if things had gone the way they should have, I don't know if I would've come here willingly. Or at all."

It was a shameful confession to make, she knew. A debt was a debt. She turned away from the stars to press her back into the terrace stones. Before her, Duni stood haloed in the torchlights from the adjoining room, the brightness of the lights threading through the dark corona of her hair like veins of gold.

"You would have come," Duni said. "Even before we made promises to each other, you wanted to leave the village and see other places. No obligation would have kept you in Jaguar Village for the rest of your life. You would have come here, and I would have been by your side."

Nyandoro felt the truth of what Duni said. She loved her family and her village, but she would've left them in a rabbit's heartbeat to see other parts of the world. Guilt twisted in her belly.

"It's not a bad thing to want more than you have," Duni said.

"It is when it ends with my family being slaughtered."

Duni made an impatient gesture. "Stop taking the blame for what happened. Bargains were made before you were born. Rain Queens already existed. You don't have as much control over your life as you thought. And that's all right."

Nyandoro twisted in self-mockery. Duni had realized in a few moments what it took her many moons to know and then to acknowledge. No, she was not in complete control of her life, and that made her want to tear the world apart. She sighed at her own foolishness. "I've missed you," she said.

Duni crossed her arms under her breasts, jerked up her chin. "Not enough to return to the village for me."

"Enough to leave you alone. This life will be hard."

"Harder if you decide to live it alone," Duni said. "As much as you hate choices being taken from you, you took mine away when you didn't ask if I wanted to be with you here."

Nyandoro swallowed thickly. She had. "If I asked you, what would you say?"

"Asked me then, or asked me now?"

"Yes." Nyandoro laughed weakly. She reached back and gripped the edges of the terrace until she felt stone cut into her skin.

"I—" Duni shook her head. "I want a partner, not someone who will make decisions for me."

Nyandoro's stomach dropped. Not even the strength of a millennia of Rain Queens could stop her from dreading the rejection coming at her like a swiftly thrown spear. She would release Duni. She would—

"I would have said yes then."

Nyandoro cracked open and the pulpy meat of her all too human feelings poured out. "And now?"

"And now..." Duni uncrossed her arms and turned away, her face hidden mostly in shadow. "I don't want to be a fool again. I don't want to be left behind like last season's wife."

The curve of Duni's cheek, her bare shoulder, and the warm slope of her hip were etched in moonlight, everything else was obscured in darkness. It would have been easy for Nyandoro to penetrate this darkness, but Duni was protecting herself. As she should. Nyandoro had laid her bare before, had made promises, and now those promises were spilled blood in the dirt.

"Stay here. Please." The words left her mouth in an unplanned rush and she felt Duni react to them, half-turning toward her. "We'd planned to be family to each other before. We can be that still." Now she was the one begging for the future she had thrown away before.

"Can we?" Duni asked.

Nyandoro's whole being trembled with Yes. She nodded, afraid of what else would fall out of her mouth if she opened it.

Duni drew a loud breath and looked around the night-darkened terrace and to the bright rooms beyond the archway where they stood. With the lateness of the day, the palace was mostly asleep. All the children had been quieted. In the half circle of smaller buildings extending around the courtyard, only a few torchlights glowed. But Nyandoro could feel the aliveness of the entire palace. The throb of its wholly feminine heartbeat.

"Show me more of this place," Duni said. "If this is to be my new home, I want to know everything."

Gladness. Relief. Nyandoro's head lifted from the sudden lightness of it all. She nodded again. "Okay."

So she showed Duni the palace and, as they walked through the wide hallways and quiet rooms, told her everything. From the moment she had left Duni slowly waking up in the room where they had made love, through the horror of her kidnapping, to finally when they saw each other in the wreckage of Nyandoro's family compound earlier that evening.

Nyandoro had braced herself for the pain of retelling it all. Those moments of terror and confusion, of new power and loneliness in the aftermath of Aminifu's death and her ascension to the throne of Rain Queen. But instead of being flayed alive by the things that happened, it felt like an unburdening. Yes, the pain was there. And it was stark and unforgiving, and she could do nothing to bring her family back. But Duni listened to her, touched her arm, hugged her waist, cried with her, and then they were wrapped in each other's arms on Nyandoro's big sleeping mat.

"I didn't tell you these things for you to feel sorry for me."

"Good. Because I don't feel sorry for you." Duni's voice was husky from crying. Her damp face pressed into the crook of Nyandoro's neck, her longer legs curled up and draped over

Nyandoro's. "I feel love for you. I think you're brave. I think you're merciful to only kill the chief who ordered your family killed." Her warm breath puffed against Nyandoro's skin. She threaded their fingers together. "I would have destroyed the whole world."

Nyandoro blinked slowly up at the arched ceiling above them. The crystalline stones gleamed in the dark. "It's a good thing this happened to me and not you then."

Fingers dug sharply into her waist. A fresh flood of tears wet her skin from where Duni's face was pressed against it. Those tears felt like her own.

Nyandoro held Duni tighter and turned them until they were face-to-face. Very carefully, she wiped away Duni's tears with her thumb, soothing the warm skin of her cheeks then her nose, her chin. The tears stopped and wide onyx eyes blinked at her. "Will you be my wife?" Nyandoro asked.

"Yes," Duni said without hesitation. "And you will be mine."

The relief rushed through Nyandoro like pleasure. She traced her thumb along Duni's plump lips and they parted, revealing a sheen of teeth, the pink wet of her tongue. "Wife."

Duni's lashes fluttered down and her mouth curved up. There was something behind that look, but Nyandoro didn't press for it. Instead, she waited for whatever it was to reveal itself.

The room was silvered with moonlight. Ocean waves whispered in the distance, and the scent of Duni's mint-rubbed skin was a growing distraction. Nyandoro breathed her in. With her eyes still averted, Duni toyed with the edges of Nyandoro's robes, her fingers lightly tracing the curve of a breast that the gapping cloth revealed. "So, I will be your wife along with all the others?"

The *something* revealed. Still, it took a moment for Nyandoro to realize what she meant. The Rain Queen's many wives, the seven who'd chosen to stay after Aminifu left.

"They are mine to care for and shelter, nothing else," she said. "You are mine to love."

"But things will change." Duni finally met her gaze and her fingers stilled their movement.

Nyandoro knew she was remembering what a naive and young girl had said to her by the village river so many moons ago.

One wife. One love. One shared future.

"Maybe they will change," Nyandoro said. "Even with this new power, I cannot see the future. What I know is that I love you, and you are my family. These things will never change, no matter who comes into our lives." This was a promise Nyandoro would keep. No matter what.

The smallest of sighs left Duni's throat. Relief. She smiled shyly and slid her leg over Nyandoro's, pushing up the cloth of her robe. "I thought I would die and never hear you say that to me again."

"What?"

"That you love me."

Although Nyandoro didn't want to admit it, that might have become true. "Well, you haven't died," she said. "And you've heard me say it."

"Yes, I have." Satisfaction thrummed through Duni's voice.

Nyandoro touched the bare expanse of Duni's back that had been tempting her all night. Appreciation hummed in her throat. The skin under her fingers radiated a seductive heat and was soft, reminding her of how Duni felt all over, like a honey flower blossom in high summer, and of how well she'd responded to Nyandoro's youthful fumblings in that long ago bed.

"I'll try not to take it personally that you haven't said the same to me." She trailed her hand up Duni's naked back and up to where the soft tunic tied at her neck.

"There is no point in me telling you what you already know," Duni said.

Nyandoro smiled at the sweet intake of Duni's breath as she untied the tunic and pulled it down slowly, revealing Duni's breasts to the moonlight and to her gaze. Her nipples were already tight with arousal, puckered and berry dark in the warm room, ready for her mouth. She dropped the tunic on the floor.

"Every woman wants to hear that she is loved," she whispered a moment before she kissed Duni's cheek.

Duni breathed softly and stretched into her touch, hands sinking into Nyandoro's waist as kisses trailed down her throat and to her shoulders. Her skin was soft and Nyandoro missed that. The blurred nights and days of her captivity had had her falling into memories of them together, loving each other, as she clung stubbornly to proof that she had something to live for besides revenge.

She mapped Duni's skin with her fingertips, stroking the invisible line from her throat to the round of her belly, the delicate underside her breasts, the wings of her ribs, but did not touch where Duni squirmed for the most.

"Nyandoro!" Duni's hands tightened in her hair, trying to guide her mouth to her breasts. But Nyandoro laughed and blew warm air against Duni's skin, slid her hands down to her hips, her thighs.

"You've been in my dreams since I knew what wanting a woman was," she whispered. She nipped Duni's throat, licked the faint hurt, and did it again and again while Duni moved restlessly in the bed. The smell of her arousal rose salty and wet from between her thighs.

"You're cruel…" Duni breathed.

"Only when I don't give you what you want right away." Her mouth hovered at Duni's collarbone. She traced it with the wet flutter of her tongue. "But I'll always take care of you." She kissed the middle of Duni's chest then licked the sweat from her skin. "Always."

Duni choked out a ragged gasp when Nyandoro's mouth closed on her nipple, and it was the sweetest thing she'd ever heard. The fingers in Nyandoro's hair gentled then slid down her neck, caressing and scratching in a mindless rhythm, then lower on her back to twist into her tunic. Duni's breath shivered out with each suck and tease from her mouth. She tasted of her bath and mint oil, her skin slick and soft. Her nipples slid under Nyandoro's tongue, and Nyandoro moaned into the sweet skin, so very grateful she was able to do this again. To feel her again and get another chance at happiness.

"I missed you," Duni murmured. "I miss feeling loved… feeling safe."

"I'm here," Nyandoro whispered against the curve of her breast. "You're safe."

She moved lower and discarded her own clothes until she and Duni were skin to skin, heat pressed to heat. Her love opened her silken thighs and Nyandoro slid her fingers between them with a trembling sigh. The wet clasp of her like a dream she'd had a thousand times, undiluted pleasure and the anticipation of even more. Nyandoro touched her and felt as if she was being touched in return, enjoying the wet slick of Duni under the sensitive pads of her fingers, around them, inhaling her scent, savoring the thick sounds of her fingers moving inside Duni's drenched quim. It was a deep and languorous fuck. A gradual teasing of Duni's pleasure to the surface and holding it there with slow and deliberate circles of her fingers.

"Ny—!" Duni's nails raked her shoulders.

Nonsense words flooded from Duni's mouth, her quim clasping and sucking wet around Nyandoro's fingers that curled up, searching for that sweet place inside. The collective knowledge of the Rain Queens was good for many things.

Duni cried out and bucked into her, hips diving up. "What—what are you doing to me?"

"Loving you..."

Moonlight spilled over Duni's luscious nakedness, her thighs spread wide, back arched, her long throat and wetly parted lips. Sweat glowed on her skin and her hair was wild around her face. She was so beautiful that Nyandoro didn't want to stop looking at her, wanted instead to keep watching the hungry thrust of her hips, the furred quim and her fingers fucking in and out, glistening wet.

Even more arousal trickled down Nyandoro's thighs at the sight. "You feel so good."

So good that her mouth watered for a taste. She dipped her head between Duni's spread thighs and latched her mouth onto the swollen pearl of her pleasure, licking as her fingers plunged slick and fast into her. Duni hissed and grabbed her head, pressing harder into Nyandoro's face.

Duni tasted of rain forests and pleasure brought out in the open. She tasted of everything Nyandoro had ever wanted in a woman. But she wanted more. Rising up, she fit her mouth once again to Duni's breast, moaning in pleasure at the firm texture of the nipple under her tongue but incredibly, she could still feel her mouth on Duni's sex, the firm slip and salt smell, but she wanted it all. Wanted to touch Duni everywhere and bring her pleasure and erase the memory of their time apart. Nyandoro breathed into her neck, nibbling along her throat and licked the curved shell her ear. Duni made wrecked, broken noises, her body's movements nearly frantic.

Yes. Just like that.

She dragged her thumb across Duni's mouth, then pushed inside, bucking her hips when the hot mouth closed around it and *sucked*. Her mind scattered. She was simply feeling. No more thoughts. No reason. And she was *everywhere*.

Rain began falling inside the bedroom. Water dripped through the ceiling and fell over Nyandoro's shoulders in warm strokes, splashed down her back and sides to fall onto Duni. Nyandoro was in every drop.

Rain slid down Duni's forehead, her cheeks, her lips, and her tongue flicked out to lick the raindrops before they fell into her mouth. She drank the rain down like she was desperate for it. And Nyandoro felt each desirous flutter and swipe of her tongue.

"So good...oh!" Duni writhed under the rain.

Lust-drunk, Nyandoro felt herself still feasting between Duni's legs, still fucking her with three fingers, tireless and strong. But she was also sucking on her nipples, rolling the hard peaks, one after another, around on her tongue. And she was falling in a thousand pieces all over Duni's warm body. She did all these things at the same time, her body split to savor each experience, the fuck, the lick, the suck, the moaning welcome of Duni's mouth on her. The pleasure from it rushed through Nyandoro's body like the most intoxicating and sweetest of wines.

Crouched over Duni, she gasped at the unexpected feel of a tongue on her quim.

Sh... It's all right. I'll take care of you the way you take care of her.

It all sounded so reasonable, so right, that she pushed back into the firm tongue licking her open from behind, then sliding into her, filling and thrusting into her body, full and gorgeous, making her moan against Duni's skin. The tongue fucked and flicked and stroked just as she did all those same things to Duni. They gasped and moaned together, the sounds of their sex a loud and wet chorus rising higher and higher.

Duni bucked and scratched Nyandoro's shoulders, crying out her name. "I love you!" she gasped. "I love you so much…"

Then they were crashing into completion together with a force powerful enough to shake the whole room. Lightning whitened the sky outside the window as the sound of the hectic pulse-beat drumming in Nyandoro's ears slowly died away. She came back to herself sprawled on her back with Duni's sweat-damp face pressed into her throat. Their breaths were loud and fast in the room.

"No wonder you can't get enough of her."

Nyandoro startled at the sound of Yemaya's voice, nearly jerking upright in the bed. But she stopped herself just in time, curving a protective arm around Duni instead and pulling her closer. The Orisha sat cross-legged just behind Duni and watched them both with a satisfied smile.

Duni seemed unaware of Yemaya's presence. She clung to Nyandoro and pressed lazy, open mouthed kisses along her neck and throat. "I love you," she whispered, her voice growing heavy with coming sleep.

Yemaya leaned closer, bringing her sea-salt scent with her, and brushed fingers along Duni's cheek. "She is good for you."

Duni made a soft noise and snuggled deeper into Nyandoro's throat, her eyes already closed. Contentment radiated from every part of her.

"I won't let her go again," Nyandoro said quietly. "I can't."

"As long as you want her by your side, she will be by your side."

Did that mean as long as they both lived? Nyandoro tightened her hand on Duni's shoulder and willed Yemaya to understand. Was it truly that simple? Even knowing what the Rain Queens before her knew—that love lasted and that it was possible to keep long-lived promises—she still had her doubts. The carnage and losses of her young life only made her brace herself for more.

Without appearing to move, Yemaya was even closer than before, white braids rippling on her shoulders as if caught in an ocean current, her eyes clear and dark. She curled her fingers around Nyandoro's hand resting on Duni's shoulder. "It is that simple."

And so, it was.

About the Author

Jamaican-born Fiona Zedde currently lives and writes in Miami, Florida. She is the author of several novellas and novels, including the Lambda Literary Award finalists *Bliss and Every Dark Desire*. Her novel, *Dangerous Pleasures*, was winner of the About.com Readers' Choice Award for Best Lesbian Novel or Memoir of 2012.

Her short fiction has appeared in various anthologies including *Necrologue: DIVA Book of the Dead and the Undead, Wicked: Sexy Tales of Legendary Lovers, Iridescence: Sensuous Shades of Lesbian Erotica, Fist of the Spider Woman,* and *Best Lesbian Romance.*

Writing under the name "Fiona Lewis," she has also published a novel of young adult fiction called *Dreaming in Color.*

Books Available from Bold Strokes Books

Best Laid Plans by Jan Gayle. Nicky and Lauren are meant for each other, but Nicky's haunting past and Lauren's societal fears threaten to derail all possibilities of a relationship. (987-1-62639-658-6)

Exchange by CF Frizzell. When Shay Maguire rode into rural Montana, she never expected to meet the woman of her dreams—or to learn Mel Baker was held hostage by legal agreement to her right-wing father. (987-1-62639-679-1)

Just Enough Light by AJ Quinn. Will a serial killer's return to Colorado destroy Kellen Ryan and Dana Kingston's chance at love, or can the search-and-rescue team save themselves? (987-1-62639-685-2)

Rise of the Rain Queen by Fiona Zedde. Nyandoro is nobody's princess. She fights, curses, fornicates, and gets into as much trouble as her brothers. But the path to a throne is not always the one we expect. (987-1-62639-592-3)

Tales from Sea Glass Inn by Karis Walsh. Over the course of a year at Cannon Beach, tourists and locals alike find solace and passion at the Sea Glass Inn. (987-1-62639-643-2)

The Color of Love by Radclyffe. Black sheep Derian Winfield needs to convince literary agent Emily May to marry her to save the Winfield Agency and solve Emily's green card problem, but Derian didn't count on falling in love. (987-1-62639-716-3)

A Reluctant Enterprise by Gun Brooke. When two women grow up learning nothing but distrust, unworthiness, and abandonment, it's no wonder they are apprehensive and fearful when an overwhelming love just won't be denied. (978-1-62639-500-8)

Above the Law by Carsen Taite. Love is the last thing on Agent Dale Nelson's mind, but reporter Lindsey Ryan's investigation could change the way she sees everything—her career, her past, and her future. (978-1-62639-558-9)

Actual Stop by Kara A. McLeod. When Special Agent Ryan O'Connor's present collides abruptly with her past, shots are fired, and the course of her life is irrevocably altered. (978-1-62639-675-3)

Embracing the Dawn by Jeannie Levig. When ex-con Jinx Tanner and business executive E. J. Bastien awaken after a one-night stand to find their lives inextricably entangled, love has its work cut out for it. (978-1-62639-576-3)

Jane's World: The Case of the Mail Order Bride by Paige Braddock. Jane's PayBuddy account gets hacked and she inadvertently purchases a mail order bride from the Eastern Bloc. (978-1-62639-494-0)

Love's Redemption by Donna K. Ford. For ex-convict Rhea Daniels and ex-priest Morgan Scott, redemption lies in the thin line between right and wrong. (978-1-62639-673-9)

The Shewstone by Jane Fletcher. The prophetic Shewstone is in Eawynn's care, but unfortunately for her, Matt is coming to steal it. (978-1-62639-554-1)

A Touch of Temptation by Julie Blair. Recent law school graduate Kate Dawson's ordained path to the perfect life gets thrown off course when handsome butch top Chris Brent initiates her to sexual pleasure. (978-1-62639-488-9)

Beneath the Waves by Ali Vali. Kai Merlin and Vivien Palmer love the water and the secrets trapped in the depths, but if Kai gives in to her feelings, it might come at a cost to her entire realm. (978-1-62639-609-8)

Girls on Campus edited by Sandy Lowe and Stacia Seaman. College: four years when rules are made to be broken. This collection is required reading for anyone looking to earn an A in sex ed. (978-1-62639-733-0)

Heart of the Pack by Jenny Frame. Human Selena Miller falls for the domineering Caden Wolfgang, but will their love survive Selena learning the Wolfgangs are werewolves? (978-1-62639-566-4)

Miss Match by Fiona Riley. Matchmaker Samantha Monteiro makes the impossible possible for everyone but herself. Is mysterious dancer Lucinda Moss her own perfect match? (978-1-62639-574-9)

Paladins of the Storm Lord by Barbara Ann Wright. Lieutenant Cordelia Ross must choose between duty and honor when a man with godlike powers forces her soldiers to provoke an alien threat. (978-1-62639-604-3)

Taking a Gamble by P.J. Trebelhorn. Storage auction buyer Cassidy Holmes and postal worker Erica Jacobs want different things out of life, but taking a gamble on love might prove lucky for them both. (978-1-62639-542-8)

The Copper Egg by Catherine Friend. Archeologist Claire Adams wants to find the buried treasure in Peru. Her ex, Sochi Castillo, wants to steal it. The last thing either of them wants is to still be in love. (978-1-62639-613-5)

The Iron Phoenix by Rebecca Harwell. Seventeen-year-old Nadya must master her unusual powers to stop a killer, prevent civil war, and rescue the girl she loves, while storms ravage her island city. (978-1-62639-744-6)

A Reunion to Remember by TJ Thomas. Reunited after a decade, Jo Adams and Rhonda Black must navigate a significant age difference, family dynamics, and their own desires and fears to explore an opportunity for love. (978-1-62639-534-3)

Built to Last by Aurora Rey. When Professor Olivia Bennett hires contractor Joss Bauer to restore her dilapidated farmhouse, she learns her heart, as much as her house, is in need of a renovation. (978-1-62639-552-7)

Capsized by Julie Cannon. What happens when a woman turns your life completely upside down? (978-1-62639-479-7)

Girls With Guns by Ali Vali, Carsen Taite, and Michelle Grubb. Three stories by three talented crime writers—Carsen Taite, Ali Vali, and Michelle Grubb—each packing her own special brand of heat. (978-1-62639-585-5)

Heartscapes by MJ Williamz. Will Odette ever recover her memory or is Jesse condemned to remember their love alone? (978-1-62639-532-9)

Murder on the Rocks by Clara Nipper. Detective Jill Rogers lives with two things on her mind: sex and murder. While an ice storm cripples Tulsa, two things stand in Jill's way: her lover and the DA. (978-1-62639-600-5)

Necromantia by Sheri Lewis Wohl. When seeing dead people is more than a movie tagline. (978-1-62639-611-1)

Salvation by I. Beacham. Claire's long-term partner now hates her, for all the wrong reasons, and she sees no future until she meets Regan, who challenges her to face the truth and find love. (978-1-62639-548-0)

A Return to Arms by Sheree Greer. When a police shooting makes national headlines, activists Folami and Toya struggle to balance their relationship and political allegiances, a struggle intensified after a fiery young artist enters their lives. (978-1-62639-681-4)